CROW

FLIGHT

Susan Cunningham

CROW

FLIGHT

AMBERJACK
PUBLISHING

IDAHO

Amberjack Publishing
1472 E. Iron Eagle Drive
Eagle, ID 83616
amberjackpublishing.com

Library of Congress Cataloging-in-Publication Data

Names: Cunningham, Susan, 1979- author.
Title: Crow flight / Susan Cunningham.
Description: New York : Amberjack Publishing, [2019] |
    Summary: High school senior Gin, who is preparing to apply
    to Harvard, and new transfer student Felix work on a school
    project that uses computer simulations to study the behavior
    of crows, but as the two grow close, Felix mysteriously
    disappears and Gin's quest to find answers turns dangerous.
Identifiers: LCCN 2018037180 (print) | LCCN 2018046861
    (ebook) | ISBN 9781948705240 (ebook) | ISBN
    9781948705165 (pbk. : alk. paper)
Subjects: | CYAC: Computer simulation–Fiction. | Crows–Fiction.
    | Love–Fiction. | High schools–Fiction. | Schools–Fiction.
Classification: LCC PZ7.1.C864 (ebook) | LCC PZ7.1.C864 Cr
    2019 (print) | DDC [Fic]–dc23
LC record available at https://lccn.loc.gov/2018037180

ISBN: 978-1-948705-16-5
E-ISBN: 9978-1-948705-24-0

For Tim, who makes life fun {

What at first glance is a common, ordinary animal we know now to be an extraordinary one. Much more than we realized is within the physical and mental grasp of birds in the family Corvidae.

— John Marzluff and Tony Angell, *Gifts of the Crow*

Slow flapping to the setting sun

By twos and threes, in wavering rows.

As twilight shadows dimly close,

The crows fly over Washington.

— John Hay, "The Crows at Washington"

One

Gin saw the white square box as soon as she walked in the kitchen. Pizza. Again.

She should calculate the limit on how much pizza one teenager could eat in a year. She wouldn't be surprised if, this year, she hit it.

Her dad turned the box slightly, aligning it with the table's edge. "Is pizza okay?" He winced. "I know it's not what Mom would do, but . . ."

"It's perfect." Gin took a large bite. Assuming a teenager could eat nine slices in the course of a day, then rounding that to ten and accounting for a few pizza-free days each month, it may be possible to hit 3,000 pieces in a year. "And I love pizza. Who doesn't?"

Her dad relaxed, placing two pepperoni slices on his paper plate. "I know this year will be hard, but it's a great opportunity for your mom."

It *was* a great opportunity for Gin's mom, who was finally getting her nurse practitioners' license while still working nights at the hospital. And though her dad wasn't the most focused parent, Gin didn't want to make things harder for him.

"I'll be busy with school and my internship." She dumped on packets of cheese and crushed red pepper and took another bite. "I have the modeling class with Professor Sandlin—that's going to take lots of time. Plus, I am a senior."

Her dad chewed slowly, methodically, then clapped his hands together. "That's right. School! And the first day is tomorrow."

Gin stopped mid-bite. "You remembered." Her dad was known for inventing programs like *Streamliner*, which senators swore by and celebrities tweeted about. He wasn't known for remembering whether his daughter had to be picked up at math team practice or needed to eat breakfast or was starting her senior year at high school.

He pulled his phone from his pocket, sheepish. "Mom had me program in all the big days. Chloe's breaks are in there, too. Anyway, can I help? Do you need school supplies? I have paper, markers, pens . . ."

"Thanks, Dad. But I'm actually all set."

Einstein leapt up on the table and meowed. Gin pulled a long string of cheese and held it out to him so he could lick away with his scratchy tongue.

"If you want, we could make an app to catalog your inventory of school supplies. It could automatically order what's needed before you run out." Her dad's pizza was poised in mid-air. With his free hand, he pulled at his straight, dark hair, which was just like Gin's, but shorter. "It'd only take a few minutes."

"Sure, that'd be nice." Considering that her main school supply was her laptop, an app wasn't necessary. But more often than not, her dad's ideas ended up being better than Gin could imagine. That was the power of computer programs. And this year, she was counting on computer programs to make up for everything else.

// Two

Freshly polished floors gleamed in the fluorescent lights. High-school students filled the halls, laughing and talking. And Gin stood at her locker, thinking.

She was already nervous about her main class of the day—Computer Simulations with Sasha Sandlin—but that wasn't until sixth period. She'd just have to distract herself until then.

Her phone buzzed—her mom must've gotten home from her night shift. *Thinking of you, honey—have a great first day. Sorry I missed you last night, but we'll get something good for dinner to celebrate. xoxo mom*

Before Gin could write back, there was a waft of perfume. "Supermodel" by Victoria's Secret.

"Happy first day of the ending of everything." Hannah leaned against the metal locker and crossed her arms as she surveyed the crowded hallway. She wore combat boots and a short plaid skirt and her blonde hair was twisted up into a series of buns. "First question of the day: do you finally feel like a senior?"

"Sure." Gin kept her locker open, creating a buffer from the river of students. "If it means you feel ready to be done."

"Or like you're ready to party. Which is exactly how I feel."

"As long as you know it's not the weekend yet. How's your schedule?" Gin grabbed her copy of *The Complete Works of William Shakespeare* for English, already worn from the pre-reading she'd done over summer break.

"Hard. Even worse, there's no boyfriend in sight. Not that I'm looking." Hannah sighed as her eyes flitted up and down the halls.

"You're always looking."

Hannah stood up straighter, face serious. "Not this year. This year is all about not looking. Because life is about so much more than having a boyfriend. Like, you know, school and family and eating three square meals a day—or is it four?"

"Five for you." A box of chocolate-dipped granola bars was already tucked in Gin's locker, in preparation for Hannah's emergency snack requests.

"And, also, finding *you* a boyfriend."

Gin shook her head. "You don't have to worry about that. Maybe that was on the list before, but my main goal for this year is to do well enough in school to—"

"I know, I know. Get into Harvard."

"Anyway, I've got *Love Fractal.*" Gin double-checked her bag—pen and notebook, laptop, two books.

"That's right. Your very own love prediction program. Better than Match, eHarmony, and Zoosk combined, but geared to the often-ignored high school student. And capable of finding both of us decent guys, right?"

"That's the plan."

"Then I'll keep not looking for a boyfriend." Hannah leaned over and glanced in the mirror stuck on Gin's locker door. She pouted, then smiled, finally ending with a serious expression. "I've got to get to class. Differential equations. Which should be vaguely fun. See you at lunch?"

Hannah left and Gin checked her bag once more, then pushed her locker closed with a click.

She walked down the hall, texting her mom, and looked up just in time to veer back and avoid running right into someone. She saw his t-shirt first—a sun-bleached red—and his wooden bead necklace, the type that everyone had worn back in middle school.

He must've been new—Gin didn't recognize him, and he definitely wasn't a freshman. She stared at him for half a second, long enough to notice that his eyes were a bright hazel and his shaggy hair a gold-brown. And long enough to feel her heart rate rise, sudden and fast.

"Sorry about that," she said. Before he could reply, she walked away.

She breathed in, trying to knead down the warmth in her stomach. He had smiled at her, easy and re-laxed, and it had seemed like he was going to say something. But her reaction to seeing him—merely *seeing* him, not even knowing a single thing about him—had thrown her.

The last thing she needed was a repeat of last year. When she'd spent hours—days, really—thinking about Liam Cook, one year ahead of her and, in spite of the one class they shared, barely aware of her. And it hadn't been for Gin's lack of trying: she used to waste half of morning break stalling at her locker so she could pass him in the hall on the way to third period. At the end of the school year, mere months before he had to leave for college, she had worked up the courage to give him a fake questionnaire for a fake report she was "writing" about student interests, just to have a reason to talk with him. In one of his answers, he used the word "apocryphal."

None of it had mattered. He had never even learned Gin's name. It shouldn't have been shocking: guys never noticed Gin. But since Gin agreed completely with Albert Einstein—or whoever had technically said it—that insanity was doing the same thing over and over, expecting different results, she had decided that this year, she would stay focused on what mattered.

A locker clanged, and Gin tightened her grip on her shoulder bag. As she rounded the corner, she glanced back. The boy, unsurprisingly, hadn't given her a second glance.

"What's for lunch?" Hannah threw her paper bag down on the table and popped open a soda, her purple nails bright against the red can.

"The usual." Since Gin's lunch was more or less hard coded into *HungerStriker*, Hannah shouldn't even have to ask.

For your 11:30 a.m. school lunch, your best choice for optimizing nutrition and taste is to have a peanut butter sandwich, a piece of fruit, and a granola bar. Not pizza.

Hannah looked in her bag and scrunched up her nose. "Well, I have leftover cauliflower enchiladas. Thanks, Mom. You know, we should go out. Off campus."

"Can't. Every dollar I have is for college. And there are no more open lunches."

"Doesn't bother *them*." Hannah pointed to three senior girls leaving through the side doors.

"They won't get caught. And if *you* get caught—"

"Don't remind me. I know." Hannah set her head on the table, which smelled like old rags and French fries, and Gin fought the urge to push her back up. Hannah had had a rough end to the summer after being dumped by Pete, her boyfriend of four months. Pete was also the reason Hannah had ditched school (and been caught) several times at the end of junior year.

Gin slid her granola bar across the table. "Here, have this."

Hannah took a bite, head still resting on the table. "We haven't even gone to all of our classes, and I'm tired of it. How many more days until summer?"

"152."

Hannah lifted her head and narrowed her eyes. "I should know better than to ask you a rhetorical question that actually has an answer." She took another bite of the bar and looked harder at Gin. "So, did your model pick that outfit?"

Outfitter had, in fact, chosen Gin's clothes. She mentally scanned through the inputs again:

Occasion: First day of senior year

Weather: High of 80, sunny and humid

Previous outfits: N/A

Recommended outfit: Gray sleeveless blouse, cropped dark jeans, off-white Converse low-tops

Gin was the first to admit she needed help with clothing: ninth and tenth grades had felt like one long morning of coming down to breakfast only to have her older sister, Chloe, send her back up to her room to change. After all, "Chloe Hartson's little sister couldn't be caught dead looking like a Lands' End model."

But then Chloe had gone to college, where she was much more interested in doubling down on hurricanes and PBRs at Sigma Chi parties than helping her younger sister choose outfits. Which meant Gin was on her own. And it seemed silly to waste time agonizing over minor decisions like what to wear. Nobel prize-winning scientists and Fortune 500 CEOs all knew the benefits of avoiding decision fatigue. But instead of limiting her wardrobe to a set of black turtlenecks and jeans, Gin had written *Outfitter* before junior year. She'd been successfully using it ever since.

"It's a good outfit." Gin finished her sandwich and moved on to her grapes. "I have a whole series of assumptions to prove it."

"Totally good outfit." Hannah shrugged, as though the outfit were anything but good. "A little plain, maybe. I could help you out sometime, if the model needs a break?"

"Models don't need breaks." Gin glanced down at her gray blouse. With her pale skin and straight hair, maybe it was a bit boring. "Anyway, it frees up my brain for the important stuff."

"Right. Since everything in high school is so important. Like . . ." Hannah glanced around the cafeteria, "the fact that Trevor McDaniel's fly is down?"

Gin laughed.

"Anyway, I bet your model couldn't predict the intriguing new guy. Now that I see him, I get the talk."

Gin followed Hannah's gaze and wasn't surprised to see the boy from the hall. "On straight probabilities, I'd guess he's a player. Or at least a jerk."

"Maybe." Hannah said, tapping her fingers on her can of soda. "Or maybe not . . . Look."

The new boy was carrying his tray with one hand and eating an apple with the other. He sat down in the first open seat, which happened to be at a table with sophomore math team members. They stared, open-mouthed. He introduced himself, then leaned back, stretching his legs out a mile in front of him, and took another bite of apple. Gin saw that his lips, which were slightly thin, were incredibly expressive.

"Hello? You still there?"

Gin blinked hard. "What? Yeah, sorry. He just—"

Hannah raised her eyebrows.

"He reminded me of someone. That's all."

"Whatever. You know you think he's cute. You could enter it in *Love Fractal*, right? Maybe you're a match."

"I could, if *Love Fractal* were ready, which it isn't. Anyway, it'd never match me with him."

"Well, it probably doesn't matter. He looks untouchable." Hannah cocked her head to the side, still watching him. "Or maybe not. Tell you what, by the end of the day, I'll have all the details."

Hannah wasn't joking. She could find out everything that anyone knew about him. Which was comforting. Once Gin was armed with the knowledge of who he really was, she could get her autonomic nervous system back under control.

The bell rang, and the cafeteria erupted in motion. Students trashed plates with half-eaten soft pretzels and pizza crusts then filed out to their next classes.

"One more class until computer modeling 101, right?" Hannah squeezed Gin's shoulder. "Good luck. Though, you've never needed luck."

Hannah took off down the hall. Gin started upstairs, then paused. The new boy was heading for the parking lot. He looked around, then pushed the heavy door open to the muggy afternoon.

Gin watched for a moment. And for some reason, one she never could've predicted with any of her models, she followed.

When she stepped outside, it was so bright that she had to squint. The doors clicked closed behind her as she walked to the edge of the sidewalk. Trying not to be too obvious, she scanned the parking lot. Sweat started to form on her brow and above her lip, and she took a deep breath of the hot air. It smelled like tar and mown grass.

There were rows of cars, gleaming in the sun. A few students milled around behind the dumpsters. Further away, students ran on the track.

No sign of him.

The practical thing to do was to go back inside. After all, it was the first day of senior year. And Gin had her most important class ever coming up. She had better things to do than stand in a parking lot. But as Gin turned towards the door, already thinking through her route to her next class, she saw a flash of red.

There, standing near the chain link fence at the edge of the parking lot, was the boy. He was still and focused, facing away from Gin, his back arched slightly. And he was staring up into a tree.

It was strange. Like he was watching something. But the tree was nothing special, just a broad, green-leafed maple.

Gin couldn't help following his gaze. Up into the tree. Through the thick leaves, glossy in the noon sun. Along the old, bent branches.

And that's when she saw them. Perched on a lower branch and nearly hidden in all the green, were two black crows. They were looking down, heads tilted, bodies still. Unafraid.

It was almost like the crows knew him. Even stranger, his mouth was moving. Like he was talking to them.

And suddenly, in a flash of black, the crows flew down and perched on his shoulders.

Gin gasped at the strange sight, her hand rushing

to her open mouth. The boy reached into his pocket, pulling out a cracker. He split it in two and gave a piece to each bird. The crows ate nimbly, their dark feathers shimmering in the sun. Then the boy gave a slight upward push of his hands, and the crows flew back up to the tree.

There was a rush of cool air, and the doors opened. Two girls walked out, and Gin's face turned red as though she'd been caught doing something wrong. She grabbed the handle of the slowly closing door and started inside.

But she managed one look back, in time to see the boy turn towards school, the crows watching from the tree.

It was odd, no doubt. The birds couldn't be wild—wild birds would never do that. But two pet crows that hung out behind school didn't seem much more probable.

Gin glanced at the time—three minutes until the next bell. She didn't want to be late, especially on the first day. Likely, there was a logical explanation for the crows. After all, there always was.

// Three

Gin's fifth period was Ancient Worldviews. She took a seat near the back, thankful for the wise counselor who had said to take an easy class. She already had assignments for two papers, ten chapters of reading, and a quiz on Friday.

The teacher stood at a blackboard that had probably been dug out of a basement somewhere, and wrote his name, Mr. Ryan, with quick bursts, his body shaking slightly with the effort. It was the first time Gin had seen a teacher use chalk in years, and the yellow dust, though messy, smelled crisp and earthy.

The bell rang, and Mr. Ryan turned around. He stood there, smiling at the class, not speaking. Seconds ticked by, and students shifted in their seats. The halls quieted. The clock above the door clicked as one minute passed and another.

Students were starting to look at each other.

But Mr. Ryan was completely at ease. He stretched slightly over one leg, out to the side, in a half-lunge. He was lean and muscled like a runner. And tall. He held a piece of chalk in one hand, rolling it between his fingers.

Another silent minute flashed by, and Gin was seriously considering raising her hand and asking whether this was actually a class.

Finally, Mr. Ryan spoke. "Welcome to Ancient Worldviews." He looked around the room, making eye contact with each student. When his eyes met Gin's, she had the distinct feeling he was looking for something. "There's no syllabus. No guide to papers you must write or books you must read. There will be plenty of work, but maybe not the type of work you're used to."

Students clapped and pumped their fists. But Gin felt her stomach tighten. The unknown was almost always worse than the known.

"We will begin class the same way each day, with a

moment of silence." He leaned to the other side, another high lunge, chalk still in hand. "Don't worry. It's not a prayer or a meditation or any weird practice that your parents will want to write the school board about. Rather, it's a moment without any noise. A moment for you to sit in your chair, and let the world stop around you. A moment when a door might open."

He hopped up on his desk, his feet dangling down to the floor. With his knit shirt and fraying jeans, he looked more like a student than a teacher.

"We're here to talk about what people thought thousands of years ago. And all of these cultures assumed the existence of something you won't discuss in any other class. Something that's impossible to measure, even with the strongest, most innovative, most technical instruments in the world. Something you might have to . . . feel." With that word, he put one hand on his chest and paused. Then he jumped to his feet and started pacing. "Who can guess what that is?"

The class was quiet for a second. Someone said, "God?"

Mr. Ryan stopped his pacing and raised his chalk. "Good start. God. And yes, many cultures believed in some sort of higher power—a god or many gods. But I'm looking for another word. Something even more basic."

Other guesses were thrown out: soul, miracles, spirit. Mr. Ryan nodded at each. But none were exactly right.

In a tapping flurry of yellow, he wrote two words on the board: material, immaterial.

"Everything you will learn in school, or have learned in school, is most likely rooted in this world." He circled 'material' several times, the chalk getting bolder each time around. "But for thousands and thousands of years, people have believed that there's a whole other world, right here. Around us, with us, in us. The *immaterial*."

He paused, and the class was silent. Gin felt the muscles in her neck tighten.

"This is a world that we can't experience with our senses. So be prepared to learn not just with your head, but with your heart." He put his hand on his chest again, leaving a faint yellow smear on his shirt.

Worlds where you couldn't measure anything sounded miserable. At the very least, it'd be harder to get a good grade. Worst-case scenario: Gin's so-called easy class would wreck her chances at Harvard—the college she'd been working to get into since she was six. Bill Gates, Mark Zuckerberg and Sasha Sandlin, the latter of whom she was finally about to meet, had all gone there. It'd be the best school for Gin—if she could get in.

Mr. Ryan held up his hands. "Now don't worry, your brain is important, too. You must reason and learn and weigh the facts. But from the start, to help understand what these ancient people thought, I want you to consider that there is more. More than the brain, more than electrical impulses we can measure."

He walked to the corner of the blackboard and wrote in small capital letters: "*The need for the immaterial is the most deeply rooted of all needs. One must have bread; but before bread, one must have the ideal.*"—*Victor Hugo*

"This quote is from a writer whose work was turned into plays, films, and a long-running musical. And so, in the spirit of the first day of school, we're going to begin with a movie. *Les Misérables.* Consider it a warm up."

Everyone murmured with excitement. Even Gin leaned back in her chair, relaxed. She could handle a movie. Maybe this class wouldn't be so bad after all.

By sixth period, Gin's stomach felt knotted up so tightly it hurt. She had waited all day—all her life, really—for this class.

Computer Simulations with Sasha Sandlin. A once-in-a-lifetime opportunity. The biggest thing Monroe High had ever offered. Considering they were in Northern Virginia, in one of the wealthiest public school districts in the nation, that was pretty good.

Sasha Sandlin had been creating computer simulations since age ten. By seventeen, she wrote a model predicting medical successes in developing countries and won the Warren Walsh Award. She did her undergrad at Harvard, got her PhD at MIT, and returned to Harvard to teach and do research. Her models were used for everything, from predicting the next hit pop song, to anticipating an opponent's moves in war.

Now she was in Washington, DC, completing a fellowship at Georgetown and teaching a class at Monroe High. And Gin was one of ten handpicked high school students who got to take her class.

Outside the classroom, Gin wiped her sweaty hands on her pants and double-checked the time. Three minutes early. Perfect.

She took another breath and walked in.

The classroom was bright with afternoon light. There were none of the typical classroom accessories: bulletin boards, plants, bookcases. Just eight tables, the SmartScreen, a teacher's desk at the front, and Ms. Sandlin, standing at the side of her desk, typing furiously on her phone. Compared to her online photos, she looked both younger and more intense.

The bell rang, and Ms. Sandlin set down her phone and perused the class, her straight hair swinging. She wore a tight skirt, cream blouse, and heels. Gin was suddenly grateful for *Outfitter*'s recommendation.

"Good afternoon, modelers." Ms. Sandlin tapped her phone, and a syllabus appeared on the screen. "And welcome to Computer Simulations 101. This is a college-level course. So it goes without saying, I will expect a lot."

Gin bit her lip, hiding a grin. *This* was exactly what she wanted. A chance to learn from one of the best in the field. Not to mention the fact that the best modeler in the class would win a summer internship at Georgetown, overseen by Ms. Sandlin.

Gin had to get it.

There were plenty of things Gin couldn't do: play sports, ease her way around a party, talk without over-sharing extraneous information. But she could work with computers. And ever since she had written her first if-then statement, she knew that creating computer simulations was what she was meant to do. Lining up logic. Bringing order to an otherwise unpredictable world.

No one else, except for maybe her dad, understood. Chloe rolled her eyes at Gin's models, and her mom would tell her to have a little fun, to let life "happen." But Gin knew better: this was work she was made for. And being an intern for Ms. Sandlin was the best possible way to get there.

Ms. Sandlin tapped the screen to reveal lines of code. "Does anyone know what this does?" she asked.

Gin thought it looked like a weather simulation, except there was an element of human behavior, too. She was studying the code, getting closer to the answer when the door opened and someone stepped in. And Gin's focus cracked.

It was the new boy—the same one from the hall and the cafeteria and the crows—standing there, in her modeling class.

Ms. Sandlin paused, glancing at her class list. "Mr. Gartner, we're glad you made it."

He threw his head back in greeting. "Sorry I'm late. They had my schedule confused."

Gin stared at the screen, as "Mr. Gartner" sat in the back of the class. Her ability to think had evaporated and she pulled her hair forward to cover her ears, which were now flaming pink.

"As you consider the model, I'm going to organize you in pairs, based on your varied strengths, modeling styles, and coding backgrounds. Table one, here on my left: Ms. Pine and Mr. Edwards. Table two, just behind, Ms. Smithson and Mr. Daniels."

As students shuffled their things into their new spots, Gin tried to determine the pattern Ms. Sandlin was using for the seating assignments. If there was one.

"Table three, up front on my right—"

That was Gin's table. She put her papers on top of her laptop, ready to move.

"Mr. Gartner and Ms. Hartson. Table four—"

Gin didn't hear anything else. She could stay at her table, in her same chair even. But the new boy was going to be sitting next to her. He was going to be her partner.

Gin stared at her laptop, as though she barely noticed when he sat down. But she felt every movement he made.

How he put a red spiral notebook on the table. How he eased back in his chair. How he pulled a pencil out from behind his ear, tapping it on the desk. Apparently, he didn't even have a laptop.

He leaned towards Gin, so close she noticed that he smelled like minty soap and the woods. Her eyes flickered to his, and he raised his eyebrows.

"Close call in the hall, right? Glad you're okay," he

whispered. Her face burned brighter. "So, you ready for this? I hear she's a stickler." He did this funny half-smile, half-grimace with his lips.

It was very, very cute. But it was also awful. In no way did Gin plan on insulting Ms. Sandlin on her first day in class—or ever.

She turned her attention back to the model on the screen. She'd been wrong about the wind coefficient. This model was definitely not for weather, but human behavior. People moving through an airport?

"Now class, does anyone want to hazard a guess as to what this model is all about?"

Gin narrowed her eyes, debating whether she had enough information to throw out a guess. The new boy—Mr. Gartner, crow boy—was writing something in his notebook, probably doodling. Then he stuck his pencil back behind his ear and tapped his fingers on his arm. Distracting.

No one was guessing, and Ms. Sandlin finally clicked to the next image. A school cafeteria.

"We're going to work on models that may seem simple, but are incredibly complex," Ms. Sandlin said. "And so, we're going to begin by modeling concepts you intuitively know."

She tapped on her keyboard and a black square covered with colored dots appeared on the screen. The dots, which must have been students, were positioned around long rectangles, or tables. Three new dots entered from a corner: one green dot, one purple dot, one red dot.

"This model predicts where students sit in the cafeteria. The green dot represents a football player, the purple dot is a student in band, and the red dot is a student who does not participate in extracurriculars."

The new dots waited in a line, as though getting food; a few seconds later, football player dot ended up at a table with a bunch of other green dots, while the band student dot made it to a table with a group of dots of all colors, including purple. The unclassified student dot lingered near an empty table, then squeezed in with the band student dot.

"Model how a school cafeteria works, and I promise you'll never eat a school lunch the same way again." Ms. Sandlin flipped to the next image and launched into her lecture.

The concepts were all ones Gin knew, but she took notes anyway. Mr. Gartner, unsurprisingly, wasn't taking notes. After a while, Gin couldn't help glancing at what he had written before. Small, messy letters, strung together to make two words: school cafeteria.

At first she thought nothing of it. But then she realized he hadn't even touched his pencil since the first few minutes of class, when Ms. Sandlin's model was still a mystery. He must've known what it was before anyone else, even Gin.

Her eyes drifted over to him, and for some reason, he glanced back. He smiled, playful. Her cheeks pinkened—again—and she turned back to the board.

As the clock pushed closer and closer to the end of class, she told herself that the rest of the week would be easier. She'd know what to expect. And she'd be prepared.

// Four

By the end of the week, Gin had eaten takeout every night for dinner, had seen her mom awake exactly once, and had found out the new boy's first name. Felix. His name meant lucky, the lucky one, a person favored by luck—and it was fitting. Everything about Felix seemed to be lucky. Like the way his hair curled perfectly over his ears. Or how he was instantly popular without seeming to care about popularity. Or how he knew every answer in modeling class even if he never volunteered one, instead preferring to write them in his spiral notebook.

Another strange thing about his name—not that she'd been obsessing about it—was that it was basically the same in twelve languages. English, German, French, Czech, Romanian . . . He could go almost anywhere in the world, and people would be able to greet him.

There were all sorts of Felixes in history, too. A bunch of saints, for instance. Like Felix the Hermit, Gin's personal favorite. Maybe because he was an oddball one, not so lucky like his name was meant to suggest. As the legend went, he could never catch a fish, which was apparently very important in ninth-century Portugal, so his parents disowned him.

He took to the hills, wandering out to a big mountain to live, alone. One dark night, he kept seeing this light on a hill and finally went out to follow it. And he found the body of some important saint—the first bishop of Barga—and he became famous himself.

The craziest part was, years later, someone figured out that the actual body that Felix the Hermit found was not the saint. It was a nine-year-old child.

Another reminder of the futility of following strange bright lights into the darkness. Which Gin definitely wasn't heeding with her searches of Felix's name.

Hannah, true to her word, had found out a lot about him. Pretty much everything reinforced Gin's initial appraisal—that Felix was exactly the sort of guy that every girl at school would like to date. He ran cross-country and windsurfed, was good at drama and newspaper and debate team, was smart without being weird. Somehow he didn't have a girl-friend.

But then, there were the strange things. First was the matter of the crows. When Gin had told Hannah what she saw, Hannah had narrowed her eyes and asked whether Gin hadn't been hanging out in the pot smokers' bathroom. But Hannah looked into it. All she had dug up so far was that Felix supposedly counted "bird watching" among his hobbies. Gin was doing her own research, stepping outside the school several times throughout the day to try to spot Felix with the birds, with no luck yet.

Second was the fact that Felix had transferred to

public school for his senior year. He'd been a prep school or homeschool student his whole life and suddenly enrolled in public school, seemingly without a clear reason.

And the strangest of all was not even about Felix, but his dad. Because Felix's dad, unlike every other dad in the greater DC area, wasn't a government worker or lawyer or financial analyst. Rather, he was the uber-wealthy owner of Odin, Inc., one of the biggest high-tech companies around. Unsurprisingly, he had gone to Harvard.

In another twist, Odin, Inc. owned dozens of companies, including the one where Gin's dad worked. It was an annoying connection, because even though *Streamliner* had been such a hit, it had barely made a dent in the Hartson family mortgage. Since her dad created the program at work, he didn't own the rights to it.

Maybe Gin would let Felix know how his father had single-handedly screwed up her father's life. An exaggeration, of course, but exaggerations could be useful when trying not to like someone.

That's when Gin realized it: she liked Felix Gartner. And of anyone to like this year, Felix Gartner was definitely not a good choice for her. She pulled up *Decider* and entered the scenario: spend senior year pining over a cute but totally out-of-her-league boy, or focus on her studies. *Decider*'s answer popped up immediately.

The clear course of action is to focus on your studies. It is most advantageous to your near and long-term future.

Exactly what she'd been trying to tell herself.

Near the end of class on Friday, Ms. Sandlin explained their first real assignment: model a predator-prey relationship between two groups of animals, such as wolves and sheep. The class had twenty minutes to start working. Gin took a deep breath and turned toward Felix, fingers poised over her laptop.

"I've always been interested in mountain lions." It was the most she'd said to him since the start of the school year. "It might be cool to see how they impact deer populations. And we could expand it to other prey, too. Or . . ." For a second, she wondered if crows had a predator—she still hadn't found a way to bring the crows up to Felix, and this could be her chance. And her thoughts turned to cats. "How about a barn cat? And a barn full of mice? Smaller scale, but interesting—and useful, too."

He glanced up at the clock. "Yeah, that's good."

"Okay." She started typing notes, angling her laptop so he could see, feeling grateful that at least they had started. "We should begin with the data matrix. Life span, reproductive rates, different hunting abilities. Maybe we can use a k-means algorithm, then set up some differential equations."

Felix twirled his pencil. "That all sounds good. But, I've actually done something like this before.

How about we work separately and combine our efforts?"

Gin's fingers froze as she searched for a response. Felix flashed a smile and slid out from behind the table. "Really sorry to do this, but I've got to check out a little early."

He walked to Ms. Sandlin's desk, said something indecipherable from where Gin was sitting, and left.

The rest of the class clamored about their brainstorming. And Gin sat at her table, staring at the notes for her first project in her most important class of the year, wondering why her group had stood up and left.

Maybe it was for the best. Because now she could classify Felix for what he really was: an immense, self-centered jerk.

The only thing left to do was to write the best model that could possibly be written. Better than whatever he could pull together.

// Five

On the Metro ride to her internship, Gin found a forward-facing seat by a window with only mildly stained fabric. The train shook, flying above ground into the bright afternoon, then diving back underground into the dark. Gin's phone buzzed—her mom had texted before her shift at the hospital.

Ginny, I hope work goes well. Noodles for dinner? I'll call in the order. Love you—Mom.

Gin texted back that noodles sounded great—anything besides pizza sounded great—and opened her laptop to start working on her cat-mouse model. She had a full forty minutes before reaching her stop. Plenty of time to get a basic framework finished.

Gin's desk at work looked out a window, straight into another brick building across the busy street. If she craned her head to the right and leaned way forward, she could almost catch a glimpse of the Washington Monument.

Gin had worked there since the summer, one of fifty interns helping the Belton Institute model economic impacts of legislation. The think tank modeled a range of scenarios for each new law, predicting things like how many jobs would be created, how many people would move into an area, how many dollars would be spent. Gin didn't write the models, but she did help check them. There were thousands and thousands of lines of code, all of which could introduce errors or inconsistencies, so she was one of a team of 100-plus that reviewed it all. If x, then y, over and over and over again.

Most of the interns left at the end of the summer, but the think tank had kept two: Gin and Lucas, a senior at a private school in the city. His dad was a government analyst, his mom was a school teacher. And he was an "It's Academic" champion and a gamer.

"You'll like what we're working on tonight," Lucas said when Gin slipped into her chair. He pushed his glasses up on his nose and shot her a big grin. His lips were plump and slightly parted—not at all like Felix's. "It's another employment scenario. But with these weird twists. It's making me think knights in battle. Or maybe Ultimate Gladiators. Except with suits."

"Sounds cool. How's Thronesville?"

Lucas looked around and scooted closer.

"I figured out a side door. In the castle land." He said it quietly and looked around again as if he were giving her top-secret information. Someone, somewhere would be very interested in what Lucas was about to say. Gin, however, did not fall into that category. "So I was exploring this hidden alleyway, and something seemed off. Maybe the way my shadow hit it. Or the pattern of moss growing. Moss, you know, has specific growth patterns depending on things like moisture and the angle of the sun and—"

"So you went in?"

He rubbed his hands together. "Yeah. I went in. And it turned into this series of tunnels. No one else was in there. It's incredible." His eyes widened and he shook his head, still in disbelief of his discovery. "I'll show you any time you want. My parents made this whole gaming room in the basement, with super comfy chairs and a drink fridge."

If Gin wanted a boyfriend just to have one, Lucas would probably be up for it. But that was a terrible thing to think. Anyway, finding the right boyfriend at the right time was the whole purpose of *Love Fractal.*

The idea for the model had come to her last fall when Hannah had sworn she'd never go on another date unless she knew the guy was right for her (that was pre-Pete). And Gin had had this flash of insight that love should be predictable.

First, people have certain characteristics they look for in dates—in high school, that might be class load and extracurriculars and social life. In other words, how much you party and whether you study and if you smoke pot after school or play football or do both.

Lots of dating software accounted for characteristics like that. But Gin's had another layer. Because she thought it was important to account for the gut-level, split-second feeling a person might have for a potential interest. And she thought that feeling could be approximated through an analysis of someone's reactions to photos of different faces.

A photo could say a lot. Not just whether the person looked more like Zac Efron or Jesse Eisenberg. Tiny signals—from the intensity of a person's smile, to the focus of their eyes, to the lift of their chin— all contained information on who the person was. And someone looking at the photograph would automatically pick up on those details, whether they knew it or not. Those crazy stories of a girl meeting a guy for the first time and saying, "I'm going to marry him," and going on to do just that, weren't all that surprising.

If John Gottman et al. could predict success probabilities of marriage, then maybe Gin could find ways to successfully match up high school students. All it would take was some good equations and the right data.

"Thanks, Lucas—that'd be fun. But this weekend isn't good, with school starting and everything."

He pushed his glasses up and rolled back to his desk. "Just let me know. By the way, I got M&M's earlier—three reds, five blues, two greens, and four browns."

"No yellows or oranges—interesting." Gin logged the data on her chart of probable M&M's combinations and got to work.

// Six

"He told you to do what? Do the project on your own?" Hannah dropped her mouth and shook her head, her hair bright blonde in the glow from Gin's desk lamp.

It was Saturday night, a good opportunity to be social according to *TimeKeeper*. Thankfully, Hannah had agreed.

Gin was sprawled out on her bed, laptop open and piles of coding notes to the side. "Maybe he had a point. It is more efficient to work separately."

Hannah threw a pillow, hitting Gin on the side of the head. "Uh-uh, don't try to defend him."

"It doesn't bug me. It's not like I care what he thinks."

"You shouldn't. Anyway, he's strange. I mean, sure, he's smart and athletic and rich . . . but how many guys actually talk to crows, right? Look, the best thing to do is to make your model really, really good."

"What do you think I've been doing?"

"Not the cat thing. No offense, Einstein, but that's not that thrilling." Hannah rubbed Einstein's head, and Einstein purred without bothering to open an eye. "I'm talking about the Love model." Hannah drew out the word "love," which made the whole thing seem silly.

And maybe it was silly. Gin wouldn't know until she finally did some testing, which she was almost ready for. She already had data on Monroe High students, everything she could access through the school's in-tranet, from yearbook photos and class lists, to team and club rosters. But she needed Lucas's help to get similar data for students at other area schools—oth-erwise, there wouldn't be a large enough pool to make decent recommendations.

"You know, it would help me a lot to try it out. Getting over Pete and everything." Hannah was lying on the floor, staring at the ceiling, feet kicked up on Gin's bed.

"It's not ready. And it would only have results from our school—I don't have the whole data pool yet."

"Whatever. Your 'not ready' is like everyone else's 'perfect.' Who knows, I could find my true love."

Gin considered it for a second. Maybe it'd be a

good distraction. Maybe she needed one last push so she could actually finish the model. Maybe it wouldn't hurt to try.

"Okay." The word just came out. Gin felt her stomach sink, already second-guessing her decision.

"Okay? Really?" Hannah jumped up. "True love, here I come."

Before Gin could change her mind, she opened the program. It began with a series of rapid-fire photos, which Hannah had to classify as 'Pleasing,' 'Unpleasing,' or 'Neutral.' The first image showed a boy with thick eyebrows, an ample nose, and a friendly smile. Hannah scrunched her nose and clicked "Unpleasing," and the next photo appeared.

When the photo analysis was done, Hannah filled out a questionnaire. And that was it. Hannah's test was complete.

"You ready?" Gin was suddenly nervous.

"Ready as ever," Hannah said.

Gin held her breath and pressed enter. Photos of three guys popped up and she stared at them for a full second. When she registered who they were, she groaned.

Hannah, on the other hand, burst out laughing. "I guess you do need to work out the kinks."

As anticipated, all three boys went to Monroe. But not a single one was Hannah's type.

There was Aidan, a player of football and of girls. Marco, a grungy computer guy who was always glued to his laptop. And Noah, who was clean cut and nice—which meant there was a 0.2 percent chance that Hannah would like him.

"Maybe I put too much emphasis on the photos. Or maybe it's the small population size." Gin paged through the guts of the model, ticking through the lines of logic, hoping some obvious issue would stand out.

Hannah was laughing so hard she started hiccupping. "No, don't feel bad. I mean, Marco might be someone you have to get to know to appreciate. And maybe Aidan has a thoughtful side that isn't meant just to get you in bed. As for Noah, nice is the new hot, isn't it? Anyway, your model could be right. That's why I need to help test it. Can't knock it 'til you try it."

Lines of logic and rows of equations flashed along Gin's screen. It could take months to figure out what had gone wrong.

"Well look at that." Hannah held up her phone. "According to my sources, Marco's at a gamer meetup. At that bar in Arlington. Want to go?"

"Are you serious? You can't be. There's no way—"

"It'll take us fifteen minutes to get there. Not bad. And at least we can drink."

Hannah passed Gin her phone, which displayed the homepage for a group called "Geekdom," open only to serious gamers. "This is so not you."

"What's not me? I like new adventures. I like bars. I know nothing about gaming. And Marco is on my list."

Gin opened *Decider* and started typing. "Let me check."

Before she had finished the inputs, Hannah pulled away the keyboard. "No way."

Gin's fingers flinched. "Not even *TimeKeeper*?"

Hannah shook her head. "Nope. It could be fate, and I'm not letting any crazy logic disrupt that."

Gin considered the options. If they left now, they could be back before eleven—which might be worth it if it meant Hannah would drop the Marco lead. "One hour," Gin said, jingling her keys. "And I'm not drinking. I'm driving."

"Obviously."

The Green Leaf was a few blocks off Wilson Street in the west side of Arlington, Virginia. Unassuming and plain, it sat between a Mexican restaurant and a Laundromat. It was hard to park: every side street was lined with cars.

The bar was on the second story, and as Gin and Hannah walked up, they heard the thump of a bass. Inside, the darkened room was packed—a few hundred people, plus tables filled with laptops. The table nearest the door had dozens of little metal rectangles and an open laptop that read, "Please sign in."

Hannah typed in their names, and two rectangles started to glow.

"A perk already—fancy nametags." Hannah placed hers at the edge of her sweater's V-neck, an ideal location for showing off her name and her cleavage. "Now, to find Marco."

Hannah wove through the crowd, and Gin tried to stay close, but soon they were separated. So instead, Gin passed the time by reading the glowing nametags and trying to estimate the most popular gamer name for the greater-DC area.

"Well, we didn't really expect that one to work out, so now we know." Hannah had her feet up on the car's dash, the seat leaned back.

Marco had been a bust, but Hannah had gotten two drinks and a phone number from a cute, blonde gamer named Clay. All in all, Hannah seemed to think it was forty minutes well spent.

"So who's next, Aidan or Noah?" Hannah drummed her fingers together.

Gin sighed. As the night had worn on, reality had settled in. Her big project was far from being complete. There was a chance—maybe a good chance—it'd never work. "It's nice of you to do this, but you don't have to."

Hannah opened her eyes wide. "But this is everything. You've been toiling away on this model for a year. I haven't done anything for a year. It's like, one-seventeenth of your whole life."

"That doesn't mean it'll work."

A stoplight flashed yellow then red, and Gin slowed to a stop. They were back in the suburbs, surrounded by acres of shopping centers and neighborhoods. The car windows were down, and the night air smelled sweet, like flowers.

"But it could be. We've got to give it a chance. And you need history, right? Well here's some history."

The light changed to green. And suddenly, an idea tumbled through Gin's brain.

"That's right," she said. "It's a real data point. Maybe I just need more."

Hannah held up a hand. "Wait a minute—that could take months. I can't try out hundreds of guys in a week. It'd be like spending all day at a huge buffet. And though I love food, I hate buffets."

Gin was tapping the steering wheel faster now. "No, not you. But history on high school relationships. Actual couples. It's all already out there." Maybe it was possible to make the model much better, without a lot more effort. "How many social media connections do you have?"

"A few thousand?"

Gin smiled. "Perfect."

When Gin got home, she knew sleep would be impossible. So she brewed a pot of coffee, changed into flannel pajama pants and her "There's no place like 127.0.0.1" t-shirt, then connected to Hannah's social media accounts and started coding.

She barely stopped for a break until five in the morning, when she took a final sip of coffee and stretched her arms overhead. Einstein was curled up tightly on one corner of her bed, but once Gin stood, he looked up and stretched too.

"Ready to see if this works?" Gin ran the program and within seconds, was looking at a spreadsheet of data—more than two thousand rows and twenty columns, all containing information that would make her model better.

"Yes!" She picked up Einstein and squeezed him, already thinking through her next steps.

That's when there was a knock at her bedroom door. Gin's mom—still wearing scrubs, her hair pulled back in a low ponytail—peeked in.

"Tell me you haven't been up all night." Gin's mom gave a slight grimace, as though she knew what the answer would be.

"Not really." Gin pushed her coffee mug behind her computer. "I mean, sort of. I had this idea, and I got started and time kind of flew."

"You know you have to sleep. It's important for your body and your brain. It's not good to be up all night. I can show you dozens of studies from medical journals that say exactly that."

Frustration crawled through Gin. After all, her mom had barely been around, much less been aware of what was going on in Gin's life. "I know, Mom. I rarely do it. Anyway, you're the one with the crazy schedule. Maybe I wanted to finally see you."

Her mom winced. She pulled out her ponytail and yawned. "Sweetie, I know I'm not here a lot right now, but I also know that you're responsible. That you can manage your time well."

"Which is exactly what I was doing." If there was one thing Gin knew about, it was time management. "Sometimes it's more efficient to go with the flow, instead of starting and stopping and starting again. At least I wasn't out partying or something."

Gin's mom's expression softened. Her eyes crinkled at the edges, making her look extra tired. Then she stood at Gin's side and put an arm around her shoulders in a quick half-hug.

"This is it—one of your models?"

Gin looked again at the white spreadsheet, the nuggets of information all neatly organized. "Kind of. It's data that feeds a model."

"Does the model do anything interesting?"

Gin leaned against her mom, suddenly feeling tired. "We'll see. I hope so."

"Try to get a little rest, okay? I'm going to sleep now—maybe if you do, too, we could wake up and hang out. Maybe watch a movie or go out for lunch."

It was a nice idea, but chances were Gin's mom would end up stretched out on the couch, studying. "Sure."

Her mom left, and Gin yawned. The model felt far away, less real than the cool sheets on her bed or the firm mattress beneath her, and before she knew it, she was sleeping.

// Seven

Two days before the cat-mouse model was due, Gin and Felix were finally meeting in the library over lunch.

The library, as usual, was freezing and Gin shivered as she walked in. The fake-wood tables were empty, the computers all on screen saver mode. She sat down near the back with stacks of books around her, making sure she still had a good view of the door. The air conditioner hummed, and the librarian swished around her desk. Felix should have been there ten minutes earlier.

Her stomach growled, too loud in the quiet room. When she was sure the librarian wasn't looking, she leaned over her bag and snuck a bite of her granola bar.

That's when she felt him there.

She looked up, surprised. So much for appearing in control and slightly annoyed.

He sat down next to her, his arms and elbows already taking up too much room on the table, and she gulped down the lump of bar and tilted her laptop towards him.

"All right," she said, clearing her throat. "Let's get going. So here you see—"

"Wait a minute. No, 'How's it going?' Or, 'Hey, Felix, how are you?'" He smiled, and Gin's eyes lingered for a second on his pretty lips.

"I said all of that about ten minutes ago. Out loud. To myself. You weren't here, remember?"

It made him laugh, and it was such a nice laugh, she couldn't help smiling back.

"Anyway, here's the framework," she said. "Then here, you can see the details."

He leaned in closer, clasping his hands together and staring at her screen.

"Yeah, I see it." Each time he moved, she caught his minty-soapy scent. "This looks good. Clever how you pulled in the different algorithms here and here."

Gin glanced at him. It *was* clever, and she appreciated that he saw it. Not everyone would, especially not so fast. After a few more minutes, she brought up the code.

He nodded as he looked through each section, sometimes saying, "Nice," or "I didn't think of that." Once, he even asked her to stop and explain her logic.

They were almost out of time, and she still had more to review, but Felix leaned back, tilting his chair up and balancing it on the back two legs.

"This is really good," he said. "You know what you're doing. So, now we just need to figure out how to combine our models. Yours operates more on the scale of weeks, right? And with a single location?"

"That's right." She didn't remind him that that was the assignment.

"That's perfect. Mine has a longer time frame with a larger scale, so I think they'll dovetail nicely together." He pulled her laptop closer. "May I?"

Suddenly he was serious, his focus sharper. He was

typing fast, downloading his model to her laptop and creating a new document to merge both. He worked so quickly, flitting from one screen to another, she had to pay close attention.

"What's this part?" she asked about a section of code that seemed to loop back on itself.

Felix grinned. "What I call a 'soul bit.' I try to insert them into every model I build. So there's a bit of unpredictability, something that transcends logic. Some real life."

It would have made Gin roll her eyes if she hadn't seen everything he'd done so far. A 'soul bit' might sound like something from a tarot card reading, but Felix clearly knew how to code. And in a way, it made sense. Algorithms for genetic changes worked better when they included a probability of mutation, or the chance that genes would change randomly.

In a few minutes, he pushed the laptop back towards her. "We'll still have to finesse the data set and make sure it's not repetitive."

There was a new input screen, asking for the starting populations of cats and mice for up to fifty different locations. Gin plugged in numbers for five locations and ran the model. Within seconds, there were graphs of population sizes at one year, five years, and ten years. Ending populations varied: in some locations, the cats and mice reached a steady state; in others, all animals disappeared.

It was good.

"Wow. This is way more robust than mine." She

plugged in another set of numbers and ran it again. "But what's driving the differences in the sites? Different behaviors?"

"Exactly." The bell rang, and Felix stood. "Well, see you in class. Nice work again. This year'll be fun."

As Gin gathered her things, she glanced out the window. And that's when she noticed them: two large black crows were sitting on the windowsill. The birds shifted their heads, watching her closely. She paused and held her breath.

She turned slowly to ask Felix why the crows were there, what they were doing. But he was already gone.

When she looked back at the window, the crows had shifted to the very edge of the windowsill. They spread their wings and, with a few powerful flaps, took off in flight.

// Eight

Ms. Sandlin was as impressed with the model as Gin had been. In fact, the project had been a success in every way except for now Gin couldn't stop thinking about Felix.

"It'd be easier if I didn't have to see him," Gin told Hannah during lunch.

"Why's it need to be easy? Just enjoy it." Hannah looked in her lunch bag and groaned. "Exactly what I can't do with this lunch. Grilled tempeh on rye. But seriously, it's your senior year. You should have fun."

"You sound like Chloe." Gin took a bite of her peanut butter and jelly sandwich, while pushing her granola bar over to Hannah. "And Chloe's enjoyment of school has already resulted in two citations for underage drinking."

"Okay then, how about this: So what if he's cute and smart?" Hannah ate half of the bar in her first bite. "Who cares? You can't let that cloud your judgment. Look, I have an idea for getting your mind off of him—if you really want to."

Gin leaned closer, waiting.

"Run the test for yourself."

"Run the test?"

"Oh come on, you know. *Love Fractal*. See who you get."

Truth was, Gin had tried the model on herself. Over and over, all through initial testing, in an effort to refine and tweak the program. She also had a secret hope that it would pair her with Liam, but of course it hadn't. And since her results constantly changed, it felt like cheating to pick the one or two matches she liked the most. She wanted to wait to run it on herself again when it was finished.

"I need more data first. And for that, I need Lucas's help."

"Exactly. Get the data, like *today*, and run it. It'll be far more fun than thinking about you-know-who. Anyway, did I tell you my plan to move on to test subject number two—Aidan Rogers? I'm going to bump into him after the next home football game. Pretend I'm interviewing him for the school paper or something."

Gin balled up her empty paper lunch bag. "You don't work at the paper."

"Which matters because . . .?"

"Just take lots of notes." Gin was looking at the cafeteria doors and noticed Felix happened to be coming to lunch. He must've felt Gin's gaze, because he glanced in her direction. She looked away before their eyes met.

"I gotta go," she said. "See you."

And before Hannah could ask why, Gin left.

Outside the cafeteria, she texted Lucas. She had told him about the project months ago and how she needed to quickly gather public information about students from other nearby schools' intranets. He was mostly finished with the program and had been waiting on the final request from her.

A few seconds later, he wrote back that he could have it to her by week's end.

Near the end of modeling class, Ms. Sandlin pulled up a screen that read "Final Project."

"The models you presented last week were a good warm up," she said. "And you'll continue to have some smaller projects through the year. But the majority of your grade will be based on your final project. This is not something you can save for the night before it's due. So begin soon. There's no time like the present."

Gin glanced at Felix's notebook, where, in small

blocky letters he had written: *No time like the present.* An ironic phrase for a modeling class, where you spent all of your time predicting the future.

"You'll be working in your same pairs," she continued.

Same pairs, Felix wrote, and looked up at Gin with a grin. Gin's face flushed, and she turned back to her laptop. The bell rang, and as everyone left, Gin studied her screen for a moment longer, getting up only after the click and slide of Felix's leather flip-flops had faded away.

// Nine

The football game Friday night started at seven. By the time Gin and Hannah arrived, it was wintry dark. The white lights from the field made everyone's faces glow. Spectators wore sweaters and windbreakers, but the players on the field steamed, sweat running through the black paint on their cheeks.

Hannah tried to pay attention to the game. But every time something of importance actually happened, she was either looking the other way or checking her phone.

Near the end of the game, Hannah got hungry. But she didn't want to leave the bleachers. "Now I have to watch," she said as she stared at the field, pen poised over her notepad. "If Aidan makes a big play, I should know."

So Gin climbed down the concrete steps and squeezed through the crowd to the snack bar. She picked up two soft pretzels and two sodas—Hannah had vodka stashed in her bag, but Gin, as usual, was driving—and headed back along the dim grassy hill. That's when she saw Felix.

She ignored the flutter in her chest and marched forward, back towards the bleachers, which also happened to mean she was walking towards Felix. And suddenly, he smiled and raised one hand in a small wave.

Her face flushed, and her breath caught in her throat. It was flattering. To be out there at a football game, with this smart, cute guy saying hi to her. Maybe—and she hesitated to even let herself think it—maybe there was a small chance he liked her. Maybe he was smart enough to be the sort of guy who actually appreciated smart girls.

Her hands were too full to wave back, but she lifted the pretzels in acknowledgment and walked towards him. The night made her feel braver. This could be the time she actually talked to him, outside of class. She could start by asking him about modeling and the crows, and they'd stand there in the chilly fall night with the stadium lights like exploding stars. Maybe he'd come back and sit with her, leaning close as they watched the game.

But for a second, his gaze looked off. Gin glanced behind her and saw who Felix was actually looking at. Caitlin Taylor, a cheerleader, was smiling and waving enthusiastically at Felix.

He hadn't even noticed Gin.

Gin made a sharp left, up the hillside. She hugged her jacket around her as best as she could while still holding the sodas and pretzels. She didn't look at Felix again, not until she had made it to the bleachers. Then she glanced back once, long enough to see him standing close to Caitlin, laughing.

Her mouth was too dry to eat her pretzel, so she set it down on the metal bleacher and tried to watch the football game. She couldn't help noticing when Caitlin returned to the track to cheer, leaving Felix in the middle of a group of popular kids, all crowded around the chain-link fence along the field.

Everyone liked Felix. Which meant that the fact that he disarmed Gin, embarrassing though it was, actually made sense. After all, who wouldn't like him?

She took a small sip of Hannah's drink—already spiked—and gave a loud cheer.

The metal bleachers were frigid through Gin's jeans, and the floodlights had gone off, turning the field a muted, shadowy green. Hannah kept her eyes on the door to the locker room, and when it finally opened, she clattered down.

Gin watched as Hannah intercepted Aidan on his way to his car. He looked surprised, but interested, smiling as he answered Hannah's questions. Hannah held her paper and pen up in position, not writing a word.

Gin headed down the bleachers, through the almost empty parking lot to her car. Felix was long gone, but she couldn't help scanning the trees for crows.

Soon Hannah was at her side. "So, they're all going to Giovanni's." She glanced at herself in Gin's side mirror, pulling her hair from behind her ears. "And he wants me to come and interview him there." She held her fingers up to make quotes around the word "interview." "What do you think?"

Gin blew on her hands. "You're serious?"

Hannah reached around in her bag and pulled out a tube of lipstick. She smeared bright red on her lips, puckered once at Gin, and winked. "Of course I'm serious. And you need to come, too. This is the stuff that senior year is made of."

Gin considered her options. Go with Hannah to Giovanni's, or go home to work on . . . something. She reached for her phone to run *TimeKeeper*—after all, this was exactly why she had programs like *TimeKeeper*. But before Gin had even opened the program, Hannah grabbed her wrist.

"No way. Just listen for a second. Remember how much fun we had in junior high playing those mystery games?"

"Ugh." Gin closed her eyes, remembering. "We were such dorks."

"Well you know what they say about dorks—they make the best lovers. Anyway, you wrote a program to do it all, and we stopped. It ruined the game."

"It solved the game." It had been a program that

Gin had been particularly proud of: clean and simple, and it worked.

"It ruined the game. And that's what all of your programs are starting to do—ruin your life. So you're not running a program to decide. You choose. You, Regina Hartson. Pick."

Gin sighed, looking up at the dark sky. "I could work on my college essays."

"You've been working on those since the eighth grade."

For a second, Gin tried to quickly analyze the options. Then she looked back at Hannah, whose eyes were bright with excitement.

"All right," she said.

"Yay!" Hannah squealed. "Who knows, maybe this isn't even about me. Maybe your model's so smart, it's setting us up to meet *your* true love tonight."

In the car, Gin turned up the heat. It was only cold air, but it made it feel like something was building. She laughed to herself at Hannah's optimism. If there was one thing she knew for sure, it was that she was not going to meet her true love at Giovanni's.

// Ten

As they walked in, there was a blast of warmth from brick ovens, and the smell of melted cheese and basil. Kids were tucked into booths and jammed around the high-top tables, making it feel more like a frat party than a pizza place.

Aidan was easy to spot: he was at a pool table in the back with a few other football players. They all wore lightweight hoodies and worn but expensive jeans. Aidan's hair was cropped, his body built, his face model-handsome.

Hannah ordered sodas, easily chatting with the guy at the counter. She always had a way with guys, but that didn't seem to help her get a good one. Like Pete. Guitar-playing, pot-smoking, cute and grungy Pete. He was an artist and firmly believed it was natural to be constantly surrounded by "fans," who always happened to be girls. That should've been Hannah's first red flag. What Gin couldn't understand was how Hannah could be smart enough to make straight As without studying but not to pick a decent guy.

Maybe *Love Fractal* could help.

Aidan was finishing up his game when Hannah ambled up to his side. "How about we play a game?" she asked. "Loser buys the next pizza."

Aidan knocked the eight ball into the side pocket. "Sounds more fun than working on that article. But we play pool a lot—you sure you're up for this?"

"Yeah, we're sure." Hannah picked up a cue. "This is the stick you use, right?"

Aidan grinned. "Don't say you haven't been warned."

It only took a few minutes for Hannah to have Aidan's attention. She'd brush up against him as she bent over to aim and put a hand on his shoulder as she asked for his advice on harder shots.

Hannah was terrible at pool. But what Aidan hadn't expected was that Gin could help clean up. Because the one and only sport Gin was good at was pool. Her Dad, though far from being cool, loved pool for the geometry and physics involved, and he'd taught Gin and Chloe to play when they were young. It was a skill that was coming in handier the older she got.

By the end of the game, Aidan had lost any interest in how well Gin was playing and was focused on Hannah. Gin sunk the eight ball, but by then, Hannah and Aidan were talking, casually leaning so close they seemed moments away from kissing.

With nothing else to do, Gin started to set up the pool table again. But before she could break the balls, she felt someone behind her. "I'll take a few shots with you," he said. "If that's okay."

The voice was familiar, but it took a second to place with all of the chatter around her.

Felix.

He grabbed a cue and chalked it. "I was watching you play—you've got some skills. I think we'd be a good match. Here, you go first." He stepped back and held out an arm.

She broke the balls and called stripes, then hit three balls in, one after another, a quick succession.

"Not to be a downer, but you might lose this game," she said. Her ears burned immediately, and she wished for the thousandth time of her life that she could keep her mouth shut around guys. "I mean, not to be too forward or anything."

"Now that's something of an assumption." Felix's smile was easy. If he had been insulted, it didn't show. "How do you figure it?"

"I've pocketed three balls already. Even if I miss the next one—which is improbable since I have a decent shot—chances are, you'll miss at least one of your hits. Most likely two. Then it'll be back to me. On pure probabilities, I've got a good shot at winning." So much for keeping her mouth shut.

"You like probabilities, don't you?"

Gin stared at the pool table. "We live in a world of rules and logic. So why not like probabilities?"

"That's fair." Felix drummed his fingers. "I like probabilities, too. But I also like improbabilities."

Gin took her next shot, which went in. Then her purple stripe rolled just shy of the side pocket, and it was his turn.

"Phew," he said, chalking his cue again. "I was worried I wouldn't even get a chance."

He took out two solids in the first hit, then two more. His moves were focused and concise. Catlike.

Finally, he missed. She took a breath and planned her shots. She had a chance of taking it all, if she could stay focused.

She hit in the red eleven and blue ten first, splitting the balls and taking each corner pocket. "Nice," he said. He gave her a thumbs-up. "You are good. Glad I didn't bet any money."

A compliment. It was disarming.

"How'd you learn to play?" he asked.

"My dad. He's something of a scientist. He may not know how to heat up canned soup or keep track of his wallet, but he knows about angles."

Felix walked closer so he was standing at her side, then leaned over with his forearms on the table. "Good thing you've got your mom to keep it all together."

"Usually. But she's working full time and going to school this year. So, I get to heat up canned soup and find wallets on my own." She felt her face warm. "Sorry. I'll find my shot."

"No, don't be sorry." Felix was quiet for a second. "My mom stays busy, too, but with ridiculous stuff like spas and beach trips. And my dad likes to keep track of things a little too much. But canned soup and wallets have nothing on angles. What angle are you going for here? Seventy degrees to pocket the purple?"

"What else?" She got in position and hit. But she hit too fast, and the spinning purple stripe shimmied away from the pocket and flew along the green felt, too far to the left.

"Close," he said. And with a series of smooth, fast shots, he pocketed all of his balls, including the eight ball. He bowed forward slightly and held his right hand out for a conciliatory shake. "Nice game. And conversation. Maybe we can play another round?"

Gin started to reach out her hand, her fingers tingling at the thought of what it would be like to touch his broad palm, his knobby fingers.

But suddenly, Caitlin was there, laughing and wrapping one arm around Felix's shoulder. "No one can beat the Felix-meister." She squeezed her body closer to Felix and gave Gin a conciliatory wink. "But you're nice to be such a good sport."

Gin pulled her hand back fast and tucked her hair behind her ear, ignoring the clenching feeling in her stomach. "Any time."

As Caitlin tugged Felix off to a group at the corner, he managed to give Gin a small wave.

The restaurant suddenly felt too warm, too loud, and she headed for the door. Outside, she walked to the edge of the building—far enough to get away from the crowd but still in a safe and well-lit area. It was the suburbs of Washington, DC, after all. She leaned against the cool brick wall and watched cars zoom down the street and people funnel in and out of bars. A breeze blew, and she shivered.

She sat there for at least fifteen minutes, studying a patch of dark sky, annoyed at herself for not checking *TimeKeeper* before she came. Obviously, it would've been better if she had gone home. She started walking back, ready to tell Hannah she wanted to leave. Before going inside, she happened to look across the street.

There was a row of elm trees, their fall leaves shining yellow in the light of a streetlamp. And in the middle, directly under one tree, was Felix. Arms at his side, looking up.

Gin searched the tree branches, her heart beating faster. It was dark and hard to see from so far away, and at first, she was sure there was nothing.

But then a patch of leaves moved. Something was

in a branch above him. She stepped forward, eyes squinting. Then she saw it.

A crow.

It hopped twice and cocked its head, watching.

Her breath stopped, and she felt a shiver reach down into her stomach. And she decided, then and there, it had been enough waiting, enough mystery. She would cross the street and stand at Felix's side and ask what, exactly, the crows were all about. She took a deep breath and looked down the street for traffic.

But as she was about to start across, the door to the pizzeria opened, and a group of laughing teenagers filed out. Gin stepped back to the brick wall so they could pass. Then she looked back across the street.

Felix and the crow were gone.

Gin stopped the car in front of Hannah's house, as Hannah finished her monologue on what Aidan was like, the half-byte version being that he was "nice but too preppy."

"You do tend to go for the grungy deadbeats more," Gin said.

Hannah giggled, her lips pressed together, stifling a smile.

"Wait a minute." Gin turned, getting a better look at Hannah. "You like him, don't you?"

Hannah scrunched her nose. "I don't know. I don't think so. Let's just say I was mildly surprised. He wasn't bad." She wound a strand of her light hair around her finger. "Anyway, I better go—thanks again for the ride."

As Hannah walked in, Gin drummed her fingers on the steering wheel. Maybe somehow, at some level, *Love Fractal* was working. Which meant maybe there was a chance it'd work for Gin, too.

When Gin got home, she saw the email from Lucas. He had sent the program. All Gin had to do was run it.

She opened it and typed in the address of the first school's intranet. After a few long minutes, a little box flashed on the screen showing it was finished.

She downloaded the data file, took a deep breath, and clicked.

It was full—rows and rows of data on students' extracurriculars, class schedules, yearbook photos. Technically, it was all public information, but it would have taken her months to gather it without the program.

And this data was only from one school.

There was no way she was going to sleep now. She rubbed her hands together, outlining the data extraction steps in her mind: clean it, graph it, split it into test and training sets, then fit the model for some good cross-validation.

To do all of that would take the entire weekend, if she was fast, efficient, and somewhat lucky.

No, not lucky. That left too much to chance. Fast and efficient would be enough.

// Eleven

It smelled like pancakes. Which meant it was Sunday.

If there was one event hardcoded into *TimeKeeper*, it was Gin's dad's pancake breakfast every Sunday. Even though he could barely heat up a microwave dinner, he could somehow make pancakes.

Gin rubbed her eyes and stretched. She should shower. She couldn't remember the last time she had worked for that long. If it weren't for the pancakes, she wouldn't be sure it was Sunday.

Saturday felt like a dream. Gin had worked all day and most of the night, careful to go to sleep before her mom's shift ended in an effort to avoid another lecture.

But it had been worth it. She had run the data in different ways and had come up with thirty-two distinct groups of students. The final step was to figure out which groups were most compatible.

Then, when someone took the *Love Fractal*'s questionnaire, they'd be placed in a group. Algorithms would search through compatible groups, finding people with a facial structure similar to the participant's preferred look, and would present those as the top matches.

Gin's stomach rumbled, and she slipped downstairs, quiet as she passed her parents' room where her mom was still sleeping.

Her dad was sitting at the table in his white undershirt and pajama bottoms, his hair sticking up in tufts. He was writing furiously in a notebook, three plates with five pancakes each already on the table.

"Hi, Dad," she finally said.

He put the notebook down and looked up. "How's my Gin-Gin this morning?"

"Good." She started in on a wedge of the still-hot pancakes, the syrup thick and sweet. "How's whatever you're working on?" She was suddenly starving and wondered if she had even had dinner the night before.

"Fine, fine. It's all very nebulous right now. But I feel it forming. Like making pancakes. When the bubbles start to burst, and you know to flip. That's what it feels like."

"That's good, right?"

"Yes, definitely." He waved his fork in the air a few times as though it helped him think. "How about you—any bubbles bursting in your work?"

"Maybe. I'm making progress on this one program."

"Very good—what's it about?" He leaned forward, his eyes suddenly lit up.

The last thing Gin wanted to talk with her dad about was a dating program designed to help her find a boyfriend. "Just something for class. But I've been meaning to tell you, Ms. Sandlin paired me up with Felix Gartner. I think his dad is the head of Odin or something."

Her dad stopped mid-bite, the syrup dripping to his plate. "Grant Gartner?"

"That's him."

"I knew Grant Gartner had a son, but I didn't know he was your age. Is he a good modeler?"

"Yes. And he's smart. The weird thing is, I think he works with crows—like trains them or something." If she couldn't work up the courage to ask Felix about the crows, she could at least ask her dad.

"Hmmm, that's interesting. I feel like I remember something about Grant Gartner keeping a crow as a pet. I'd have to look it up."

"Maybe it's like a weird hobby?"

Her dad snorted. "If there's one thing I know about Grant Gartner, it's that he's a man who doesn't do hobbies. If he has crows, there's a purpose to them. But this boy—Francis?"

"Felix."

"Felix. Is he a good partner? A team player?"

"Yes, he's fine."

"Good." Her dad looked up, thinking. "Grant Gartner. Someone should study that man's mind. Somehow he always manages to be one step ahead of everyone else. Like today—there's another article here . . ."

He flipped through the paper and pointed to a story on the front page of the business section. *Odin unveils Amethyst 2.0.* Gin glanced through the article—it was all about Odin's latest steps to create a mobile phone that used quantum cryptography. Several companies had announced similar technologies months earlier, but somehow Odin beat them to the production line.

"Grant Gartner is the sort of man who gets what he wants. Who knows—his son might be, too." He rubbed his hands together. "More pancakes?"

She shook her head. She never wanted more pancakes. She'd only made it through a whole stack twice. Anyway, hearing her dad talk about the Gartners made her feel unsettled.

"I'm going to get back to work." He stood, patting his stomach. "That bubble is growing. And if I'm near my whiteboard, it just might pop."

Gin cleaned up, setting her mom's plate of pancakes at the side of the stove. Most likely, they wouldn't be eaten until dinner.

By early evening, Gin's head hurt. The new and improved *Love Fractal* was ready for testing. If she wanted, she could outline a testing protocol. But her brain was full. And she was tired of staring at her computer screen.

TimeKeeper's first recommendation was to go for a walk to clear her mind, but it was drizzly and cold. So she took recommendation two; she texted Hannah.

Hannah wrote back right away, saying she was about to meet Aidan at a coffee shop to "really interview" him this time—whatever that meant—and that she'd update Gin later.

There was nothing else to do. Gin tried a movie, but even that couldn't hold her attention. She was suddenly antsy, and she started scrolling through *Love Fractal*, scanning the code, glancing at the photos.

She clicked through the photos from her school, and it didn't take long to come across him. Felix. With his easy smile and shaggy hair.

And before Gin knew what she was doing, she had started the model.

Headshots popped up, and she rated them. Pleasant, pleasant, neutral, unpleasant. The questionnaire opened, and she answered the questions honestly as though she were seeing them for the first time.

Soon, the model was processing her answers. Thirty percent, fifty percent, ninety percent complete.

It felt like a dream, seeing the progress bar move along. Like she hadn't just run this program she'd worked on for so long, this program that would hopefully change her life.

And then, it was finished.

Finished. Results were waiting at the click of a button. Not just any results, but *her* results with the new, expanded, statistically significant data set. She hadn't planned on taking the test so soon. But she just had.

She bit her lip, hard. Her finger was poised above the mouse. One click, and she'd know.

She should wait to look. It'd be better to run the program on herself after the testing was finished. These results likely wouldn't be valid. Seeing them could even skew her efforts to finish the program.

Then again, maybe it wouldn't hurt anything. Maybe she *should* see her results. Maybe it would even help.

With a deep breath, she clicked.

And there, on her screen, were three photos. Three guys. And her heart dropped.

She stared at the photos, trying to figure out why she felt disappointed. To begin with, none were from Monroe, which wasn't a surprise now that she had data from nine local high schools. But somehow, she had hoped to know at least one.

And second, these guys weren't exactly what she'd hoped for. It was hard to put her finger on why. They sounded smart enough: one on math team, two in all honors classes. And they were relatively cute.

She looked harder at their photos, willing herself to feel something. A bit of attraction, maybe. But there was nothing, not even a spark.

Maybe that was normal. When Hannah first saw her matches, she had laughed. And now she liked Aidan. Once Gin spent some time with these guys, she might be surprised.

She closed the program and, without another thought, started reading ahead for physics.

A few chapters in, there was a knock at Gin's door, and her mom peeked in.

"I got ice cream. And was thinking of ordering that new movie—the one with Daniel Radcliffe. Want to watch? It's not *Harry Potter*, but it'll be fun."

Gin left her book open but pushed it to the end of her bed. Ice cream and a movie sounded surprisingly good.

"Okay. I guess I could use a break."

It wasn't until they were halfway through the movie, and Gin had eaten two bowls of ice cream that everything finally made sense: Gin wasn't disappointed because of how the guys looked or who they were.

It was about who they weren't.

None of them were Felix.

After school on Monday, Gin sat against the cool brick building, waiting for Hannah. It was one of those sharp, blue, late-October afternoons, when everything was shiny. The tips of bird wings, the pale limbs on trees, the chrome on cars. Students got on buses, sports teams jogged to the athletic fields, the marching band streamed out of the band room with flashing instruments.

"Hey." Hannah stood there, looking down. "You look lost in your thoughts. Or maybe just lost?"

Gin stood, brushing off her pants. "No, I'm good. Let's go."

"Actually, would you mind if I got a ride with Aidan? He has a break before practice and was going to show me this old music store in town. Apparently, he plays guitar."

Gin's mouth dropped. "No way. You mean, this is actually happening?"

Hannah tossed her hair and laughed. "Hard to say. There's something about him that's . . . attractive.

And I don't just mean he's cute, you know? But I still have Noah to think about. I'm taking this seriously. This is actual research."

"Okay, do your research. I've got to finish the model anyway. But if *Love Fractal* works, it'd be incredible." That was an understatement. A fully functioning dating model might be the thing that got Gin into Harvard, possibly with a scholarship so she could afford it.

Aidan walked out of the front doors, and Hannah squeezed Gin's hand. "All right, I'm outta here." Then she was off, headed towards Aidan, her face set to her casually interested look.

As Gin pulled her bag over her shoulder, an old, white 4Runner drove by, duct-taped and dented and totally out of place among the student body's fleet of Range Rovers and Audis.

Gin glanced up at the driver and couldn't help shaking her head. Leave it to Felix—the richest boy in school—to drive a clunker.

Felix looked in Gin's direction, and their eyes met for a second. He raised his eyebrows, as if saying hi, but she busied herself with her phone. When she finally looked back up, the car was gone.

// Twelve

It was Tuesday night, almost Thanksgiving break. Homecoming had come and gone and not surprisingly, no one had asked Gin to go. *Decider* helped her keep the dance in perspective—*Focus on the big picture now, and there will be time for fun later.*

Maybe by prom, she'd have hit it off with one of the guys from her results.

Hannah had gone to homecoming with Aidan. A casual date, nothing serious—which by Hannah's standards could definitely mean she was falling for him.

Outside, it was cold and gray, the best weather for studying, and Gin had resolved to stay holed up in her room. College applications weren't due for another month, but she wanted to have everything ready early. Between the applications and her computer simulations, it felt like most of her work was focused on a future life.

Which probably wouldn't be approved by crazy Mr. Ryan and his Ancient-but-not-obsolete Worldviews class. Not that he was actually crazy. Or that she disliked the class. She found it fascinating. Like the other day, as part of a unit on Asian history, they were talking about haiku, the sparse, 5-7-5 poetry invented by a Buddhist monk. It was all about using a few words to express a moment in time. Not past or future, but something in the present. Not the idea of an experience, but the experience itself.

Which was ironic since reading someone's haiku was reading his idea of the experience, but Gin didn't point that out.

Mr. Ryan had written one on the board in his yellow chalk:

Old Pond.
A frog jumps in—
Plop.

They had talked about the poem for a while in class. How it contrasted stillness and action. The frog as a sign of spring. What an old pond actually was. How it made them feel. Gin had raised her hand to point out that the words didn't fit the 5-7-5 pattern, to which Mr. Ryan reminded her that the poem was originally written in Japanese.

She YouTubed the poem when she got home and found an old video that started with a low frog ribbit, moved to a strange burst of swing music, then showcased a woman reading the poem in Japanese: Furu ike ya; kawazu tobikomu; mizu no oto. That was followed by sounds of water dripping as the English version of the poem was read in a low, toadish voice.

It was odd, but Gin couldn't help watching it a few times, whispering the words to herself. As though she were there at the side of the old pond, watching the frog leap in, hearing the sound of water.

TimeKeeper buzzed—time to reedit college essays—but before starting, she scratched something out on a piece of paper. It didn't have the right number of syllables, but she wasn't counting:

Raven black sky.
Night flutter of leaves.
Satellite soars.

// Thirteen

The sky was gray and the sun was low. It was the day after Thanksgiving and Gin still felt full from the pre-made turkey dinner her mom had heated up. Chloe hadn't come home, instead electing to video call from her boyfriend's house in Rhode Island, where she was spending break. At least, Gin's mom said, it was better than staying at the Alpha Phi house for the week.

For some reason after dinner, Gin decided to ride her bike. The old blue Schwinn was heavy and rusted but still functional. The wind kicked up as she left her neighborhood, and she almost turned back. But then it calmed, the sun nudging itself out from behind the cloud cover. Gin pedaled through neighborhoods and a wooded park, along sidewalks and winding paths, until she found herself at her old elementary school.

She rode up the grassy hill to the brick building and stopped at the top, the playground and wide field below her.

Her body was warm from the exertion, her breath exploding in iced puffs as she leaned over her handlebars. The dried grass was pale yellow and brown, and the ground was edged by shadows of bare oaks.

She stood, prepared to ride home, and that's when she noticed the flash of feathers.

Black. Soft in the sky. Catching the afternoon light. Pushing back the air, like smoothing a child's hair.

A crow.

Flying fast, up and around, as though it were flying with a purpose.

She scanned the sky, the field, and then she froze, mouth opened, unable to believe what she was looking at it.

Because down in the middle of the field, was Felix.

He looked smaller in the big open space. But still exactly like himself. Shaggy, gold-brown hair. Jeans, low on his hips. The bottom of a pale yellow t-shirt just visible under his forest green fleece. Instead of his sandals, he wore old tennis shoes. She had never seen him wear tennis shoes.

But the most amazing part was his focus. It was like every bit of his body was tense, ready. His feet firmly planted, back straight, one hand at his side and one held halfway up in the air. Eyes narrowed. Lips barely opened.

She followed his gaze—he was watching the crow. And when she saw what was happening, she gasped. Because the bird was coming right to him. It got closer and closer, and for a strange second, she worried that the bird was going to attack, to heave its body into Felix and pierce him with its thick beak.

But there was no attack. Instead, just as the crow was within reach, Felix stretched his right hand further up, and the bird flew to his fingers. As though it were completely ordinary to walk out to field, raise a hand, and have a bird fly down to you.

The crow stayed there, perched on Felix's right hand, totally, unimaginably relaxed. Felix moved the crow to his shoulder, then pet its head.

Gin bit her lip, gripped the handlebars harder. This—whatever it was—was what she'd been wanting to ask about. And it was *crazy*. Felix was strange, but in a popular, athletic sort of way. Not like this. To be out here with a crow sitting on his hand. Like an animal whisperer or circus act.

Felix squatted down, crow still on his shoulder, to a black mesh box near his feet. He opened it, reached in, and took out another crow.

With a crow on each hand, he held his arms up to the sky and whistled. Immediately, both crows took off, flying a long wide arc to the right, around the field. Wings easing up and back, up and back. Black bodies like holes in the sky.

It was beautiful. Why had she never watched birds like this before? After reaching the end of the field, the crows angled back and flew towards him, making a loop.

He turned, following the crows' flight, and that's when he saw her. Her heart beat fast, her face turned bright red, like a flag, and all she wanted to do was leave.

The birds flew so close overhead she swore she felt the rustle of their feathers, and Felix raised his hand, almost tentative—if anything Felix did could be considered tentative—to wave. And then, he smiled.

She couldn't help it. Her hand shot up in a wave, and before she knew it, she was riding towards him.

As though everything in the universe had set itself up to create this moment: her flying downhill, bumping over the wintry dirt, bike jolting beneath her, and him standing there, a crow on each shoulder.

She pulled her brakes hard, the thin pads rubbing the steel rims, and put her left foot down while staying on the bike. She tried to act as though it were comfortable standing like that—body leaned over the bike frame, arms rested on the handlebars, everything balanced on one foot—when in reality, it felt extremely awkward.

"Hey." There was no silliness or charm in his voice. He sounded nice.

"Hey." The quiet wrapped around them for a second. This field, tucked away from busy roads and surrounded by trees, felt as still as the Old Pond. And Gin felt like the frog, poised to jump.

"So . . . you like crows?" It was not at all how she had planned to broach the topic.

The smile hit his eyes first, then the corners of his lips angled up, those lips that were somehow always slightly puckered. And he grinned.

He crossed his arms and in that second, with a crow on each shoulder, he looked like some strange medieval prince. Or a king. Someone from an old Norse legend, who ran around with crows and wolves and conquered lands with his bare hands.

She breathed in deep, and it smelled like wet ground and geese and gray skies.

"Yes, I like crows." His answer didn't sound silly or condescending but seemed genuine. "Actually, I train them. Want to see?"

She tried to consider the offer, to tease out what *Decider* would say. *Situation: In a strange field with a strange boy and his trained crows. Decision: Stay or go?* But instead, she set her bike down on the ground. The bike's left pedal sunk slightly in the dirt and her pants scraped along the chain ring, leaving a narrow smear of grease, but it didn't even bother her.

She stood by Felix's side, close enough to see what he was doing, but not too close to scare the crows. Because she was certain she would scare them. They were right there on his shoulders, and she was so near, she could reach out and touch them. Glossy bodies like bundles of energy. Stocky with compact muscles. Onyx eyes that blended in with their midnight feathers but caught the light and shone.

The crow closest to her tilted its head to the right and held Gin's gaze.

"This is Maggie." Felix pointed to the bird that was watching Gin. "And this is Frederick." He pronounced it "Free-derick."

"Maggie and Free-derick," she repeated. "Good to meet you both."

"They were doing some simple flights. But we're about to practice retrieval. It'll only take a few minutes. Ready?"

At first, she thought he was talking to the birds, but

his eyes, with their flecks of green and gold, were still locked on hers. "Ready."

He straightened his body and touched each bird on the head. They immediately stilled. He whistled two low tones—*Phee-Phaa*—and the birds were off. Wings beating fast, moving them farther and farther away, until they had disappeared over the trees at the far edge of the field.

There was a breeze, soft and cool, and Gin pulled her sweatshirt around her tighter. Her nose felt iced, and her hands ached. A plane flew across the sky and for a second, she imagined the rows of people tucked neatly inside, watching movies and sipping sodas. No idea they were flying over a boy training crows.

She waited a second longer and turned back to Felix. His eyes were set on the horizon.

"Are they supposed to disappear like that?" she asked.

He moved a little closer. "Are you worried?"

Her face flushed, and she felt the muscles in her body tighten. "No, not worried. Just curious."

He stepped closer again, so he was standing right next to her, their feet and legs and hips inches apart, and watched the sky. "They'll be back. They're both old pros at this." He looked back at her, eyebrows furrowed. "You must think it's really strange?"

It *was* strange. But instead of telling him that, she just shrugged.

"My dad travels a lot for work," he continued. "And my mom has her own stuff going on. So I've always had copious free time. So much free time, I learned to work words like 'copious' into sentences. And I worked with the crows. It's kind of a family thing. My dad trains them, too. He started it all. Frederick is almost as old as I am." He stopped talking and pulled his hand through his hair. "But that's a lot of information I'm sure you don't care about."

"No, I don't mind, it's interesting."

"Interesting. I like that." He looked at her closer and reached a hand out. For a full second, she had no idea what he was about to do. And suddenly, his hand was on her cheek.

It felt like every sensor in her body had pooled in that one spot. A jolt ran through her, as though his touch had reached down to squeeze her stomach and tighten her throat. She could barely breathe. She couldn't move. Like her brain had stopped processing.

He pulled his hand away. "Got it. Mud splatter. That's what you get for biking down a wet hill."

She put her hand to her face and felt the heat still there. "Thanks."

"And here they come," he said.

She turned to watch, the sleeve of her jacket brushing against his.

The crows were flying straight for Felix, their bodies dipping and rising with each stretch and release of their wings. Contractions, like a heartbeat. In a bustle of movement, they were there.

Gin stepped back and lifted her face up, feeling the wind from their wings. In another second, the crows were perched on Felix's shoulders.

Felix held his hands up in front of the birds, and they both dropped something from their beaks.

"See?" He opened his palms flat to show two small blue bells.

Gin picked one up, felt the cool metal in her hand. She shook it, but it didn't make a sound. "Magic bells that only birds can hear?"

"Just broken. So they don't ring. The birds like them for the shine and the color. And believe it or not, different colors can mean different things." He jammed his hands in his pockets.

She liked how it felt, standing there with him, crows perched on shoulders and all.

"That's amazing. I didn't know anyone could do this. I mean, training crows? Where do you even start?"

He laughed. "Where you start everything: at the beginning. Want to see some more?"

And before she could answer, he whistled again, the crows taking off in a dark, cool wind.

The sun had nearly set, leaving the sky gold-blue at the horizon and navy above. The first planets were popping out, turned on by the darkening air. Rogue wisps of cloud, pink just minutes before, were fading to charcoal.

The crows had worked for more than an hour. Gin's nose was nearly frozen, and she kept squeezing her hands to keep them warm. She should go. But she didn't want to.

"I love your Pata-Gucci, by the way," she said. It was meant as a joke—Hannah was always calling Patagonia "Pata-Gucci," and it was funny when she did. But from Gin, it seemed to fall flat.

"What, this?" Felix pulled at the bottom of his fleece. "You must be cold. You want it?" Before she could protest, he was pulling off the fleece and holding it out to her.

"No, I was joking. You know. Patagonia's so expensive and all. It was a bad joke. Put it back on—I'm cold just looking at you."

"Really, I don't want it. I only need one fleece, and my crazy mom who buys all this stuff just got me another. Don't ask me why she buys Patagonia. I guess so I can fit in with the cool kids. You know, every mother's dream?"

It was funny. Thinking about him having to wear something to be cool.

The fleece was flying in the air, towards her. Before she could plan an appropriate reaction, her hands went up, and she caught it. She held it to her face, warming herself, and couldn't help breathing in the smell of him.

"You'll be cold." She said it quietly, suddenly wanting to keep the fleece. It *was* warm.

He shook his head. "No way. It's good for me. It builds up endurance for the elements. You know, like how they go from hot tubs to snow fields in Sweden. Seriously, the fleece is yours. If you try to give it back now, I'll leave it on the field for some dog or kinder-gartener to find."

She pulled the fleece over her head, wondering what all of this was. The talking. The fleece. The crows on his shoulders—Beatrix and Rufus now. She swam in his fleece, even with all of her layers. But she was definitely warmer. In the process of pulling it on, she lost the rubber band holding her ponytail. When she couldn't find it on the shadowy ground, she pulled her hands through her hair, shaking it out.

She caught him watching her, and when their eyes met, he smiled. "You look warmer already. You wear it well."

She flushed at the compliment and turned to watch a group of starlings settle into the oak trees around them. Chattering and chirping. Beatrix and Rufus seemed to watch, too, cocking their heads one way then another. It smelled like night.

"All right, buddies." Felix's voice was soft and kind, like he was talking to a baby. "Time to go home. Good work today."

He put the two crows in the box with Maggie and Frederick, secured the Velcro tabs, and gingerly picked it up. The birds rustled inside but didn't com-plain.

"Can I give you a ride?" he asked.

She almost said yes. She wanted to—to sit in his car, with the crows, with him. But there was the matter of her bike. And the fact that he wasn't in her results. And the reality that she'd likely never be in his.

Maybe in some alternate universe it could work.

One where she wasn't so smart and quirky and he wasn't so cool and easygoing.

"No," she said. "I'm good."

"All right. Well, be safe. Good to see you, Gin." He smiled, and the last bits of light hung on his cheeks and his teeth and his eyes.

She turned and picked up her bike, forcing herself to look away. "You too."

He started up the hill, then paused. "Oh, and, about the crows. Most people have no idea what I do with my spare time. And it might help me out if we kept it that way, you know?"

She did kind of know. And she wasn't about to go tell everyone about this afternoon. Except maybe Hannah. But how could she explain any of this? It'd be like trying to describe the ocean to someone who had never been. How waves rose and crashed. The sand and salt and wind. Whipping your hair, stinging your eyes, sticking to your mouth.

"So you like crows," she said. "No big deal, right? Nothing that anyone else would even care about."

"Thanks." He grinned, the sort of smile that was impossible not to return. "See you at school."

She watched for a second as he walked towards the parking lot, which was still empty except for his car. That old, beat up 4Runner, tucked in the corner of the expansive blacktop.

Then she pushed her bike forward, and after two steps, she was up, pedaling hard, pedaling home.

// Fourteen

Mr. Ryan stood at the blackboard, rolling a piece of chalk between his fingers. Gin had grown to like the chalk—the sound of words knocking on the board, the soft swish of the eraser, the bits of yellow dust everywhere.

He turned back to the class. "Anyone?"

As always, he had written the quote in the upper right corner. "*What is the sound of one hand clapping?*" —*Zen Koan.*

Gin typed it in her notes. But she wasn't thinking about one hand, or clapping, or class. She was thinking about Felix and the crows.

Gin had told Hannah everything. Saying it out loud made it seem even more odd. But Hannah pointed out that all rich people were somewhat strange—who else had time for something like training crows?

Gin had wanted to ask Felix more about it at school, but modeling class had been busy with lectures and anyway, he had more or less asked her not to talk about it. And the crows felt almost sacred, like if she brought them up at school, she'd be ruining whatever had happened on that field. So she didn't bring them up.

Instead, she filled up every crevice in her schedule with researching crows. She watched videos, read scientific studies, even ordered books about the birds. She did all of that while also wearing Felix's fleece. The bit about the fleece had put Hannah over the edge—"He likes you, it's so obvious," she had said.

But to Gin, nothing was obvious. She didn't want to get her hopes up when there was nothing but circumstantial evidence.

Anyway, crows were fascinating. Like how they could do complex cognitive tasks. Or how they worked together to hunt. Or how they mourned when another crow died. That last one was really strange. If one crow, say, got hit by a car and died, then dozens of other crows would gather around the body. They'd stay for a moment, silent. And eventually, they'd caw together and fly away. Like a tribute. There was probably a more scientific explanation—maybe they were taking note of the death to increase their own chances of survival. But every person who had witnessed a "crow funeral" swore there was something deeper going on.

Gin started seeing crows everywhere. The crow that flew over her house each night. The group of crows that hung out near the school's dumpsters. Crows settling into trees or hopping down sidewalks or flapping up to street signs and peering down at her.

She also read through dozens of articles about Grant Gartner—his inventions, his businesses, his charitable efforts. In only one article did he mention crows. It was an interview from twelve years earlier with a small, local newspaper, and when asked what he did for fun, Grant Gartner said that he trained crows. "Who knows," he had said at the end, "maybe their skills will come in handy one day."

It was that statement that stuck with Gin, rolling over and over in her mind. The crows were obviously well trained. Maybe they were being used for something. The question was what.

"Come on, class. Take a guess." Mr. Ryan looked to one side of the class, then the other, waiting.

Gin stared back at the quote. One hand clapping was a non-existent sound. Like drumming without a drum. The sound of air, which was like waves of sound, like light. Maybe the sound of one hand clapping was a bright, yellow light. Or the sound of someone's thoughts. Or . . .

A few students volunteered answers and Mr. Ryan nodded at each one. Finally, when the class's ideas were exhausted, he held a hand out. "The sound of one hand clapping," he said as he waved his lone hand in the air.

The class laughed. And Gin held her hand under her desk, opening and closing it, slowly.

In modeling class, they got their next assignment. This model would be due the week before winter break, which meant they had exactly two weeks to build it. It was a fun one, Ms. Sandlin said, because it was all about predicting something very hard to predict—weather.

"Don't worry, even the experts can't get this one right," she said after a few kids groaned. "You'll be judged on your logic, creativity, and effort, as always."

They only had a few minutes to talk about it. Gin

stared at her computer, suddenly nervous. She had barely talked with Felix after that day on the field. He was always so easygoing, and despite that—or maybe because of it—she seemed to clam up around him.

"So, maybe we should meet and work on this one?" Felix tapped his pencil on his open notebook. Gin could see the sum total of his notes from the day: the erf function, the molecular structure of a catenane, and a note to look up 'purple frogs.' "I've never even attempted to model weather. Unless you've already done it. Then we can totally work separately."

"No, I haven't," she said too quickly. "We should meet. Maybe the library after school?"

"The library doesn't sound very weather-conducive."

"So what are you thinking—like a lab at NOAA? I don't know anyone there, but maybe you have an in?"

He tucked his pencil behind his ear and looked at her, *really* looked at her. She felt herself blushing, but she didn't look away.

"I just meant that maybe we could meet somewhere we actually experience weather." He motioned towards the window, where trees were shifting in the breeze. "You know, wind and water, sun and sky."

It almost sounded like a date. "Sure. Like where? The library has good windows."

He smiled, wide. "You know, this afternoon's actually going to be warm. How about the river?"

"The river? What, like the Potomac?"

He closed his notebook and sat up straighter, energized. "Exactly. There's a park near the Roosevelt

Bridge, with a little pull off by the river. Let's meet there after school, near the boat ramp."

Gin knew exactly which park he was talking about—she had gone there last summer once with Hannah and Pete. It was a cool place. And maybe he was right. Maybe the best way to model weather was to start by experiencing it. Like graphing data, but in a sensory way.

The bell rang, and Felix was still sitting there, eyebrows raised, waiting.

"That works."

Felix tapped his notebook on the desk. "Sweet." He stood and leaned over slightly so he was closer to her. It was overwhelming, like she could feel the energy rolling off of him.

"All right." She closed her laptop and added the event to her phone. "See you at 3:30."

But Gin didn't get there right at 3:30. Traffic was heavy, and by the time she reached the parking lot, it was almost four. She got out of her car and squinted in the sun. The water glinted, thousands of small waves rippling blue, and a breeze pulled at her hair. Across the river, she could see the white Capitol dome, and further back, the Washington Monument, stately and smooth.

Felix's car was parked to one side, but Felix was nowhere to be seen. In fact, no one was there.

She glanced around the parking lot again and walked to the river's edge. It smelled vaguely like fish and mud. Little waves lapped against the concrete boat ramp, one after another, and she squatted down and touched the water. It was icy cold.

Something flashed way out on the river and she stood up for a better look. A windsurfer was bobbing in the waves. She could see the white and blue sail, the metal bar gleaming in the sun. The rider wore a full-body wet suit and leaned back, legs slightly bent, arms strong.

A slight shift in the board's sail set it off, skimming across the water, cutting through the choppier waves. Beautiful.

And somehow—maybe it was from the rider's easy stance, or the wet curls against his neck—she realized it was Felix. It made her catch her breath. He zipped along the water, then slowed and looked back to shore. That's when he noticed her and waved. She waved back, and before her hand was down at her side, he was angling the board to zigzag back to shore.

Once he was close, he hopped into the water and waded up the boat ramp, resting the board's sail down on the grassy bank and squeezing the water out of his hair. "Hey. Glad you made it. Give me one sec, okay?" he said, bounding off to his car.

Within seconds, he was back, wearing a black puffy jacket and flip-flops, still-wet hair curling out from under an indigo beanie. He was holding his note-book, a chocolate bar, and a towel.

"I figured you got stuck in traffic. So I got out on the water for a second. Conditions are great." He took a bite of the chocolate and held it out to her. "Want some?"

She shook her head: *HungerStriker* had recommended a granola bar before she left school, and she was still full. And nervous.

He finished eating and wiped his hands together. "If you want, I can take you on the water. I have an extra wet suit."

For a second, she could imagine it—being out there in the wind, speeding along the glittery river. "Nah," she said. "It looks cold. And isn't the water . . . dirty?"

"It's not bad, really. The wet suit keeps you warm, and as long as you shower when you're done, you're fine." He laid the towel out on the concrete boat ramp, and sat on one side of it, cross-legged. "Here, want to sit?"

She sat next to him, the concrete cold even through the towel, and hugged her knees to her chest.

"It's crazy to think about it, isn't it?" He was staring out at the river, and they sat there for a moment, in the quiet.

"What?" she asked after it was clear he wasn't going to say more.

"Oh, you know . . . this. The weather stuff we're supposed to model. It seems kind of impossible. To try to build something that accounts for all of it: all of these drops of water and atoms of oxygen and energy from the sun."

Gin pressed her face into her knees for warmth. Even with the sun on her back, the wind was chilly.

"But then, being out there, it hit me." He was leaning back, his elbows resting on the boat ramp, feet crossed and almost touching the water. "The trick is to make it overly simple."

The wind stilled. With the water and the sun and Felix so close, what was impossible was the act of thinking.

"So how'd you get into it?" she asked.

"What, windsurfing?"

"Well, yeah, that too. But I meant modeling. Did you do it at your last school?"

Felix sat up and stretched his arms overhead. "Ahh, modeling. Guess we must be pretty weird to love predicting the unpredictable, right?" He smiled at Gin, and she met his gaze for a moment, then stared at the water and took a deep breath. "I think it was my dad who first got me into writing code. I was maybe four."

"Four?"

"Yeah, is that young? Maybe I was five. It was normal at our house. I guess anything seems normal when you're little."

A seagull floated near them, banking hard to the left to catch a breeze. Felix picked up a handful of pebbles and threw them, one by one, into the river. The breeze ruffled his drying hair.

"I started with basic code, lots of 'if-then' logic, and moved on to making models for fun. Things like whether my dad would be mean or nice when he got home from a business trip, or whether my mom would extend her vacation at the spa." He looked at her and shrugged. "It was all kind of a joke. Then Dad got me a tutor—"

"You had a tutor? Like a once a week thing?"

He found a smooth rock and skipped it across the water. Seven hits. "No. The other type. The type that teaches you Latin and classical literature and physics and calculus, all when you're ten." He turned to his side, propped up on one arm, facing her. His body was fully relaxed. She kept her arms tight around her knees. "I was at this weird point where the private school saw I had potential, and my dad wanted to maximize it. Just like his portfolio. Take something good and make it the best." At the word "best," he pumped his hand in the air for emphasis. "It worked for a few years, and then I got sick of it. So back to private school I went."

"That sounds kind of . . . miserable."

"At the time it was. To realize that I could never, ever live up to my dad's expectations." He looked back out at the river, his face serious. "But once I really got that, it was like the whole world opened up. Total freedom. Because I didn't have to care about him anymore, you know?"

He pulled off his beanie and shook out his hair, bits of water flying in all directions.

"So what about the modeling part?" Gin finally asked.

"Oh right," he said. "Modeling. That was the best part of the tutor. He taught me a bunch of it.

Eventually I started doing more complicated work. And it just grew from there."

He sat up and scooted towards Gin. "Anyway, enough of my story. How about you?"

Gin picked up a stick and touched it to the water. "Oh, you know. Father who's a crazy computer scientist, the type who creates programs to teach his daughters everything from reading to how to find the right school bus home. Mother who's a nurse at the ER and keeps everything together at home."

He cocked his head, eyes serious. "Yeah? That's kind of cool. Where's your dad do his research?"

A knot formed in her stomach. If she was going to tell Felix that his dad had messed up her dad's life, this was her chance. "Some think tank group. Actually, one that your dad owns. My dad works on apps. *Streamliner* is his big one."

"Whoa, no way. *Streamliner*? My dad loves that thing. I swear, he's said like three times that it's incredible. Which, from him, is basically giving it a Nobel prize."

"It changed a lot of people's lives. Just not ours. Since my dad was a company employee, it's not like it made us rich. If he'd been out on his own, we'd be living the high life. You know, fancy house, maids, crazy trips . . ." She glanced at Felix, embarrassed to realize she was probably describing his life.

He leaned back on his hands, legs stretched out before him, feet nearly touching the water. "Oh yeah, I know all about that. But I wouldn't necessarily call it the high life. More of the distracted life. Anyway, I want to hear about your mom, too. What hospital does she work at? I've had a few emergencies—split chin in third grade, broken arm in fifth, a few near-disasters in junior high. Maybe she patched me up."

"Arlington General."

"Never been there. But now I know who to call the next time I decide to take my skateboard down the steps at the Capitol." He nudged her with his shoulder. A quick touch, but enough to make her catch her breath. "With all that logic, you were practically fated for predicting the future."

The wind was picking up again, and the sun slipped behind a cloud, making everything darker for a second. When it popped back out, it was so bright she had to squint.

"I don't know about that. My sister Chloe's not a modeler. She's more of a professional partier. And it's different now—Chloe's at college, and my mom's working or studying all the time."

It was the most she'd said about her family to anyone—even Hannah—for a long time.

"That's fair. And trust me, I'm the first to say things often aren't as good as they seem." His eyes were lit up in the sun, and for a minute, the only sound was the water pushing against the bank.

Finally, he rubbed his hands together. "Anyway, as for windsurfing, which you kind of asked about, and which I love to talk about—I got into that a few years ago. My friend was learning, so I tried it. When I got out on the water and felt the wind tense on the sail, it was incredible. I never looked back."

"That's cool." It had been cool watching him out there. She could imagine that it felt even better. "So you like to write computer models, to windsurf, and to train crows."

"Guess that pretty much covers it." He looked up at the sky, breathing deep. "So about this model—I feel inspired after being out here. What about you?"

"Water, sun, wind, land. I guess I have the basics." In a small way, it was a start. Maybe she could put numbers and assumptions to the whip of wind, or the darkening sky, or the coolness of the air.

"Good. Let's meet again soon, maybe at my house? But if we're good for today, I think I'll get back out on the water. You sure you don't want to try?"

She shook her head. "Next time." The sun was a little lower now, and when she stood up, her shadow was long, reaching out into the river.

"I'll hold you to it."

Felix pushed his board back in the river as she walked to her car. She sat inside and put the keys in but didn't turn the ignition. Instead, she watched. How he ran out into the water, and swam, one arm on his board. How he climbed up, his wet suit dripping, and tugged the sail in close, closer until he had caught the wind.

To catch the wind. It sounded impossible. But it was beautiful.

// Fifteen

If Gin had had any doubts that Felix was rich, they were now gone.

The day after their "work session" at the river, she had agreed to meet Felix at his house. Which meant first driving through the rolling, wealthy woods of Great Falls, Virginia, where old trees spread their branches, and everything had a hefty price tag. The Gartner estate was likely the priciest, with its immense brick wall and iron gate that Gin had to be buzzed into. The house itself was massive and modern, made of steel and rock and wood and glass. The living room, which was the size of a small home itself, had window walls and stretches of smooth leather couches and low, empty tables.

When the maid had shown her in, she kept looking for signs of something strange—bird cages or rows of blue bells. But the house was so nice, so put together, it looked like something from a magazine. It didn't look like anyone—much less someone who trained crows—lived there.

Gin and Felix were supposed to be working on the weather model. But so far, they hadn't even broached the topic—all they'd done was sit in the living room. Or rather, Gin sat, and Felix lounged. Laying back on the couch, one long leg off the side, the other bent up. His flip-flops were off, his hands were behind his head, and his shirt was hiked up just enough to show a thin line of his stomach.

A cloud passed by, blocking the sun and darkening

the living room, and Gin thought cloud cover was as good a place to start as any. She was about to tell Felix, when he spoke.

"So, Gin, what do you want?" His eyes were still closed, body still fully reclined.

"What do I want?" All thoughts of cloud cover vanished.

He opened his eyes to look at her once, then promptly closed them. "Yeah. What do you *really* want?"

"Now? In life? For the next twenty years?"

He smiled wider. "Just, whenever."

Gin bit her lip and rubbed her forehead. What *did* she want? The question settled in her, weighty for a second. Until she remembered she knew exactly what she wanted. "I want us to finish up our model. So I—we—can do well in this class. And then I can go to Harvard."

"Harvard, that seems right. Smart school for a smart girl. You know, my dad went to Harvard, and sometimes interviews prospective students. If you want, I could see if he could help."

Gin's mouth dropped open—she had never expected Grant Gartner would have the time to even consider helping someone like her. "Really? That'd be great." It was more than great. Even though she was smart, getting into a school like Harvard demanded more than smart—you had to be special, and most likely, to have connections.

"So, Harvard . . ." Felix's eyes were still closed, his lips smiling. "And then what?"

"Get a good job," she said. "Work on computer models, ones that are good and make a difference. And make money. You know, the normal stuff."

He turned to his side and looked at her. "I don't believe you."

She sat taller, hands on her knees, feeling suddenly indignant. "What, that I want to work on models? Because that's been my dream since I was, like, five. Or that I need money? Because I can show you my bank account. And there's not much in it."

He pushed himself up and pulled one knee to his chest, setting his chin on it. "No, I just don't believe that's *all* you want."

She narrowed her eyes, her body tightening with annoyance. "I guess it'd be nice if I didn't have to worry about any of it." She could feel the heat build in her face. "If I could float through life, riding yachts and vacationing in Europe."

"Okay, that's fair." He stretched his arms out in front of him and sat up straighter. "And you're right, money is important. But the thing is, a lot of time, too much of it makes people less happy. Take my father's friends, for instance, who have loads of money and end up stressing about which plane to buy or whether their private beach will erode an inch."

He was focused now, body tensed. Obviously, this was important to him, but he was sounding like an arrogant jerk.

"That's not the same as someone struggling to pay their bills or buy shoes for their kids," she said. This was another side of Felix she hadn't seen—the privileged, out-of-touch-with-reality side—and she didn't like it.

"No, totally not the same. You're right. It's all . . . relative." He rubbed his chin, thinking. "Sometimes it feels like everyone thinks being rich is the same as being happy. And it's not. Here, I want to read you something."

He leapt to his feet and took three long strides to one of the built-in cabinets on the back wall. He ran his finger along the book spines, pulling a large, black book off the shelf.

"The Bible?" Gin asked.

"Precisely. Don't worry, I'm not about to preach. It's just one of the best documented, really old books out there. And there's this story in here." He flipped through, fast, until he was about halfway in.

Then he leaned back on the couch and held the book up, his long arms resting against his legs. He glanced up at Gin, cocked one eyebrow, and started to read.

"'The words of the Teacher, son of David, king in Jerusalem.'" He looked back at Gin and shrugged. "Just the intro, you know? Anyway. 'Meaningless! Meaningless!' says the Teacher. 'Utterly meaningless! Everything is meaningless.' What does man gain from all his labor at which he toils under the sun? . . .'"

At first, she wanted to roll her eyes. But then she started watching him. How his long eyelashes swooped out over his cheeks. How his wide hands almost engulfed the book.

She had heard the story before, she thought. This

man, a king, had everything in the world that anyone could possibly want. Gold and jewels, women, rich food, satisfying work, palaces. He made it his mission to try all of it and see what fulfilled him. But nothing was good enough.

After reading for ten minutes, Felix stopped and looked at her, apologetic. "I'm boring you, right?"

She squeezed her eyes shut, stretched her arms up, and made herself focus. "No. Definitely not boring." She opened her eyes and glanced at Felix.

He grinned, and she felt her face flush, but she held his gaze for a few seconds longer. Then he closed the book and tossed it on the table.

"You get it, right? This guy goes after everything that can possibly make him happy. And none of it is enough."

A clock chimed, low and quiet, somewhere in the hall.

"Nothing, at least when it comes to stuff, is ever enough. For anyone." Felix leaned forward, his eyes bright with intensity. "I mean, the *Bible* tells us that. And everything else we do reinforces it. So you can keep chasing it—getting more and more stuff, like cars and accomplishments and bits of paper." He reached in his back pocket, pulled out four $50 bills, and waved them in the air. "Or you can be different. Like, in the present. Figure out what really matters. That's part of why I build models. To remember that there's no point trying to figure out the future. Because you'll never get it right. What matters is this moment. Right now. The only place you can be."

He sunk back into the couch and propped his feet up on the coffee table. "So now, Gin, I ask you again. What do you want?

Sunlight hit his eyes, playing the colors off each other—cedar and grass and plains and lakes.

And before she could change her mind, take back her choice and ask for something more clever, more substantial, she said it. "An orange soda."

He clapped his hands together and jumped up to his feet. "Yes! That's good. And that, we can do. Let's go."

Felix's house backed up to the woods, with a large, wraparound porch that, like the living room, was spacious enough to be a small house itself. There were well-placed fire pits, a tasteful stone bar, and modern-looking lounge chairs and swings.

Gin had given up on even thinking about the model and watched the woods instead. Birds flitted among the branches and rustled down in the piles of brown leaves. The sky was clear, a late-afternoon wintry blue. The air was crisp on her cheeks and smelled like wood fires and snow. She had a sudden and clear memory from when she was in kindergarten, of squatting down at the edge of a creek and poking a stick into the mud, hands icy cold because she had left her mittens at home.

A group of geese flew past, their easy arrow shape

high overhead, and she took a sip of her soda—a fancy tangerine one, with natural sugar and a pretty glass bottle.

"Lifestyle of the rich and famous." Felix held his arms out, then let his hands dangle over the rail. His body was a couple feet from hers, but it felt close in the vast woods. "Where you can buy beautiful vistas and enjoy them all alone."

"Or with your very own modeling friend," she said.

He laughed. "We should add that to the neighborhood's brochure. Enjoy these views with your high school honors class modeling buddy."

The sun lowered, buttering the woods below and pulling a hazy pink glow up above the treetops. Swallows swooped. Somewhere further away, crows cawed.

"Hear them?" Felix asked.

Suddenly Gin understood. She wasn't hearing a group of random crows in a tree somewhere, but Felix's crows. The ones he had trained.

"I can introduce you, if you'd like?" His eyes were expectant, his face hopeful.

She had millions of questions about the crows—what exactly could they do? Why was Felix's dad training them? Were they actually just a hobby?

"Okay." The word bubbled up through her.

And he took her hand and pulled her away, playful. As they started to walk, he didn't let go.

Her insides welled up, and her mouth was suddenly dry. She chewed on her bottom lip, breathing deep to steady herself. It felt electric, Felix's hand holding hers. His hand was nice. Solid and strong. Calloused along the inside of his thumb. Warm. This hand that wrote models and trained crows and tamed the wind with a windsurfing sail.

They were walking back toward the side of the porch, down the steps, and into the yard. And as much as she wanted to see the crows, she didn't want their walk to end.

Something shifted. A cloud slid over the sun, darkening the woods, and there was the soft hum of an engine.

Felix let got of her hand and walked back around the porch to the side of the house. Her hand felt too cold, and she tucked it into the pocket of her sweater.

He came back, his face pale, worried.

"Sorry," he said. "My dad's here. And he's kind of funny about guests. I'll have to show you the crows another time."

"It's okay. I should get going anyway." She said the words quickly as if convincing herself.

"But we still have to finish our model." Felix's voice was soft as though his dad could hear them. "We'll make sure that happens. Soon. And the crows, they want to see you, too."

There was a flicker of an apology in his gaze.

He led her to the side gate and she slipped out, walking along the brick walkway to her car. Ahead of her, the trees at the horizon were black silhouettes on the pale sky. She opened her car door and glanced back at the brightly lit house, where she could see Felix entering the living room.

She closed the door with a thud, and put her hand—the hand he had just held—to her mouth. She closed her eyes and breathed in deep. Then she turned the ignition. Her headlights carved out a clear path in the quiet night, and she followed it home.

// Sixteen

Rain beat against Gin's bedroom window in waves. Her homework was finished, except for one more exercise for Ancient Worldviews. Meditation.

Everyone in the class had to meditate—or sit still and try not to think, whatever they wanted to call it—every day until winter break. The class had groaned when they heard the assignment, but Mr. Ryan promised it'd be easy. After the week, they'd write a few paragraphs about the experience.

"Regular meditation," he had said, "changes you."

It was only fifteen minutes a day. Akin to exercise for the brain. A few months ago, Gin could've done the assignment without a second thought.

But now, it was nearly impossible. Granted, she had a lot to think about—college applications, Ms. Sandlin's computer simulations class, *Love Fractal*, school. But the hardest thing to stop thinking about was Felix.

She'd start the meditation off well enough. Maybe a line of code or a sentence for her college essays would drift through her mind, all easily set aside.

And then, Felix would appear. It probably didn't help that she was wearing his fleece. But each time he popped into her mind, it was so vivid. His pretty lips. The back of his neck. His beaded necklace. The crows.

And once he was there, in her brain, stretching through her chest and into her fingertips and toes, it was impossible to get him out. It was like another one of Mr. Ryan's practices. One cold afternoon, they had sat outside on the empty metal bleachers, and he told them to think about anything they wanted, anything at all, except for a pink polar bear. And of course, in trying not to think about the pink polar bear, everyone found their thoughts littered with just that.

Felix was the same. Gin would steady her mind, clear it, and he'd be there again. She'd stand up, take a sip of water, try again. Maybe last another minute. And he'd be back, infusing her thoughts with his nonchalant smile, his happy eyes.

A bucket of rain hit the window. There was a low roll of thunder, and the lights flickered. She gave up on the meditation, pulled a blanket over her lap, and called Hannah.

"Are you calling me because your time model told you to?" Hannah had picked up on the first ring. "Because I have to finish this paper. Like, right now."

"Hi, Hannah."

"I'm not joking. This is serious. I actually have to do some work this year. So, is this for real?"

Gin sighed. "This is for real. I haven't checked *TimeKeeper* all day, if that makes you feel better."

"Oh. Good. So what's up?"

Einstein jumped up on the bed and circled a few times, settling back down by Gin's feet. "Nothing. I'm just . . . tired of it all. Classes and work and the models."

What she wanted to do was to talk about Felix. Parse out what had happened, what he did or didn't mean by the hand holding, whether having trained crows meant his family was bona fide crazy. But now, with Hannah there on the phone, it felt silly. He had held her hand, that was all. It wasn't like he had asked her out, or kissed her, or . . .

"Yeah, I totally get it. Senior slump, right? Well, I know something that will cheer you up. Because it means your love model is working. Really working. You won't believe what Aidan did the other day."

And just like that, Hannah launched into a story about Aidan. And, in a roundabout way, it made Gin feel a bit better.

Gin and Felix met again at his house the following Saturday morning. Felix promised they'd have the entire day to work. And this time no one else would be there. Not his dad, who was working. Or his mom, who was at a tropical beach somewhere. "That's what she always does in the winter," he said with an *I-don't-care* smile.

When Gin arrived, a maid opened the door, but

then Felix was there, leading her upstairs. The wide wooden stairs were like the rest of the house: open and modern, perfect and cold.

At the top of the stairs was Felix's room, which was more of a suite. There was a massive king-sized bed, a leather couch, a huge television, and a hanging chair that was situated perfectly near an immense window wall, overlooking the woods. The woods looked different from high up in the house; the faraway trees were almost like toys. She could see the long driveway with her gray Honda Accord, technically her mom's, as well as a separate building that she hadn't noticed from the driveway. She looked harder at the building, which appeared to be a barn, and that's when she saw the immense, cage-like structure next to it.

"Is that—"

"Where the crows live." Felix stood by her. Just then, a crow—a small black smudge from where they were—flew up and around. "I'll show you after we get a little work done, right? Here, you take the fun chair." He pushed the hanging chair towards her.

She folded herself inside it, her legs crisscrossed in front of her and laptop ready. The chair wrapped around her, like a cocoon, and limited her view to one window and the floor in front of her, where Felix was already sprawled out with a notebook, pencil, and laptop. It made everything feel more reasonable. Like Felix was an ordinary guy with a little room and a twin bed in the corner.

"Okay, Gin the model-maker. Where do we start with this one?"

Gin tapped her fingers on her keyboard, light, to help her think.

"I started last night. So maybe you go first, for practice?"

He looked up and grinned. "As long as you know that this class is way more important to you than it'll ever be to me, right?"

"That's a given."

"Okay." He lay on his back, hands on his chest. "Well, let's talk about weather, first. Think about Chicago and Buffalo, the classic example. Chicago's to the west of Lake Michigan, Buffalo's to the east of Lake Erie. They're both at the same latitude, with similar temperatures. And yet, Chicago gets half the amount of snow that Buffalo does. Big difference, right? So weather is very location specific. We have to remember that."

It was a good example. Gin had read about it in one of the weather books.

"Maybe we start with the data, all easy to get from big government sites. We can use linear regressions to map out how the variables interact. And then use stepwise regression to figure out which of the variables—maybe five or ten—best predict the weather."

He sat up and looked at her. "You're not saying anything. Does it all sound crazy?"

Her face flushed slightly, and she shook her head. Truth was, Felix's line of logic was similar to her own, only he seemed to think through it in seconds, while it had taken her an hour to get to the same place.

"No, actually," she said. "That's what I was thinking, too. And I downloaded some data last night."

"All right." Felix rolled over to his stomach and opened his laptop. "Let's get started."

They worked quietly, clicking through the data and running equations. It was surprisingly comfortable.

Gin had gone to the library the day before to check out a climate book with collections of scientific papers, and after an hour on her laptop, she started to thumb through it.

"Ahh, a weather book," Felix said. "Can I see?"

Before she knew what was happening, he was sliding into the cocoon chair with her, his side pressed next to hers. She swore she felt sparks everywhere their bodies met, from her shoulders down to her arms, through her hips and thighs. Her left side touched his right. So close, she could barely breathe.

The chair expanded to fit him, but then shot their bodies back together, pressing them even closer. He kept his legs out, feet steady on the floor, and Gin had no choice but to set her left knee over his thigh.

It was all she could do to continue to flip through the book as though it were perfectly commonplace for her to be wedged into a hanging chair next to a boy. Not that she could comprehend anything in the book now. Felix Gartner was sitting right next to her. So close, she could feel his arm flex and relax each time he wrote a word, his stomach tense when he leaned forward.

"Wait, that's a good one." He turned the page back over. "El Niño, La Niña. That interplay of ocean and air temperatures near the equator." He nudged her with his elbow, playful. "We have to know whether we're talking El Niño or La Niña, right?"

She laughed. "Yes. El Niño, La Niña. Maybe we can throw in an abuela or two?"

"Precisely," he said.

They worked all morning, breaking at noon when yet another maid brought in a platter of sandwiches, chips, fruit, and still-warm chocolate chip cookies. Between mouthfuls, they crafted the model framework and started in on the details.

After lunch, Gin sat back in the chair, guessing Felix would spread out somewhere else. But he sat next to her again. Her stomach flip-flopped with the closeness, and it took twenty minutes before she could focus again. But she did focus, and by late afternoon, they had made incredible progress. The model would rely on six core variables: temperature, humidity, the previous day's weather to the west, time of year, wind speed, and wind direction. They'd try several "extreme" variables, things like intensity of that year's wildfire season or recent traffic levels, and see which of those had an impact. And, Felix would code in his soul bits.

All things considered, they were in better shape than she had expected.

Felix stretched. His notebook slipped down to the floor, and the fabric chair shook with the movement. "I need a break. You?"

It was four. They had worked for almost six hours. Intense, focused, brain-work. *TimeKeeper* would definitely say it was good to take a break. Even five minutes would do wonders.

"Yes. Let's break." Gin unfolded herself from the

chair. She was actually excited to use Felix's bathroom again: it looked like something out of a penthouse in a fancy hotel, with its marble floors, huge soaking tub, stone shower, and big mirrors.

When she washed her hands, she could catch a bit of his scent, the mellow soapy part. If he smelled like a color, it'd be green. When she came out, he handed her a fancy soda.

"Orange work again?"

She took a sip. "Definitely."

She started to head back for the chair when he stood behind her and tugged the bottom hem of her shirt, playful. "Uh-uh, we need a real break." He directed her to the door and took off down the stairs. "Come on, I'll show you the crows."

// Seventeen

Outside, it was damp and cold. But Gin barely noticed. Because the crows were near.

She could hear them, cawing and cackling, as she and Felix followed the gravel footpath that ran along the edge of the woods. The closer they got, the stranger it all felt. Captive crows, carefully trained. She wasn't even sure if it was safe.

"So, are the crows like pets?"

"I guess. I mean, it's not like having a hamster. They're some of the smartest animals around, like orangutans and dolphins. Crows do have a relatively small cerebral cortex. But a crow's forebrain is overdeveloped, packed tight with cells that help with memory, planning, problem solving. My dad studies crows for his artificial intelligence work."

It was the first reference Felix had made to the crows having an actual purpose, and it made Gin's skin prickle. She racked her brain for Odin technologies that involved artificial intelligence, but none came to mind.

Around the barn and bordering the woods as far as Gin could see, there were a series of thin metal poles, so high they towered above the treetops. The poles held up a thin mesh that looked like a very fine net. If that was the aviary, then it was huge—its own forest.

The barn, with its distressed wood and weathered metal, was fancier than Gin's home. But she wasn't interested in the barn. Because they were almost there.

The caws grew louder as Felix slid open the large barn door. He held his arm out. "After you."

Inside it was warm and smelled slightly of animal droppings and hay. Gin had to pause for a second to let her eyes adjust. Felix slid the barn door shut and opened a second door into a mesh cage, as wide and tall as the barn itself.

And finally Gin saw them. Crows everywhere, fluttering and swooping and diving. Dozens of them. Hundreds maybe. They sat on branches and roosts throughout the aviary, cawing and cackling, their sounds rising up and filling the space.

They swooped near Felix, sometimes landing briefly on his shoulder, and taking off again. They hopped up nearby branches and tilted their smooth heads one way then another, as if to get a closer look at Gin.

"They're checking you out," Felix said.

"Wow," she whispered.

"Here, take this." He handed her a thick cracker. "Just hold it up."

She lifted her right arm, tentative. The two birds closest to her peered down, examining the cracker. She breathed slowly, trying to stay still.

And in a soft, black flurry and a whoosh of air, one bird dropped down.

She felt it before she understood. A gentle pressure on her curled fingers. A jostling of the cracker.

The crow was perched on her hand.

It was lighter than she expected, but powerful. She could feel each smooth, hard toe wrapped around her finger. Each movement the bird made rippled through her hand. The bird was folding and unfolding its feathers, arching and tilting its head. It pecked at the cracker again, crumbs flying through the air, and opened up its beak with a loud caw.

"Whoa." Gin had a sudden image of herself tied to dozens of crows, so many that they actually lifted her off the ground, pulling her up in flight. It was a crazy thought, so unlike her. Maybe that's what these creatures did, grew wild ideas in your mind.

"That's Catherine. As in Catherine the Great. She's one of the best. It's cool that she's the one that came to you." Felix reached in his pocket and pulled out a small blue bell. "Here, she likes to play catch."

He shook the bell once—no sound, but a flash of light—and Gin could feel Catherine shift. Energized and focused, her lightweight body lowered to a crouch. Felix tossed the bell up in the air, and in one swift motion, Catherine took off. She flew fast, higher and higher. Gin lost sight of the bell, but apparently, Catherine didn't: she held her wings out taut and swooped through the air. In a second, Catherine was on Felix's hand, the blue bell in her beak.

"That's amazing," Gin said. "But how smart are they, really?"

"It's hard to say exactly. But they're pretty smart. They have so many different calls, it's like a whole language. They're very social. They can use tools and figure out puzzles. You ever hear Aesop's fable about the crow and the glass of water?"

Gin shook her head. She was having a hard time remembering anything at the moment.

"Here, I'll show you." He moved Catherine to his shoulder and walked to the back of the aviary, then outside another mesh door. There was a large, grassy lawn filled with towering trees. The netting was still there, but it stretched so high, it felt limitless.

"Can they get out of here?"

Felix shook his head, looking up. "Looks like they could, right? But they can't. It's all enclosed by a special mesh, light and strong, with the ability to fix itself. One of my dad's inventions. But that's a story for another day."

"It seems like it goes on for miles."

"It does. At least for a few hundred acres or so. My dad spares no expense when it comes to the crows. And he has plenty of expense to spare."

Felix walked to what looked to be a shed, only much fancier than any shed Gin had seen before, and returned with a small bag and a foot-long plastic tube filled halfway with water. He shook the bag, smiling. "Mincemeat. Their favorite."

He put a piece of meat on a little foam disk and dropped the disk into the plastic tube, where it floated on the water. He gave a low whistle, and Catherine fluttered off his shoulder and landed near the plastic tube. She examined the meat, which was too low in the tube for her to reach. Then she flew to a pile of small rocks, brought one back to the tube, and dropped it in.

The water with the floating meat rose a bit. It was still too low for Catherine to reach, but she was closer. Before Gin could blink, Catherine was off for another rock.

That's when Gin remembered the fable: a thirsty crow finds a half-full glass of water. He can't reach the water, so drops rocks in until the water rises and is high enough for him to drink. Gin had always thought the story was a lesson in creative thinking, not an actual phenomenon.

One after another, Catherine brought rocks and dropped them in, the meat rising higher and higher. Finally, the meat within reach, Catherine tilted her beak in and gulped it down.

"Wow!" Gin said, clapping.

"Here's another one." Felix positioned a touch

screen on a table. "Pattern recognition." Catherine pecked at it and a circle appeared. With another peck, two simple pictures appeared—a cake and a television screen. Catherine touched the cake, then two more shapes appeared, this time a tire and a gift box. She pecked the tire.

"She's choosing the round shape," Felix said. "She never misses. It's a level of thinking that toddlers and orangutans can do."

After four sets of shapes, all of which Catherine sorted correctly, a pellet came out from a dispenser. Catherine ate it fast, then flew back up to Felix's hand. "Good girl." Felix glanced sideways at Gin, as though to gauge her reaction. "Pretty cool, huh?"

It *was* cool. And also strange and somewhat unbelievable.

"I had no idea crows were this smart." Gin looked back up at the aviary. Everything the crows did—from pruning each other's feathers to watching the activity around them—seemed to take on a new purpose.

"Most people don't. They're used to being misunderstood."

"And your dad uses all of this for artificial intelligence . . . how?"

Felix's face turned serious. "If I told you, I'd have to kill you." Then he grinned. "Only joking. But the truth is, even I don't know all the details. I just know about the crow-bots."

"Crow-bots?"

"Crow-sized robots. They're scattered throughout the aviary. They're programmed with simple behav-

ioral rules, then through machine-learning algorithms, they become more and more like actual
crows." He stepped back to get a better view of the
space above, and pointed to the side. "See, there's
one right there."

Perched on the lower branches of a tree was a crow.
It blended in well—Gin never would have noticed it
without Felix's direction. But now that she was looking at it, she could see it was different. Its body was
bulkier, feathers slightly awkward. When it blinked its
eyes and turned its head, it looked almost mechani-
cal. Definitely not perfect, but it was fascinating.

"Do the other crows know?" Her voice had turned
quiet, as though she was afraid to scare the crow-bot
away.

"Of course. They can sense that it isn't alive. It's not
a perfect experiment for lots of other reasons, including that the crow-bots can't really fly. We have to position them around the aviary. And the real crows don't
ever incorporate a crow-bot into their groups. But
they will interact with it, and that's how it learns. My
dad hasn't gotten as much information from the
whole thing as he'd like. But it's still interesting. Here,
I'll show you one of the crow-bots that isn't engaged."

She followed him back inside to a side room, neatly
organized with drills, tools, and several computers.
There were boxes of thin metal wire and bags of black
feathers. And on one counter, what looked at first to
be a dead crow was lying on its side.

"You can hold it." He gingerly picked up the crow-
bot and passed it to her.

Gin's first reaction was that it was surprisingly light and soft, though she could feel the metal structure just under the carefully placed feathers. Close up, it was clearly not a real crow. But it looked more realistic than she would've thought.

Felix typed on the computer, and the crow-bot shifted in her hands, blinking its eyes and opening its mouth. Gin started, her heart suddenly racing, palms sweating, and nearly dropped it.

"Sorry, sorry." Felix held his hands up, grinning. "I know it's unsettling. I couldn't help it."

The crow-bot moved its wings, pushing out into Gin's hands, and she set it back on the counter and stepped away. "Weird," she said. "But amazing."

They watched for a few minutes as it cycled through a series of behaviors: cawing, opening its beak wide as though begging for food, hopping awkwardly to one side, haltingly flapping its wings. It wasn't perfect. But suddenly, the crows made a lot more sense.

"Okay," Felix said. "Enough of the pretend crows. Now, let's take you to the nursery."

They headed to the other side of the aviary, where natural light poured in through a sunroof. A heat lamp shone on a wide tree stump, which held a large nest of twigs and branches. Felix pulled Gin forward—it was still like magic, his hand touching hers—and she peered inside the nest.

Four baby birds lay snugged up together. Their bodies were covered in fluff, their necks just strong enough to lift their heads.

"Oh," she said, putting her free hand to her mouth. "They're so . . . little."

A crow flew up and perched on the side of the nest, eyeing Felix and Gin.

"That's their dad." Felix dropped Gin's hand to point to the crow perching near the nest. "Rufus. And Mandy is their mom." He crouched down to look more closely at the babies. "We actually breed them to cultivate certain characteristics. Cute, aren't they?"

If Gin could put together a logical thought, she'd ask Felix more. But all she could do was nod. "How old are they?"

"A week. Here, want to hold one?"

He scooped up one of the baby birds, so gently it barely moved, and brought it close to his face. "Hey, little one," he said, softly. Then he placed the bird in Gin's hands. It was warm and light, a small bundle of feathers. It looked up at her, opened its mouth, and gave a small chirp.

Gin looked at Felix in surprise, and Felix laughed. "He likes you." The way he said it made her stomach jump. She stared at the bird, face flushed.

Then Rufus flapped his wings and cawed.

"Okay, okay. Time to go back, buddy." Felix took the bird from Gin's hand and placed it back into the nest. "And we should probably get going, too, right?"

The crows chattered as they left, a farewell of sorts. Throaty clicks and soft cuckles, rising and falling. Like music. The crow-bot was still perched on the low branch, and instead of watching Gin and Felix leave, it watched the other birds.

They sat outside the barn for a minute, the wooden step cold, the air darkening. Gin asked about the crows, question after question. Felix was happy to answer, telling her how each crow nest was built from more than 1,500 twigs and branches, and how there were legends and stories about crows in almost every culture, and how wild crows sometimes brought trinkets to people they liked. She tried a few more questions about the crow-bots, but he didn't have much information. Clearly, that was his dad's special project.

It was nearly dark when they started walking back to the house. Partway there, Felix stopped suddenly. "Oh, man."

The front door opened, and a man stood there. He was lit from the back, but even from yards away, Gin could make out his cropped silvery hair, thin silver glasses, black turtleneck, and jeans.

"Guess you're meeting my dad. Sorry in advance for anything he says, or does, or just who he is," Felix mumbled. They walked up the steps, and Felix stiffened.

"Felix," his dad said, without even looking at Gin. "Were you out in the aviary? I don't remember you asking if you could go, much less bring a friend. It's critical that the birds have time without people to rest between shifts. And I'll be working them tonight."

He put one hand on Felix's shoulder, stopping him in the doorway. Felix kept his eyes straight ahead.

His dad gripped his shoulder harder. "We just had a talk about responsibility. Or have you forgotten already?"

Felix looked up, sullen. "We weren't out there long."

His dad loosened his grip and gave Felix a pat. He

stood like an army sergeant, feet slightly apart, arms crossed over his chest. And Gin knew her own dad had been right: this was not a man who did anything for fun.

"Well. I don't want it to happen again." His dad cleared his throat. "Marcel has dinner waiting. She wasn't aware you'd have a friend joining."

Felix looked at Gin and frowned. "Gin can't join, she has to go. But Dad, this is Gin, my partner in computer modeling. She's the one I told you about, who's applying to Harvard. Gin, this is my dad, Grant Gartner."

"Hello, Gin," his dad said, giving her a thin-lipped smile. "Felix says you're an accomplished modeler."

"That's a nice compliment." Gin tried to keep her voice confident. "I definitely enjoy it."

He nodded, and a few seconds of silence passed.

Gin cleared her throat. It was clearly time for her to go. "Well, it's good to meet you, Mr. Gartner. I'll just head up to grab my bags."

"That won't be necessary. Marcel has already collected your things." He opened the door wider so she could see her shoulder bag there to the side.

It was strange, for someone else to collect her things. But that was probably what life was like when you were rich. Someone picking up after you, cooking your meals, taking care of any tasks that weren't worth your time. The ultimate *Streamliner* scenario.

As she stepped outside, she looked back at Felix. His face was serious now, the playfulness from earlier completely gone.

She walked through the shadowy yard, the first planets bright overhead. When she got to her car, she glanced back once more, but the big wooden door was already shut.

// Eighteen

The city was ready for the holidays. There were twinkly lights, snowflake banners, and the clang of Salvation Army bells at every street corner. And of course, the huge Christmas tree near the White House. It was enough to make Gin's walk from the Metro to work feel festive and warm, despite the blustery, cheek-stinging wind.

At the office, a pretty, red holiday cup of coffee was waiting—it must've been from Lucas, who had gotten in the habit of bringing Gin coffee. He always bought Starbucks, which was Gin's coffee shop of choice, a preference based entirely on consistency. Lucas wasn't at his desk, and as Gin's computer powered up, she sipped the warm drink and stared out the window. It was steely gray outside, the air frosty as though it could snow.

"Hey, whatcha thinking?" Lucas asked. Even though it was still the weekend, he was dressed for the workday: plaid button-down shirt, solid tie, two pens in his shirt pocket, khaki pants that were pulled up too high.

Gin searched for an answer that didn't include the

word "Felix." Because he had pretty much been all she'd thought about since working at his house the day before. Finally, she just shrugged.

"I've started on today's file," Lucas said. "I highlighted my half green and yours yellow, so we won't duplicate."

"Thanks." She took another sip of her coffee; maybe the caffeine would help her focus. "And thanks for the drink. What do I owe you?"

"Nothing. It's on me this time. Interns have to stick together, right? Anyway, I'm still trying to convince you to come over and try Thronesville. You know, even though more and more girls are gaming, your gender is still underrepresented in the field. Which means you could get some good perks if you started."

"And coffee is supposed to help how?"

Lucas held up a finger. "It reminds you that gamers are thoughtful people. And that, therefore, you should be a gamer, too."

"Decent logic. Trust me, I'm thinking about it. I'm just up to my ears in my modeling class and schoolwork and my own model—which, by the way, really benefited from that program you wrote. So, thanks again."

"Any time. How is *Love Fractal* anyway?"

"Definitely not finished. But getting closer."

"Well, I know lots of gamers who could use a little, you know, help in the romance area. So maybe you could test it out on them?"

It was an interesting idea: take one subpopulation, gamers, and see who they matched with. It'd be an excellent test group.

"That could be cool. I'll let you know when it's ready," she said. "And then maybe we can make sure their prospective dates aren't like the square root of -1."

Lucas gave a half-laugh, half-snort, the type that was both awkward and endearing. Suddenly Gin wondered who, if anyone, Lucas would be matched with.

"You know, when *Love Fractal*'s done, I can run it on you if you want?"

He paused for a second, fingers frozen over his keyboard, and scrunched up his nose. "Um, maybe."

"What—you don't want to see if your true love is out there?"

Lucas tapped his cheek and pushed his glasses up. "It's more that I don't know if I'm ready. My mom always says that guys like me are best after college. You know, that we age well."

Besides the fact that Lucas was probably right—guys like him often were appreciated more a few years down the road—there was another truth in his insight. A great match could fail if the timing was off, while a so-so one could take off if the timing was good. Gin was suddenly thinking of her model—she had accounted for length of time since someone's last relationship, but maybe there was a second timing layer she could add.

Truth was, *Love Fractal* was getting overwhelming. With so many variables, so many little shifts and causal effects, sometimes it seemed impossible to predict anything.

But she remembered what she and Felix had done

with the weather model. Kept it simple. Accounted for only the main variables.

Maybe that was enough.

When Gin got to school Monday morning, Hannah was already sitting in front of Gin's locker, slumped forward.

"Hey," Gin said, nudging her.

Hannah looked up, her eyes red and makeup a mess.

"Whoa, what's the matter?" Gin slid down next to her. The floor and the lockers were cold. It was frigid outside—single digits—and from the weather reports, it wasn't getting warmer any time soon.

Hannah shook her head and rolled her eyes. "Nothing is wrong. Not really. At least, nothing real."

Gin leaned closer so they were shoulder to shoulder. "Well, something's going on. It doesn't take a computer model to see that."

Hannah sighed. "It's nothing you couldn't have guessed. Aidan is an ass. With a capital *A*. And to be honest, I'm not surprised. Maybe the model thing had me more interested in him than I should've been, you know?"

"Oh, Hannah, I'm so sorry." Gin's stomach fell. Mostly because Hannah was upset, but also a little bit because now *Love Fractal* was 0 for 2. "What happened?"

"The usual. Hot football guy decides it's best to

date several girls at once. Apparently, it increases your attractiveness when you have a girl or two in the wings. Exponentially. I can see the graph. One girlfriend, and you stay steady, but with two, your attractiveness goes up. Which makes more girls like you, and so it goes up again. It feeds itself, you know?"

"But you guys were good together. And he liked you."

"Yeah, well, tell him that. Apparently, he likes that soccer player, Liv, better."

"So he's dating her? Are you sure?"

"Oh, I'm sure." Hannah nodded, her eyes wide. "I went to his house last night. Just to say hi. I walked right in, which I've done before plenty of times, because his parents work late, and the door's always open. Anyway, he was with her. Silly me, thinking he'd want to hang out with me when all he wanted was another girl."

"Did you see them . . . you know?"

"No. I did, however, see them both without their shirts on."

Gin put an arm around Hannah's shoulder. "Oh, Hannah. I'm sorry. That's awful."

Hannah pushed her face into her knees, her unwashed hair falling forward. "Ugh, how stupid."

Gin squeezed tighter. "You know, he's a jerk. He definitely doesn't deserve you. And I'm sorry the model has been so off. I wish you had called me."

"I knew you were working. And I needed to deal for a little, you know?" She reached over and lifted the flap of Gin's bag. "Any chance you have a granola bar in there? Or chocolate? I'm starving."

"Absolutely." Gin handed Hannah a bar. "So, we should go out Saturday night. I bet the 9:30 Club has a good show. You might meet someone. We'll try the old-fashioned way."

Hannah wiped her eyes. "Okay. Maybe. But first, I'm going to try for Noah."

"Noah?" Gin shook her head. "He's definitely not your type. Anyway, I've got more data now—we could run the model again with a bigger pool of candidates."

Hannah threw the crumpled wrapper at Gin. "Come on, now. You know you don't change an experiment midstream. Anyway, give yourself some credit. You're smart. And your model says Noah might be a match. If he's not, he could still be a good friend. You know what they say about nice guys."

"No, I don't."

"Then, you'll just have to wait and find out." Hannah stood up, stretched, and pulled her jacket back in place. She almost looked like nothing had ever been wrong. Even her smudged mascara could somehow pass as stylish. But her eyes were still damp, and her face was slightly pale. "See you at lunch."

Gin watched her go, striding down the hall, trying to act like she owned it.

// Nineteen

Gin and Felix worked on the weather model all week. They wrote sections separately, emailing bits of code back and forth, and spent afternoons in the library finishing it up.

By all accounts, it ended up being a success. Ms. Sandlin gave them a 97 percent, the highest grade in the class. And Gin had finally started to understand Felix's "soul bits," which were sort of like the Monte Carlo Method of introducing randomness, only more random.

The only issue was that they couldn't get the model to work. It did predict weather—just not accurately. It'd call for wind and cold, but the next day would be warm. Or it'd predict rain for three days, and every day would be dry as a bone.

"I don't get it." Gin was scrolling through the code, Felix twirling his pencil. Ms. Sandlin was giving them class time to work on their big projects, but Gin and Felix still hadn't started. "I've been inputting actual weather data to see if somehow the model will auto-correct, but it's not working."

"I was playing around with it too." Felix started doodling in his notebook, which was so full of blank pages, Gin wondered how he remembered anything from class. "I think we have the right basics. But maybe it's *too* basic. Or, maybe actual weather has been too similar. Like, we need some major weather event or something."

"Anyway . . ." She put her finger on his notepad

to stop his drawing—but he traced around it. The touch of the pencil along the curve of her fingertip was so intense, she nearly pulled her finger away. "We have to figure out our big project. I have a few ideas."

"Let's hear them." His pencil moved to another corner of the page. Her finger throbbed.

She tried to think through her list of ideas, but suddenly, none seemed that good.

"You know, I don't think well in school at all." Felix looked up at her, eyebrows furrowed. "All of these lights and desks and people. We should work outside."

Gin leaned back and folded her arms over her chest. "You want to windsurf."

He grinned. "Sure, I want to do that, too. But we don't have to meet at the river. Just outside. Where things move and you can smell the earth and you feel . . . alive."

Gin glanced at the clock. They only had ten minutes left, and she could use the time to review for her history test. "Okay, fine. We'll meet outside. But we have to pick a topic and start working. How about tomorrow?"

"It's a date." He closed his notebook and she tried not to blush.

When the bell rang, Ms. Sandlin stood. "Winter break is almost here, which means it's nearly time for our final project check-ins. Bring your topic and preliminary research."

It was so soon it made Gin want to groan. Felix,

however, didn't seem to care—he was the first one out the door.

// Twenty

That night, Gin tried to brainstorm for the final modeling project. But her mind felt like mush. She had a bowl of vegetable soup—her mom had made a Crock-Pot full while Gin was at school, a blessed break from takeout—and she ran the weather model.

The prediction was a surprise. The model showed snow. Up to eight inches by the next morning. Enough to shut down the whole city for at least a day.

She felt a leap of excitement—a snow day!—and then remembered the prediction was coming from their weather model. She looked online and found no other sites were predicting snow. Not even a flurry.

"Stupid model." Gin said as she raised her window to check. The sky was dark and full of stars, not a cloud in sight.

A single crow flew by, and Gin thought about messaging Felix. Something funny, like how the model predicted snow so there probably wouldn't be a single flake this winter.

But instead, she messaged with Hannah, who was happily watching a movie and ignoring a paper that was due the next day. Then, Gin went to bed, snuggled under her covers, wearing Felix's fleece and her plaid pajama pants.

When Gin woke, it felt different. It was warm. Quiet. The sun hadn't risen, but she opened her curtains anyway and looked out. And gasped.

It was snowing. Hard. Snowflakes fell in clumps, so fast and thick, they turned the night sky gray-white. A flat pillow smoothed over roads, yards, cars. Lines of white were carefully balanced on every tree limb. Bushes had become puffs of marshmallow.

Nothing moved. It was as though the whole world had stopped.

She lifted her window and stuck her head outside, letting the icy snowflakes land and melt, dampening her face.

The model had been right. It hadn't predicted anything correctly, except the one thing no one else could.

She opened her laptop—the "Surprise Superstorm of the Year" was already being covered online. Local schools and government offices were closed, and it was strongly recommended that everyone stay indoors.

"They should have checked with our model," Gin said out loud, then laughed. She started to reach for *TimeKeeper*, as she had a whole day to plan now that schools were closed. But it was all so out of the ordinary, there was no way her program would work. So instead, she lay back and watched the snow swirl through the night sky.

She woke to her phone buzzing and sun beaming through her window. It was eleven in the morning. She couldn't remember the last time she'd slept that late. Usually, sleeping past eight made her feel frantic, as though she'd missed too much of the day already.

Outside, it looked like a snow globe village. Sloping roofs were iced with snow, like gingerbread houses. Yards, sidewalks, and roads all merged together in one white surface.

There were a few signs of life. The street, though free of tire tracks, had footprints down the middle, and people had been shoveling driveways and clearing off cars. Kids down the street were building snowmen and throwing snowballs.

She checked her phone. Felix had texted: *Score one for our weather model! Can you meet? I'm almost at the field, and I've got the crows.*

She wrote back that she'd see him there soon and started pulling on layers—long johns, fleece pants, a wool sweater. There was no time for *Outfitter*, and anyway, there weren't that many options for this weather. She clamored downstairs for a quick bowl of cereal, and after digging her snow boots out of a box in the basement, she popped her head into her dad's study.

When routine was broken, her dad could either be something of a mess or strangely happy. Today he was in his armchair, eyes closed, hands folded over his chest. A large whiteboard was pulled up next to him, already covered with colorful words and symbols. She guessed he was happy.

"I'm going for a walk," she said.

He opened his eyes. "Okay." He didn't blink for a few seconds, as though his mind was turning through some important concept. Then he held up a finger. "How about pancakes when you get home?"

"Pancakes? But it's not Sunday. That's, like, anathema."

He nodded slowly. "You're right. It is illogical. And not within our routine. But nothing today fits within routine. So pancakes, therefore, make perfect sense. And by then Mom should be up."

"Okay, pancakes. I'll be back in a few hours."

He closed his eyes again and settled back in his chair, a faint smile on his lips.

The snow was so light, it puffed out with each kick of Gin's boots. The clouds were clearing, and every now and then the sun would burst forward, making icy flakes glint and tree limbs shine.

There were a few other people out walking, but not many, and by the time Gin got to the field, it felt like the whole world had emptied. It was quiet. No revving engines or horns or squealing brakes.

She saw the crows first. Just like last time. Glossy

black bodies slipping through the sky, high above the snow. She stood upon the hill overlooking the field, watching as two of the crows flew away, flapping hard and fast. When they were gone, the field was almost empty.

Except for Felix. There was a line of footsteps through the snow to where he stood. His body was straight and still, hands at his sides, eyes focused on the horizon.

He wore a down coat, tall snow boots, and gray gloves. And a charcoal wooly hat that covered his ears except for the bottom tips, which, even from high on the hill, looked red from the cold.

There was movement above the trees at the edge of the field. The crows were coming back, focused and fast. Within seconds, they flew to Felix's hands, and he moved them to his shoulders. Then he blew on his hands for warmth.

Gin started down. The movement must've caught his eye, because he turned, his hand popping up in a wave. He was walking towards her, fast, the crows balanced on each shoulder. She paused to take him in— how strange he looked in this frosted white world.

"You made it," he said. "I was getting worried."

"Don't worry. I love snow. And anyway, my dad has an emergency GPS tracker on my phone, so I could never get lost."

They were several feet away from each other, but with all of the white space around them, she swore it was closer.

"Good dad." He reached out to squeeze her hand.

One second, but enough to send a surge of warmth through her body. "So we did it, right? Predicted the unpredictable."

"I know." Her breath was a white cloud and it felt as though her core temperature had shot up five degrees. "I almost called NOAA to see if they wanted rights to our work. But I figured that'd be too much, too soon."

"Yeah. They aren't ready for us yet." He leaned closer, grinning.

"How'd you even get here?" It should've been her first question. Because no one was out on the roads.

"My dad had to get to the office, so he had our streets plowed, all the way up to the main roads that they've cleared. And my car, though it might not look like it, is built like a tank. Plus, I have chains."

Gin shook her head in disbelief, though she should've known the Gartners wouldn't slow down for a snow day. One of the crows on Felix's shoulders, Beatrix, it looked like, flapped her wings and cawed.

"Want to see them work? They still have to find some bells." He stepped back, opening a space between them, and Gin immediately felt colder.

"Absolutely. Beatrix and Frederick, right?" Funny how in a short time with the crows, they all started to look unique.

"You got it. And Maggie and Rufus are in the box. Ready for some magic?"

"You know I am. As long as we're brainstorming—"

"About our final project. Should be easy now that we have one working model, right?" He shifted the birds to his hands. "Let's start the brainstorming now. What do you have?"

Before she could answer, Felix whistled. The crows flapped up, and Gin marveled again at the power in such small packages of feather and bone and blood.

She waited for the birds to get across the field, above the treetops. "Okay. My school ideas first: predict how many kids fail out each year; predict how many kids get into Ivy League schools; predict how many kids get so stressed they fall apart before college even starts . . ." She snuck a look at him out of the corner of her eye. He was smiling.

"Good. I like those. Especially the last one. What else?"

"Modeling traffic jams on the Beltway. I mean, if we could make that model work, or find some pattern everyone else has missed, we could be rich. Or I could be rich, and you'd be richer."

"True." Felix watched the sky, thinking. "It'd be fun to try. Especially to account for the use of the model itself. Once people start following what it says, traffic patterns would change. The trick would be to keep the model from making its own traffic jams. It could self-adjust for every user."

"That would be cool." She was already thinking through the logic.

"So which is your favorite?"

"That's the problem." Gin hugged her arms to herself for warmth. "Nothing feels right. Maybe that doesn't matter. But I was hoping to find one that felt . . . exciting. How about you—do you have ideas?"

Felix shrugged. "We could model the success of golfers in different conditions and on different courses. All big CEO's would love that one. Or model wind direction and speed for windsurfers. Or . . . I don't know, it's the same thing. Lots of ideas. None of them that striking."

The crows flapped back over the trees. They were each carrying something shiny in their beaks. Gin turned her head up to watch, the cold air stinging her eyes.

The birds flew down to Felix's shoulders, and as suddenly as they had appeared, Gin knew exactly what to do. "Crows," she whispered.

"What about them?" Felix opened his hands for the bells, and the crows dropped them in.

"It's obvious, isn't it?" Gin's voice was almost bubbly now. "What we should model? Crows."

A wind pushed through as Felix paused. "The crows, huh? You'd want to do that?"

She nodded, fast.

He put one gloved hand to his chin. "It could be good. How about their movements? Like a model on flocking behavior. But with smarter animals, not the typical starlings or pigeons. And my dad tracks everything they do, so we have all the data we'd need."

"Wait—you already have data?" This was better than Gin had hoped.

In reply, he pointed to Frederick's leg, which had a slender black band. It was so small, Gin hadn't noticed it before. "Everything they do is tracked, the data logged. I don't know why I didn't think of this earlier. Must be that rule about not noticing the things you're closest to. We'd leave out information from the crow-bots, of course. But we can look at how the real crows fly, when they stop, how their groups come together and disperse. No one's modeled crow flocking behavior before, so it'd definitely be unique."

"It could be good."

"Really good." He turned to her and they stood there for another frosty breath. It was incredible. A model like this, one that hadn't been done before, with unique data—it was exactly the sort of opportunity Gin needed.

Without warning, Felix threw his hands up in the air, jostling the birds on his shoulders, but not enough for them to fly off. "We should celebrate!" he yelled. He kneeled down in the snow by the black box, and took the other two birds out, one on each hand, and held them out towards Gin. "Here, take these guys."

Maggie and Rufus shifted to Gin's gloved hands, and she was surprised again at how light they were, almost like air. "Hey guys," she said quietly, and the birds turned their heads sideways to watch her.

"Okay," Felix said. "On the count of three, push up and shout 'fly.' Got it?"

Gin tensed her arms and nodded.

"One, two, three—"

Gin pushed up with her hands, and shouted "Fly," as Felix whistled. All four birds took off, but this time they weren't going to the end of the field—they were going up, higher and higher. When they became little dots in the sky, they separated and started circling down, loop after loop after loop.

"Wow," Gin whispered. "It's like they're dancing. It's so . . ."

"Beautiful." But Felix wasn't watching the birds. He was looking at Gin. He stepped closer, and reached out one gloved hand to hold her hand, tight.

She shuddered from the sensation. All she wanted was to lean into him, to kiss him, to touch her lips to his. But instead, she looked up to the sky, where the crows floated, effortless and smooth.

The streets were plowed by late afternoon, and temperatures warmed, melting the ice. School was on for the next day. It had been a fluke storm. Apparently, that's what their weather model was good at—flukes.

Gin was looking over *Love Fractal* that night when she heard a tap at her window. She ignored it at first. But it happened again. And again.

She stared at the white shade, which was already drawn shut. Her heart beat faster, and the house seemed to still.

Tap, tap-tap. Tap . . . tap, tap, tap. It was probably a tree. No need to be afraid. Never mind that she'd never heard a tree tap at her window before. She'd take a look to be sure.

She pulled the shade up, and it took a second for

her eyes to adjust to the night. Then she saw it: a crow, perched on her windowsill.

She jumped back, her hand flying up to her mouth, and she nearly yelled out in surprise. She told herself to stay calm: it was only a crow. Harmless.

She took a deep breath and kneeled down. Crows didn't just come to her windowsill. It had to be one of Felix's.

The bird ruffled its wings and tilted its head. Catherine. And she was holding something in her beak: a small white paper triangle.

Catherine tapped again, seemingly with no plan of leaving. So with her heart beating fast in her chest, Gin slowly pushed up the window, until Catherine was right there in front of her.

The cold night air poured in and Gin waited, unsure of what to do next. Was she supposed to take the paper triangle from Catherine? Or give a whistle, so she would fly home?

But then Catherine dropped the white triangle down on the windowsill. Gin picked it up and unfolded it. In the middle, in small letters that were all capitalized, was a single line.

Want to go to the city Friday night? To start the project?—Felix

It was a note. An impossibly unlikely note—not a text or an email, but a handwritten note delivered by a crow. She wanted to laugh.

Instead, she found a pen and wrote back: *Yes!! I'd love to!!*

There was nothing clever she could think of to

add—it was all too strange—so she folded the note back up and held it out on her open palm, as if she were giving a horse a treat. Catherine picked it up with her beak, and with a sweep of her wings, pushed off into the darkness.

Gin watched her go, soaring through the sky, and for a moment, it felt as though Gin's heart was soaring along, too.

// Twenty-One

Hannah came over Friday night to make sure Gin looked nice. Which, by Hannah's standards, could mean anything: a leather skirt, ripped shirt, and knee socks, or maybe a neon jumpsuit with dark glasses. Usually, Gin would use *Outfitter*, but *Outfitter*'s suggestions didn't seem right, and besides that, Gin was nervous.

She told herself there was no need to be nervous. Even opened her biology textbook to the section about hormones and the fight-or-flight response to remind herself that it was only chemicals.

But nothing helped. Especially since Hannah was sure Felix liked Gin. Actually *liked* her. As soon as Gin had told her about the hand-holding and the snow day and the crow message, Hannah had no doubt. But Gin saw it differently: she and Felix had to hang out since they were partners in class, and Felix holding her hand was likely no big deal since he often traveled to Europe where kissing cheeks and holding hands were part of life. And, of course, there was Caitlin—clearly, Felix had been interested in her at the football game, and clearly, she was more interesting than Gin.

Anyway, Felix was just so . . . much. And no matter what logic Gin used, she couldn't find a line of reasoning in which Felix would actually like *her*.

Regardless, there was something more important than how unlikely it was that Felix Gartner liked her—there was a chance *Love Fractal* was working. Hannah was actually hitting it off with Noah. After meeting for coffee, they'd been out twice. The best part was that Noah was different, really different, from any guy Hannah had ever dated.

If the model worked for Hannah, maybe it would work for Gin. And it hadn't matched her with Felix.

"Now hold still." Hannah put sticky lip gloss on Gin's lips and stepped back. "Okay, see what you think."

When Gin looked in the mirror, she gasped. Her hair was shiny and dark, her eyes shimmered, her lips were bright and glossy, and even her cheeks were faintly flushed. Her outfit, though it had come from her closet, looked brand new: Hannah had dressed her in gray cargo pants and low boots and a fitted shirt, a combination *Outfitter* had never put together. It was like Gin had transformed into someone else.

"Wow," she said. "I look . . . good."

Hannah laughed. "Of course you do. You always

do, but a little makeup and the right outfit go a long way."

"Thanks, Hannah." Gin hugged her, tight.

"Anytime—you know I love this stuff. By the way, your hair looks great. Have you been growing it out?"

Gin turned her head again, and saw that Hannah was right. Her hair had always been shoulder-length—practical and easy. But recently, she had kept forgetting to get it cut, and now it fell below her collarbone.

The doorbell rang, and Gin took a deep breath. She started to pull on her jacket, but Hannah grabbed it.

"No, wait. Let him see you first like this. Sans jacket. You can put it on downstairs."

Gin rolled her eyes but did as she was told. On the way to the door, she peeked in her dad's office. He was leaned back in his chair, twirling a dry erase marker in his hand.

"Bye, Dad," she called. "I'm leaving now. Hannah will take off in a second."

He glanced up, confused for a second. "Was that the doorbell?"

"I'm going downtown with Felix. For our project, remember?"

"Did you text Mom?"

"I always text Mom."

"Okay, good. Have fun."

Gin glanced up the stairs to be sure Hannah wasn't sitting there, waiting for the show, then she opened the door.

Felix, wearing jeans and a flannel shirt, stood on the front step. He was smiling so wide, Gin couldn't help but smile back.

"Hey." He watched her for a second. "You look really nice."

"Oh, thanks." She started to put on her jacket, and he took it from her and held it up. As she slipped into it, his hand touched her shoulders. It made her catch her breath.

They stepped out into the wintry night, and he opened the passenger door of a new, shiny SUV that Gin hadn't seen before. It had tinted windows and a leather interior, and when she sat down, her seat was toasty warm.

"Is this new?" she asked after he had shut her door and climbed in the driver's side.

"It's my dad's. One of many. I thought I'd bring it since we're going into the city, and I wanted to be sure your parents didn't worry."

Leave it to Felix to be thoughtful like that. She looked out the window as they drove, trying to distract herself from everything bubbling up in her chest. That's when she noticed how the trees and bushes were dark except where a street lamp turned them a shadowy gray.

"Isn't it weird how color works?" Gin immediately cringed. What was really weird was to start a conversation like that. She made a mental note to build a conversation model, something that would tell you the best thing to say in any situation. She'd call it *Commentator*.

But Felix wasn't phased. "And how does color work?"

There was no going back now. All she could do was embrace it. "You know, how something has the potential to be a certain color, or lots of colors, but it's no color at all unless light is shining on it. Like in dark caves, where light never enters, does color exist? Because there's no light to absorb and reflect."

"Right. Like, the potential for color is always there, but color itself—only in the light." He was serious, not teasing. "So when we all go to sleep, our clothes, our sheets, everything becomes a non-color."

"Exactly." Gin felt much more relaxed. Leave it to Felix to make any conversation seem normal.

Traffic was a mess for everyone coming out of the city. Luckily, Felix and Gin were going into it. Before long, they were driving over the Potomac, towards the bright lights of Washington, DC. The city wasn't one that towered—height restrictions kept properties from sprawling up into the sky—and Gin could see the Washington Monument, the Capitol building, and the National Cathedral in the distance.

"The crows are somewhere in there?" Gin asked.

"That's what their trackers say." Felix handed her his phone. It showed a map of the city with four blinking red dots.

It was strange, these crows scattered through the city, on their own. She wondered if the training had a connection with Grant Gartner's artificial intelligence work, but couldn't guess what that would be. "And they always come home?"

"Yeah. Always." Felix took the exit after the bridge. "My dad works with them at least once a week, rotating them, so they're all used to it. He's working with them tonight. That's why they're here."

"So what does he have them do here? I mean, why even come to the city?"

Felix shrugged. His face glowed from the lights outside, contrasting with the dark car, the black river, the night sky. "Why do anything? It's for his research, I guess. He's always done it. And the work is the only hobby he has, the only thing he does that's relaxing, so I don't ask too many questions."

Gin stared at the map with the little glowing dots. Nothing about this "hobby" fit with what she'd seen of Felix's dad. But tonight was strange enough without analyzing Grant Gartner.

"Here's the thing. I've watched my dad do this before, and usually the crows cover a wide area until maybe nine, then settle into a smaller area for an hour or two, before my dad takes them home. Which means we don't have to look for them right away."

Before Gin could ask what they were going to do in the meantime, Felix leaned over, one hand still on the steering wheel, and gave her a quick look. "So, how about dinner? I know some good spots."

It was feeling more and more like a date. "Sounds good." She tried to keep her voice casual, as though going out to dinner with a good-looking guy was something she did all the time, and wiped her clammy hands on her pants.

"Then the next question is where to go. There's the

nice option, with fancy menus and foaming sauces and fresh-off-the-boat fish that's the rage in Tokyo." He glanced at her again. "Or, we could hit up something more . . . authentic."

"Authentic sounds good." Not to mention cheaper. She wasn't planning on spending all her internship money on one dinner, even if it was with Felix Gartner.

"I know just the place. As long as you like Chinese?"

He could have said pizza and she would've happily agreed. Soon they were winding through the city's one-way streets, with their brick row houses and old oak trees and people walking to bars and restaurants. A few turns later, Felix parked off an alleyway. He slipped out of the car so fast, Gin was still searching for the door handle when he opened her door.

He held a hand out to her. It made her blush, but she took it, the thrill of his touch startling her again. He shut the door with a flourish and did a funny half-spin, and ended up standing right by her side, close. Then he took her hand again, firmer this time.

"You're going to love this." He leaned so close she felt his breath, warm on her cheek.

Truth was, she already did.

The first set of row houses they came to contained businesses: a drug store, a liquor outlet, a pet store, a bar. In the middle of the building, they walked down a set of concrete steps to a wooden door with no sign—just a piece of paper taped to the front, with Chinese characters written in black sharpie. Felix pulled open the door and bells tingled.

Inside, the restaurant was small and simple, with plain wooden tables and old wooden floors. But it was packed: nearly every table was filled with diners. It smelled good, too: like ginger and garlic and hot, seasoned broth. Cooks clattered in the kitchen, and an aquarium glowed along one wall. A small table at the front had a running fountain shaped like a mountain and a statue of a golden cat with one perpetually waving arm.

A woman greeted Felix with a fast handshake, saying something in Chinese. Felix answered her, his words not as smooth, but all Chinese. Gin looked at him in surprise.

Apparently, Felix had said something funny, because the woman laughed. "Come, come," she said, ushering them to a small table near the window. As soon as they sat, a waiter was pouring hot tea, the warm liquid streaming down from the metal pot. Then he left with a slight bow.

"You speak Chinese?" Gin whispered.

"There'd be no perks of private school and tutors if I didn't, right?"

Gin shook her head and stared at the menu, all in Chinese. She wasn't even sure if she was holding it the right way. "Well, I've been happily educated in the public school system, which means I have no idea what this says."

Felix bit his lip. He hadn't even glanced at the menu—he was watching her. "Anything you don't like?"

She started reaching for her phone to check *HungerStriker*—there was a special mode for situations like this—but instead, she shook her head.

"Then I'll order. If it's okay with you?"

A waiter came, and Felix gave his order in Chinese, one sentence after another, until Gin was worried they'd have enough food for ten. The waiter smiled and nodded as though Felix was choosing all of the best dishes.

After the waiter bustled back to the kitchen, Gin picked up her cup of tea, warming her hands.

"So, you come here often?" she asked.

"Often enough." Felix drank his cup of tea in two gulps. "There's always some sort of dinner prepared at home, but if I'm out windsurfing late or just walking the city, then this is where I usually come. How about you—do you have favorite places in town?"

"Anything except pizza." He raised his eyebrows, and she shook her head. "Don't ask."

"Well, I'm not a big pizza fan either. Unless it's Giovanni's. And the entire football team and cheerleading squad is there." Felix sighed. "Just kidding. Obviously."

"I thought you liked them. I mean, they like you."

"I don't mind them. But none of them are my type, you know?"

"Then why do you . . ." She stopped herself, unsure of what her question would sound like.

"Why do I act like I like them?" Felix grimaced. "Well, I think being nice to everyone is the right thing to do. Even football players have hearts, you know?" He gave her a sad, sappy look, and she couldn't help laughing.

"And I guess, it seems like the best way to get through school without making a big deal of it. You know, just be friends with everyone. Then they stay off your back. It only takes a few bad incidents in elementary school to realize there's power in not having enemies."

On one hand, it was disconcerting. On the other, she liked him all the more for it. "So it's all an act?"

"I don't know. That makes it sound terrible, like something my dad would do. And I don't mean it like that. They're not bad people."

She waited for him to say more, and when he didn't, she scoured her chest for the courage to ask the question she'd been wanting to ask for weeks. "And the girls, too? You know you could date any of them in a heartbeat." She flushed as she said it.

"I guess they're not bad. But they're all the same. You know, they're in the bell curve. In that big section with 95 percent of everyone. They don't really stand out."

Before Gin could ask how girls like Caitlin—who was not only smart and nice, but also incredibly gorgeous—could not stand out, a large bowl of soup appeared before them, trailing a ribbon of hot, rising steam. The soup was actually crackling and spitting, and Gin's mouth opened in surprise.

"Sizzling rice soup," he said, ladling it in her bowl. "A specialty here. You'll love it."

And not surprisingly, she did.

// Twenty-Two

The city streets shone, damp from the burst of rain that had fallen while they ate. It was early in the evening, still fairly warm, and with the mist, everything felt quivery and fresh.

Gin and Felix were walking through a grassy area near the Kennedy Center. How they'd even gotten there was a mystery to Gin: she'd been too focused on Felix.

Dinner had been delicious. Even better, they had talked about everything—modeling, of course, and school and family and music and books. She'd even told him about *Love Fractal.* He liked her logic, and he had laughed when she described Hannah's matches, and then her own matches. And though he was confident it would be a huge success, he swore that he'd never let a program pick who he dated.

He had slipped someone a credit card before a bill even came but promised she could help cover the next time. The next time. Those words rang in her chest like a gong.

Even the fortune in her cookie, which she'd normally joke about, had seemed so right that she tucked it in her pocket to save. *A new interest is at your fingertips. Seize the moment!*

They still had an hour and a half before the crows settled down and became easier to track visually. So Felix was taking Gin to two more stops. But he refused to tell her where.

Gin tried to guess, thinking of all the places in DC

that Felix might like. Only, she had no idea how to narrow the list down. But she didn't have to puzzle through it long, because soon they were cresting a small hill, Felix pointing ahead to the glowing marble statue of Abraham Lincoln himself. "There he is. Stop number one."

The Lincoln Memorial. The immense statue looked solemn and stately in its white stone box with towering columns and rows of steps. In a way, it was like a huge, tiered cake. Gin had visited it a few times as a girl, and remembered feeling that the steps were endless, the carved man like a giant.

"You like Lincoln?"

"I do." Felix started jogging towards the memorial, motioning Gin to follow. "Come on, I'll show you."

They reached the moon-white steps and Felix didn't slow, racing up two and three steps at a time. Gin, however, was full from their dinner and tired from the first sprint, and her jog slowed to a walk. When she finally made it up, Felix was sitting at the base of Lincoln's shoe. She leaned over to catch her breath.

"He was a simple man, you know. The stories are all true. Log cabin. Hardworking." Felix's voice rang out in the structure. They were surprisingly alone. Gin stood up and looked around, deciding that it was much more fun to visit at night when there weren't hordes of people taking photos and jostling around.

Felix leapt to his feet and grabbed her hand, leading her to Lincoln's side. They looked up at him—his thick wavy hair, kind eyes, steady mouth, long limbs, all frozen in smooth, white stone.

"Ostentatious, isn't it?" Felix's tone was suddenly harsh.

"Wait, what?" Gin asked. "You mean, the Memorial? Or Lincoln himself?"

Felix reached his arms out wide, as if to encompass the massive marble and stone structure. "The Memorial, of course. Lincoln, no doubt, deserved a memorial. And maybe he should've been honored in a big way. But back in the early 1900s, when this was designed, lots of people thought it was too much. That it didn't come close to representing who Lincoln was." He looked harder at Lincoln as though Lincoln understood. "It just goes to show how easy it is to mess things up with money. I mean, if they really wanted to represent Lincoln, they should have made something to show how he was only a man. One man, like any one of us. Maybe that would make us all dream bigger."

Gin closed her eyes, breathing in the night air. She touched a finger to Lincoln's cold marble leg. And she wondered for the first time what Lincoln himself would think of such a statue. "You have a point."

Felix took her hand, starting to lead her back down the steps. "Then let's go to stop two—dessert."

"Dessert" was not what Gin imagined. She had pictured a cozy coffee shop or a late-night bakery or even a street food vendor. Instead, they were standing in front of a church. Not a church like the National Cathedral, with sprawling gardens and stained glass and spires. This church was plain and dumpy, like all of the nearby buildings. There were beat up Fiats and old Chevrolets parked in front, tough-looking men standing at the corners, and alleyways on either side that were littered with blanket-wrapped homeless people and trash-filled shopping carts.

"Is this safe?" she whispered as they walked in.

"Absolutely." Felix clapped his hands, enthusiastic as ever. "I mean, in relative terms, of course. But I come here every week, and I've never had a problem."

The inside was bright, but as worn as the outside. It smelled like sweat and bleach and canned peas. And it was full of people. Sitting along the hallways, standing in corners. And Gin realized that this church was also a soup kitchen.

Felix seemed right at home. As he walked down the hall, he gave at least a dozen high fives. Everyone, it seemed, knew him.

Soon they were in a large room filled with tables. A slender man wearing a white robe came up and shook Felix's hand.

"Hey Felix, my man," he said. It took Gin a second to sync his casual words with his formal appearance. "Glad you're here. And you brought company?"

"Hi, Father Mark," Felix answered. "This is my friend, Gin. We came for dessert."

"Good to meet you, Gin." He held a hand out, his face calm and happy, the wooden cross around his neck swinging as he leaned forward.

Gin shook his hand, surprised to see he was young and fit. Cute, even. But the robe made it all feel slightly silly, like he was wrapped up in a sheet.

"We're mostly done for the night, so no need to help out. Just enjoy the food. Banana pudding is on the menu." Father Mark leaned closer and whispered, "I had two servings, it was so good."

Felix laughed and pulled Gin to the food line, which was comprised of a row of plastic tables manned by scraggly men and women. When Gin and Felix reached the first woman, she leaned over and tousled Felix's hair, then let out a deep, low belly laugh.

"How you been, Felix? Felix the cat. You here for dinner? And you finally brought a friend for us to meet?"

"No dinner, just dessert. And, yes ma'am, I did bring a friend—this is Gin. Gin, meet Rosa. She works here every Friday."

"Got that right. But just for a little longer, 'til my real gig comes up." She winked at Gin and sent them down the line. "Hey Freddie," she called. "Be sure and hook up Felix and his friend now, okay?"

There could be no doubt that Freddie hooked

them up: he ladled so much banana pudding in their bowls they had enough for a small party. Felix led the way to a table in the corner, where a man with stringy brown hair ate alone.

"Hey Rick, this is my friend Gin," Felix said as they sat down.

Rick didn't look up.

"Rick isn't real talkative," Felix continued. "But he's still cool. Right, Rick?"

Felix dug into his pudding, stopping to introduce Gin to whoever came up. Which seemed like everyone.

"You must come here all the time," Gin said during a break between visitors. "But is this okay, just to come and eat? I thought you had to be, you know . . . homeless." She whispered the last word.

Felix smiled. "True, usually the people who come to eat are homeless. But, everyone is welcome. And it's good for others to eat, you know? Keeps it more human. I come and volunteer once a week, sometimes more. And I eat every time. It's Father Mark's rule—you come not just to serve, but to let others serve you."

It was a dichotomy he was showing her, from the Lincoln Memorial to the soup kitchen, and Gin was trying to unknot the whole thing in her chest. All she was sure of was that Felix should be taking Ancient Worldviews. He could probably teach it.

"Come on, almost time to find the crows. You going to eat all that?" He held his spoon over her pudding.

Gin pushed the bowl closer to him. "Let's share."

And then she was eating banana pudding, creamy and sweet, in the middle of a soup kitchen, surrounded by men and women who probably hadn't had a fair shake in months or years, maybe their whole lives, with one of the richest boys in the city. And the weirdest part was, it didn't even feel that weird.

The night was starting to seem epic. Gin could already tell it'd be one of those experiences that branded itself onto her brain, her neurons hardwiring themselves to it, letting all sorts of thoughts travel near, over and over, so she would never forget it.

"I think we got one." Felix was holding his receiver up in the air, watching a green light flash. "Come on, we're close."

They were in an exclusive part of DC with polished row houses and old trees and lines of Audis and Mercedes and BMWs. Gin felt like she had just been on her first real tour of the city; in a few quick hours, they had sampled the socioeconomic extremes.

She smelled dinner grilling somewhere and imagined a wealthy couple with friends over. Relaxing after work, not even thinking of all the Rosas and Ricks a few miles away.

Suddenly, Felix stopped. He put a hand in front of her so she'd stop too, and held the receiver up higher.

"She should be right here. Just listen and look," he

whispered. He pulled Gin close to his side, and at first, all she could hear was his breathing. If she was braver, she'd wind her fingers in between his, squeeze his hand, lean her head against his shoulder.

Instead, she looked for the crow.

There was the swish of cars in the distance, layered in with muted city sounds: a truck backing up, a honking horn. Street lamps glimmered in the bare tree branches.

She scanned the houses with their painted trim and heavy doors. Then she saw it. Half a block down on the ledge of a second-story window, there was something small and dark. It blended in with the shadows, so that it was nearly imperceptible. And it was almost as still as a statue.

Almost. Because when it shifted, its dark beak shone. A crow.

She grabbed Felix's arm tight. "There," she whispered. "I see her."

Felix followed her gaze, and when he saw the bird, he took Gin's hand and started walking down the sidewalk. Step by step, closer and closer, Felix's receiver flashing all the way. "Yep," he whispered. "That's Maggie."

It was fascinating at first, seeing Maggie out there in the city. No net or cage to hold her, just perched on the windowsill. But the longer Gin watched, the stranger it all felt. Because Maggie was unimaginably still. Sometimes she shifted and hopped to one side of the window ledge. But mostly, she stood there. As though she were there for a specific reason.

"What's she doing?" Gin whispered. "Is she okay?"

Felix shook his head. "I don't know."

They watched for a full ten minutes, which felt like an eternity. It was so long that Gin was getting worried a neighbor might see them and call the police. Finally, they crept closer, out from behind the tree where they'd been mostly hidden. And that's when Maggie noticed them.

She turned her head, flapped her wings and hopped a few times.

"She's excited to see us," Felix said.

Maggie glanced back at the window, as if deciding whether to stay or leave. Then, with a burst of black feathers, she flew down to the tree and perched above them.

"Hey girl," Felix said. "How are you?"

As if in answer, Maggie cocked her head, watching.

"She's waiting for me to put my hand up," he said quietly. "If I did, she'd come here. But I don't want to interrupt her work. Because it seems like work, doesn't it?"

Gin could hear the confusion in his voice. He thought this was strange, too.

"What does your father do with them at night? When he takes them out?" she asked.

Felix shook his head. "I guess I don't know." He looked quickly around the street, as if expecting his father to suddenly appear. "I thought he let them fly around the city for a while, like a joy ride, then had them stay in one area to practice retrievals or things like that. That he just wanted to get them out around the big buildings and traffic and everything. But with Maggie . . . it's like there's something more."

They watched the bird a minute longer. Eventually, Maggie flew back up to the window ledge. She stayed there for another five minutes. And then she took off, paddling her powerful wings through the air.

As Maggie left, she held her beak slightly open, as though carrying something. When she passed close to a street lamp, there was a glimmer in her beak. A tiny spark in the night. Enough for Gin to see what she was holding.

A small blue bell.

On the drive home, Felix was in good spirits. He had been impressed by Maggie's abilities—to stay still for so long was something that surprised even him. But he was also confused. He listed all the explanations for why she could've been at that window, trying to guess what his dad was hoping to accomplish with that training. The most plausible explanation, he decided, was that she was practicing a new retrieval process.

"You got the address, right?" Gin asked. She was trying to form her own theory for why Maggie had been there. Maybe it helped Grant Gartner study the crows' learning process. He could be tracking how long it took Maggie to process environmental clues. It was a stretch, but she didn't have any other ideas.

Felix handed her his phone. "Absolutely. Right here in my notes. You can look it up now. Or later. Maybe it's time for some music?"

He turned up his speakers, and Gin rolled the window partway down and leaned back, forgetting about Maggie for the moment. The wintry air swirled through the car as they flew through the night, out of the city. Felix tapped the steering wheel in time with the music, pausing now and then to glance at her. When their eyes met, they'd smile.

"Hey," she said. "The plane parking lot."

They were driving right by it, the parking lot where you could stop and sit under the planes taking off from Reagan National. Felix pulled hard to the right, and before she knew it, they were parked by the edge of the river, a line of planes with flashing red and white lights circling in the sky above.

"Come on." He hopped out of the car and grabbed a thick wool blanket from the back. He climbed up on the hood and held a hand out to Gin.

"Come on . . . where? You want me to come up there?" The parking lot was mostly empty, but it still felt silly to climb up on a car.

"Um, yes."

There was nothing else to do but to take his hand.

"Here, this will help." He spread the blanket out on the hood.

She slid down, leaning carefully back against the cold windshield. He settled in right next to her, their bodies touching. Felix pulled the free side of the blanket over them both, tugging her even closer.

It was suddenly warm—only Gin's face was still cool.

The sky seemed bigger, the city bright along the horizon. The river rippled like static and troughs of tiny waves caught the city light and let it go, over and over. Gin could hear the lapping water, close, and the rush of traffic, far.

Then the plane came. Like an earthquake, low and rumbly. The sound was building behind them, but before she had a chance to look back, the plane was overhead. It was so close, it looked massive. Its immense silver body was straight and heavy. Impossible how it hung in the sky.

"Wow," she whispered and leaned against Felix's chest. Their hands met, almost by accident, and he wove his fingers through hers. For a full three seconds, the ground shook.

She could feel him looking at her, and she turned her face towards his. His face shone bright, his eyes glowed, and his mouth was set, confident. But something about him seemed tentative, like he was waiting. His lips parted, and she felt an urge to reach out and trace them, first the top, then the bottom.

Instead, her brain listed out reasons to look away. One: she needed to keep her focus on school, and Felix was obviously a distraction. Two: it was unlikely he liked her, and she was probably setting herself up to be let down. And three: *Love Fractal* certainly hadn't put them together. But even if all of that was true, it suddenly felt like none of it mattered.

"Gin," he whispered. He pulled one hand out from

under the blanket and touched the side of her face, pushing a few strands of her hair back behind her ear, running a finger down her jaw to her chin. She could feel the warmth of his breath.

"Yes?" she whispered back.

"I . . ." He narrowed his eyes as though searching for the right words. "I . . ." He leaned closer and closer. Until his eyes closed. And his lips were near hers.

And then they were kissing.

Kissing. Gin's whole body felt flooded, as though electricity ran through her, every bit of her suddenly alive. From her burning lips down to her tingling fingertips and into her warm, flip-flopping gut, she felt it: Felix was who she wanted.

She didn't pause or reassess or reevaluate. Instead, she leaned closer to him, her body against his, and she touched his cheek, his hair.

He kissed her harder, like he'd been waiting for this. And all she could think was that this was what it was like to feel his lips. Soft and tender and fiery.

He wrapped his arm under her waist, pulling her closer still, and the warmth and the night and the sky and his lips made her feel like she was slipping through a dream. She'd never felt this before, not even close, and she didn't understand how it could suddenly appear.

Unless it had always been there.

But there was no time to think, to analyze, because they were still kissing. And so for that moment, she turned her brain off and did the only thing she could do: kiss him back.

They kissed through a dozen more planes then finally lay there, watching the sky and each other. Felix couldn't stop grinning, and neither could Gin. Later, as they drove home along the dark, woodsy, suburban roads, Felix held her hand tight, their forearms resting on the console.

The whole night had been magical. Gin couldn't make sense of it, so instead, she hummed along with the music, stole one look after another at Felix, put her window down for a minute at a time, letting the air freeze her face.

When they reached her house, he turned the car off, and they sat for a second, in the quiet.

"So . . ." he finally said.

"So . . . That was, um, fun?" She smiled at him, and he smiled back, and then they were laughing.

He shook his head and shifted in his seat so he was looking straight at her. "Really fun. Something I've wanted to do for a long time."

She narrowed her eyes, her mouth opened in surprise. "Wait, what?"

He held her gaze. "I've liked you for a while, Gin. And I want to, you know, spend time together. Watch some more planes, maybe . . ."

They started to laugh again, and he sighed, tugging

at his shaggy hair and letting it shift back into place. "I guess, what I'm wondering is, whether you'd be up for it? To hang out again?"

She nodded, fast. "Yes. Any time."

He let out a breath as though relieved and leaned close again, his face inches from hers. "Okay. We'll make a date."

And then they were kissing again, deliciously kissing. And Gin never wanted it to end.

Gin waved to Felix from the door, watching the lights of his SUV until they disappeared down the street. Inside her house, she stood for a second, feeling the night wash through her again. She put one hand to her mouth, remembering the feel of his lips, the closeness of his body.

"Hey, honey."

Gin looked up, startled. Her mom was sitting on the couch in fleece pajamas, her hair in a messy ponytail, her glasses on, a textbook open on her lap.

"Did you have a good night?"

There weren't enough words for the night she had just had. "Yeah, it was good. It took a little longer than we thought to find the crows—that's what our whole project is on, these crows that Felix trains—and so we ended up walking around the city a little and grabbing something to eat." She was talking too fast, trying hard not to grin stupidly.

"That sounds good. And you stayed in the safe parts of the city?"

"Yes, Mom." Gin rolled her eyes, but didn't ask her mom to clarify her definition of safe. "I thought you were at work tonight."

"I was, but someone needed to swap shifts last minute, and frankly, I can use the time to study." Her mom pushed her glasses up on her head. "But tell me about Felix—he's Grant Gartner's son, right? He must be pretty . . . wealthy?"

"Yes. But Felix is down-to-earth. Not like his dad. I mean, Felix is smart and all, but he's pretty relaxed." Gin walked into the kitchen and grabbed a snack, so her mom wouldn't see her smiling like crazy.

"It's no big deal," Gin continued, walking back to the living room. She stood at the bottom of the stairs and ate a handful of chips. "We're just partners for that computer modeling class. It's a good thing, too, because he's actually a good programmer. Anyway, I should probably go to bed. Need my sleep and all, right?"

"Right. Me too. Well, see you in the morning, hon."

Gin bounded up the steps, and only when she was in her room, door tightly shut, did she pump her arms, jump up and down, and silently scream, "Yes!"

Then in an old notebook she used for recording funny quotes and random ideas, she wrote one line.

Senior year goal No. 1: Find (and kiss) a boyfriend. Check.

// Twenty-Three

When Gin got to school on Monday, Felix was waiting at her locker. He was looking the other way, so she took a moment to watch him: how he leaned against the metal door, his notebook tucked under one arm and his pencil behind his ear.

So this was real.

Technically, she shouldn't have been surprised. They had messaged all Sunday and even talked on the phone that night. But she hadn't even told Hannah. She had wanted to wait until school, mostly to see if he would pretend like it didn't happen or say it was all a mistake. She'd still tell Hannah if that happened, but she'd rather have the whole story—better not to gush on like an idiot only to be dumped the next day.

When he saw her, he smiled and walked straight for her. Definitely no mistake.

"Hey." He nudged her shoulder with his and put his arm around her.

And she knew then, with 100 percent certainty, that even if she tweaked and corrected and revamped *Love Fractal*, and it still never matched her with Felix, she would choose this, choose now.

"Hey." Her cheeks warmed and her heart pounded. The way he was looking at her made her want to kiss him and laugh at the same time. "What?" she finally said.

"Nothing." He leaned close, touching his head to hers. "Just glad you're here."

As she opened her locker and organized her bag,

he stayed there the whole time. She felt like she should say something, but she didn't know what to say, and truth was, it was entirely comfortable just to be there. Together.

"So, the crows want to see you." He was watching her, still grinning. "Maggie said so. After her big night on the town, she wanted to tell you about it."

"Okay." Gin matched his smile. Their mouths would be so tired from all the smiling, they may never kiss again. "I'd like to see them, too. You know, to catch up."

They started walking down the hall, Felix's arm around her shoulder again, a comfortable fit.

"Today?" he asked.

"That'd be nice."

"It's a date. You, me, the crows. Maybe we'll even find some time for that project."

When they reached Gin's English class, they stood facing each other. "I guess I should go to class," he said. "Unless you think I can follow you around all day. I could hold your bag. And your hand?" He took her hand and made his eyes look sad and stunningly cute.

She managed to shake her head.

"That's what I thought. Okay, I'll see you soon." He kissed her on the cheek, light and soft, and left. Partway down the hall, he turned and waved. She waved back and, before she knew it, she was sitting in her chair, listening to a lecture. She couldn't even remember walking into class and taking a seat.

School was entirely different with Felix. He met her at break, and again at lunch. Gin had texted Hannah so she wouldn't be too surprised, but it didn't feel weird. If anything, it felt more normal. Like Gin and Felix had always been together. In modeling class, they worked on their crow program. It was so fun, it felt like class was over in five minutes.

After the last bell, Gin waited outside for Felix. He was going to give her a ride to his house and bring her back to school to get her car. Totally inefficient, but inefficiencies were no match for more time with him.

Hannah showed up first and gave Gin an excited, jumpy hug. "Okay, so I need more details," she said. "When did this happen? And how? He's so into you. I knew he at least kind of liked you, but this is . . . real."

"Saturday. Obviously your outfit helped. We went out for our modeling project, but I guess it turned into a date." Gin couldn't help how the words bubbled out, matching Hannah's enthusiasm. "This is good, right? I mean, it seems like it's working."

"I'd say it's working," Hannah squeezed Gin's arm, hard. "Well, have fun. Felix seems great. Even if his family is, you know, a little out there. Whose isn't?"

Gin looked up, and the beat up 4Runner was there, Felix waving from the driver's seat.

"There's no hope now—you're in this," Hannah said.

Hannah was right. Gin was in this. No matter what.

"I'll see you later?" Gin asked as she walked to his car.

"Yeah. Call me tonight."

"Even if *TimeKeeper* doesn't tell me to?"

"Especially if *TimeKeeper* doesn't tell you to."

Gin pulled open the door and slid down into the creaky passenger seat—she definitely liked the 4Runner more than the fancy SUV. As soon as she was inside, Felix took her hand, pulled it to his lips, and kissed it. She'd never grow tired of his lips.

"So, I thought we'd make one stop before the crows," he said.

"Okay. What is it?"

"A surprise." When she frowned, he held up his hands as though it were out of his control. "And on the way, I want to hear more about you. You know—what you like, what you dislike, what you really think of school."

"Like a life history?"

"No, no. Just some intel. On Regina Hartson. Starting with . . . what's your favorite color?"

She laughed, checking his face to see if he actually wanted her to answer. Apparently, he did. "Um, most days blue. Pretty typical, I know, considering that 30 to 40 percent of Americans choose blue as their favorite color. But majorities are there for a reason. And, sometimes, my favorite color is orange." Too much information yet again, but somehow with Felix, it didn't seem to matter.

"Okay, got it, blue—like most Americans—and orange. Favorite food?"

"Popcorn."

"Popcorn?"

"The homemade kind, with lots of butter and salt. It's the only thing my dad can cook besides pancakes. When my sister and I were little, he'd show us the kernels in the pot, and we'd each have to guess how many there were and what percentage would pop. Then he'd make this huge bowl, and before eating it, we'd count every piece of popcorn and see who was closest. Once I guessed both numbers exactly. It was like a miracle."

"That's crazy. And fun. Can we do it?"

"Absolutely. So how about you, what's your favorite food?"

Felix shook his head. "Uh-uh. Still my turn. What's your favorite book?"

Gin scrunched her nose. "What's up with all of these favorites? You know, it's actually hard to pick one favorite, because different things can be favorites for different situations. So maybe my favorite book for a quick, fun read is Sherlock Holmes—"

"Somehow I didn't peg you as an Arthur Conan Doyle fan."

"Yeah, well that's the point. I might love that for certain situations, but it's not like it's my all-time favorite. That's too hard. Although right now, *Franny and Zooey* is at the top of my list."

"Good book. Fits well with your analytical-yet-seeking side."

"My what?"

Felix held up a hand. "Next question: what inspires you?"

"What inspires me?" She felt her face warm—it felt so personal, not to mention the fact that she'd never asked herself that question.

"Yes. What *inspires* you?"

She glanced at him and noticed how his wooden bead necklace seemed shiny in the sun. It looked like eighty beads altogether. Maybe ninety.

"I guess . . . numbers."

"Numbers?" He was curious, not teasing, but it still made her blush.

"I mean, not the numbers themselves, but what they represent." She was talking fast, trying to explain. "Counting. Measuring. Putting an order to things. It's like language, the basis of all our communication. And higher math. And physics. And all of the principles the world runs on. I mean, atoms are made of certain numbers of protons and electrons—the very numbers define which element they are."

Felix was quiet for a second, his face thoughtful.

"That's cool. I hadn't thought about it that way. But you're right. So, numbers . . . I like it. Anything else inspire you?"

Gin looked out the window. They were on the highway now, and she still had no idea where he was taking her. The sun was lower, lengthening shadows and turning the air a creamy gold.

"Sure, other things do. Like sunsets. All of those colors, the different wavelengths of light, the thought of the earth spinning. And trees. I mean, they're fractals, so that's pretty cool. And the sound of one hand clapping. I learned that in Mr. Ryan's class."

He laughed, and the light glinted off his teeth. "Okay," she said in her most serious voice. "Now it's really your turn. What inspires you? Feel free to add in favorite color, food, book."

"All right, I'll answer a few. I like the color green, my favorite food is hot dogs, and my favorite book is—*Oliver Twist* and *Siddhartha* and *The Lord of the Rings*." He said the titles fast so they ran together.

"And what inspires you?"

He rolled the windows down a bit, letting the cool air in. "Crows, definitely. But you already knew that. Following your heart, using your instinct—that stuff is major. And authentic people. You know, the ones who are real, genuine. Like you. And, the last thing that inspires me is what we're about to do."

When they first reached the river, Gin thought they were going to sit there and watch the sunset, which would be fitting, since she had just said she liked sunsets. But Felix opened the back of his 4Runner and pulled out two long, rolled up pieces of plastic. Soon he was blowing them up with a pump.

"Inflatable stand up paddleboards," he said. "You'll like it. It's easier to learn than windsurfing. And it gets you out on the water."

"But it's freezing."

He stepped towards her, so close she had to lean up against the car, hemmed in by him. Then he stepped closer still, their jackets touching, his feet on either side of hers, and put his hands on her shoulders.

"It's cold, I know. But I have a wet suit for you. And I promise, the chances of falling in are very, very small. And I also promise that you'll love it. Okay?"

She sighed, trying to think of a reason she couldn't do it, but there weren't any that came to mind, especially not with him so close. Finally, she nodded.

Felix smiled wide, leaned in, and kissed her. And it was like she was already swimming.

She could plug this paddleboarding option into *Decider*, but the answer wouldn't matter. She already knew that she'd do it. Maybe, when it came to Felix, she'd never be able to turn down any of his ideas. And maybe that was okay.

As soon as she pushed out on the water, she was certain it was a mistake. The wind was cold and strong, chapping her face and whipping her hair. The waves had looked small from shore, but seemed to grow once she was in their midst. The wide board bobbled. It felt insubstantial, like all it would take was a gust of wind to send her overboard, into the murky, cold river.

She made herself breathe slowly, in and out, telling herself that the worst thing that could happen was that she fell in. And even that wouldn't be a big deal, because she was wearing a wet suit and a life jacket, and Felix was with her. Nothing to worry about. At least, that's what she tried to make her brain understand, so it, in turn, could tell her body.

Felix gave her pointers. How to stand with her knees slightly bent, weight centered; how to reach out and paddle, leaning into the water; how to switch the paddle from one side to another so she'd move in a straight line. He took off to show her, and within seconds, he was gliding over the water, his board smooth, his back and arms and legs flexed, effortlessly balanced.

"See," he said. Water dripped from his paddle and glittered with the light. "Use your instinct. Your body knows where center is."

Gin gritted her teeth, determined. She kept her knees slightly bent, her stomach tensed, her paddle poised, her eyes straight ahead. She focused on using her instinct, whatever that meant. It couldn't be *that* hard.

And, as it turned out, it wasn't. It took some time to get the feel of it, and she wasn't nearly as fast as Felix, but soon she was gliding over the water. The little waves bounced her up and down, but it wasn't enough to throw her off.

"Fun, isn't it?" he shouted.

That's when she realized she was smiling.

// Twenty-Four

"So, what's the verdict—did you like it?" Felix brushed his hands together after eating his last pizza pocket and took a long gulp of milk.

"Yes." Gin pushed her plate away, finally full. She'd been so hungry after paddleboarding, she had polished off more pizza pockets than Felix. "Though I would've liked it more without the fall."

She had fallen in, once, as they were paddling back to shore. Even through the wet suit, the water was so icy it took her breath away. But Felix was there in a second, jumping in and helping her back up. When they got to shore, she had dried off and changed in the back of his 4Runner. Then he blasted the heat in the car and held her, letting his body warm hers. That's how they saw the sunset. Definitely her best one yet.

"Everyone falls in."

"That's not what you said earlier."

"The probability of falling in at any given time is very small. But everyone falls in at least once." He finished his glass of milk and set it on the table, hard. Then he took Gin's hand, gently tugging her out of the kitchen. "Come on, let's see the crows. They've been waiting for you."

The aviary was so dark, it was like staring into a cave. Felix turned on some little tiny lights spaced around the walls, and Gin felt like she was under a star-filled sky.

Soon Gin's eyes adjusted, and she could see dark silhouettes of the birds: three, ten, dozens of them, perched all around. She followed Felix until they were standing under a tree. He leaned back against it, still holding her hand, and pulled her body close to his, so she could feel the rise and fall of his breath.

There was a rustle of wings and a loud, harsh ke-awww. Catherine was right above them, settling on a branch. Her feathers were plumped out, and she tilted her head left and right, as though inspecting them. Finally, she made a quiet, low, chuck-chuck-chuck sound.

Felix laughed. "Catherine's trying to figure us out, I think. She's never seen me like this. You know, so close to someone."

"Interesting." Gin wasn't sure which part was the most interesting: Catherine's apparent thought process, or the fact that Felix hadn't been like this, in this spot, with anyone else. "You think they can reason like that?"

"Well, you know they're smart, right?"

"Right."

"So smart that they can recognize faces and figure out puzzles." He rubbed his thumb over her hand and it made her whole body feel squeezed together.

"Right." The word came out almost breathless, and she cleared her throat.

"So don't you think they could recognize other things, like emotions?"

"What are you saying? That all this makes you emotional?"

He grinned, his lips dark in the shadows. "Well, something like that." He was watching her intently and shifted his hands so they were around her waist. She placed one hand on his arm, and, with the other hand, she touched his cheek. His eyes were so focused, almost serious, and before she could catch her breath, try to slow down her heart, he was leaning in and kissing her.

She lifted her hand higher, traced one finger over his eyebrow, pushed her hand through his hair. And then they were pulling each other down, until they were kneeling on the ground, facing each other, kissing. Bodies pressed close. His arms around her waist. Her arms around his shoulders. Reaching for more of him.

Without warning, a loud, powerful "caw-caw" suddenly rang out. Gin and Felix jumped. And they sat back on their heels, looking sheepish, as though they had just been caught by their parents.

"That was a real crow, right? Not a crow-bot?" Gin looked up into the dark trees, worried for a moment.

"Yes. Real crow. The crow-bots are resting in the workroom for the night. Too much crow-bot time, and the real ones get annoyed."

"Then that was pretty funny."

"Wanna try again?" Felix was still holding her hands, and he pulled her closer, but she nudged him back. She wanted a second to catch her breath and think. To be sure her mind was part of all of it.

"How about if we talk about our project for a minute?" It was the only thing she could think of. "After all, that's why I came over. Right?"

"You didn't come over for this?" He leaned closer. The warmth from his breath was intoxicating. It pulled her in, and she had to force herself to lean back, further from him. She hugged her knees to her chest and looked down for a second, then met his gaze.

"Maybe there was more than one reason."

"Thought so. But okay. We can talk about our project." He settled back against the tree and held his arm out to the side, and she nestled in close to his chest. He was wearing a dark gray fleece and brown cargo pants, blending right in with the aviary's woods. "So, we're studying crows. Modeling their flight behavior and how they interact in the aviary. All to create a simulation—an agent based model, most likely—to study flocking behavior of a more intelligent species of bird. Does that about cover it?"

"I guess it does." They hadn't done an agent based model in class yet, and she was looking forward to trying one. They'd set up rules for the crows as individuals, then the program would let a group of individuals interact. Gin and Felix would track what happened, looking for new behaviors that emerged at the group level. "I think it's going to be good."

"Absolutely. This model will be good. And in case you were worried about the data part, let me reassure you on that point." He stood up and bounded over to a wooden panel in the wall. After pressing a hidden button, the panel opened, revealing an entire room filled with computers and screens and drives. Lights blinking. Two chairs, each at a console. Like a command center for a small airport or army.

"Whoa. That's incredible." Gin walked over, standing just outside the room, as if stepping in would set off dozens of alarms. "What is it?"

"This is part one of our big project: data collection. Did I mention my dad's a little anal about the crows? He's kept all the data about all of their behaviors for years. We have everything we'd ever need to know right here. Where they've flown and perched and slept every second of their lives. This is data central."

Gin shivered. "This is . . . I mean . . . This can't just be a hobby."

Felix looked over the computers. "I guess the data feeds into his AI program. Or maybe it helps him train the crows better."

"Are you sure? I mean, did you ever figure out why Maggie had stopped at that house?" The feeling Gin had when they saw Maggie in the city bubbled up in her chest again. This all seemed to be something . . . bigger.

"Maybe she was casing the house so my dad could send in a team of burglars later." Felix raised his eyebrows. "You know, since he needs some extra cash and all."

"Okay, okay, I guess it's silly." Gin shook her head. "I was just trying to figure out how it connected to the AI program. Or some other research project. Or . . ."

"You sound worried. But you shouldn't be. My dad is smart, but Maggie's a crow. That's it. Nothing crazy high tech. But you should look for yourself. I'll send the raw data on their movements to you." He sat down at one of the computers and started typing. "I'm putting it on my super secure file sharing site and sending you the link right . . . now."

"I'm sure you're right. It's probably nothing. It's just so different." The hard drives blinked, and it seemed like they were reiterating her point. Because the computers weren't regular PCs, amped up with lots of memory and storage. At least two were top-of-the-line gaming computers, no longer reliant on SSD or DRAM, but using a hybrid storage technology that was supposed to come out in a few years. "And these computers . . ."

"Right? The crows may not be high tech, but the computers are. Anyway, we should start playing around with the data for our project." He was back at her side, tugging her hand, pulling her into the aviary. "Plus, if you're following hunches now, I'm all for it."

That's when Gin realized that was exactly all it had been—a hunch. A feeling or a guess based entirely on intuition, not facts.

"So, I guess we have step one of our model creation covered?" Felix pulled her in tight, resting his chin on her head.

Their final project, and the trained crows, and Mr. Gartner's strange interests felt miles away. "Yeah, all covered."

"So maybe we'll start now with our night observations? Like, what the birds do on a typical evening."

"Sounds good to me." They were still for a few minutes, watching, when one of the crows—Frederick, maybe, ruffled his feathers and tucked his head down.

"You get that?" Felix whispered.

Gin nodded.

And before she could say anything else, they were kissing.

// Twenty-Five

The last week before winter break was frigid and windy, the skies like slate and the trees leafless and sharp. Monday night, after all the kissing in the aviary, Gin had gone home and finalized her college applications, including the one for Harvard. The applications had been ready for weeks, and she was certain they were as good as they were going to get. Plus, she wanted to have plenty of time over break for Felix. And so, without overthinking it, she pressed submit, seven times.

The rest of the week had been all about the crow model. Felix and Gin started after school and worked until almost midnight for three days in a row. The work was fast and furious and good. With an agent based model, they'd have less upfront coding. But they'd have a lot more to do after the model was created, examining all of the scenarios and figuring out which ones, if any, showed an emergent trend.

Most flocking models relied on three rules of inter-action: alignment, or how a bird would naturally keep moving in the direction other birds were moving; separation, or how a bird would shift to avoid other birds that got too close; and cohesion, or how a bird would move towards nearby birds. Gin and Felix decided to start with those rules, then add others based on what the data showed.

They already had an example flocking model to play around with. It was beautiful to watch: at first, the computer screen would be splattered randomly with hundreds of "birds," all represented by little kite shapes. The birds were all heading in different directions, none of them coordinated. But slowly, as the birds moved around the screen, they began to align, moving together in the same direction, flying as if in a wave. Flocking. Order arising out of chaos.

It took her breath away every time.

Since Felix and Gin's model would use a group of more intelligent birds—crows—there was a chance that a new pattern would emerge. And their model was coming together amazingly fast. Felix felt it, too. As they were working, he kept pausing, shaking his head, and whispering things like, "Wow. This is good," or, "Now this is better than I ever expected." And they'd work some more.

Their styles complimented each other. Felix, with his crazy fast thought process and unyielding logic and "bits of soul" he always wove in. And Gin, with her attention to detail and strong analytics and sense of how all the parts fit together. It felt like they were meant to be a team, meant to do this together.

But as much as Gin loved the modeling, she also loved the breaks from modeling. When, without warning, Felix would tug her close, his face so near she could feel his breath, and they'd kiss. His hands would move to her hips, thumbs pressed tight to her waist; her hands would settle at the small of his back or on his chest or in his hair. Then one of them would pull back for a second, and they'd both grin, and then they'd write some more code, the logic falling out of them as though it had always existed, and they were hanging it up, like laundry on a line.

They worked at his house so they could take crow breaks, when they'd layer on their jackets and hats and gloves, and walk out over the dormant lawn, which was either crunchy with frost or slick with mud, and sit in the aviary. The more Gin knew about the crows, with their quick wits and astounding intelligence, the more beautiful they became. Watching, waiting, learning. Smarter than pets. Smarter than young children.

Smart enough to be doing something.

Gin couldn't shake the idea that the crows were part of something bigger, had some sort of a purpose. The AI research was the most logical connection—after all, crows were one of the most intelligent animals around. But it seemed like there was another layer. Though if that were the case, surely Felix would know about it. Unless his relationship with his father was so bad they barely talked about anything, even the crows.

The data didn't help. She had looked at it a few times, trying to find some pattern, something that suggested what—if anything—the crows could be doing. She had even researched trained animals: homing pigeons had been used to carry messages in wars, while turkey vultures could sniff out rotting corpses from thousands of feet away. Even the U.S. Navy used dolphins to find land mines planted in the oceans and to patrol harbors for unauthorized swimmers; the dolphins would then tag either with a buoy to alert officials.

But there was nothing about crows. So she stopped trying to figure it all out. She was thinking enough as it was—about the model, about the last bit of classwork she had to do before break, about Felix. Mostly Felix.

Funny thing was, with all of that thinking, she wasn't even using her other models, the ones that could help her maximize her time. She had stopped using *Outfitter* altogether—instead, she'd pull on outfits that she thought Felix would like, or that he had already complimented, or that just felt right. There was no need for *TimeKeeper*, because all of her time, like her thoughts, was consumed with the crow model and homework and, of course, Felix. And *Decider* felt almost obsolete, as though there were no decisions to make.

That, in itself, was an odd sensation. There had always been decisions to weigh, paths to consider. But with her college applications sent off and her relationship with Felix solidifying, it was like there was nothing else to choose.

On the last day before winter break, they had a check-in on their final project with Ms. Sandlin. Gin and Felix went last. After they explained the basics, Ms. Sandlin stared at their model framework and data summary, drumming her fingers.

"Well." Ms. Sandlin leaned forward and folded her hands neatly on the table. "This is one of the best starts I've seen. Certainly in this class. Maybe in any of my classes."

Gin and Felix grinned at each other.

"I'd go as far as to say that this model may rival many that are produced professionally, by teams of people with support staff. Your work is creative, intriguing, well supported. And it could lead to fascinating conclusions."

It was all Gin could do to not leap up and scream with excitement.

"Of course, you still have more to do. But if you keep it up, I believe this is going to be quite successful." She paused to take her glasses off, touching the frame to her lips. "Can I ask how you came up with this idea?"

Felix leaned back in his chair, relaxed as ever. "Sure. It's a family hobby—I mean, the crows are. So we had a good data source that we thought was unique. And once Gin saw the crows out in a field, training, she thought they'd be a good subject for the model. And I agreed."

"Very interesting." Ms. Sandlin was looking at the model again, scrolling fast through screens of data and code.

The bell rang. "Wait one second," Ms. Sandlin said to Gin and Felix, then stood.

"Have a wonderful winter break," she said as students shuffled out the door. "Don't forget to continue work on your models. Remember, it's the majority of your final grade."

Soon Felix and Gin were the only students left.

"Now." Ms. Sandlin was suddenly intense. "I cannot emphasize how impressed I am. It'd be one thing to simply write a flocking model. But this idea, modeling flocking behavior in a more intelligent species, with all of the implications that could have . . . it's quite good. With this work, I have no doubt that you should both be able to join my summer internship program."

Gin put her hand to her mouth. It couldn't get better than this.

"I'll see you after break. I especially look forward to the next check-in."

As soon as they were out the door, Felix turned to Gin and lifted her up in a big bear hug. "Don't you love the crows now?"

"Yes," she said. "I do."

After school, Gin had to work, and Felix was heading to the river, but they met by her locker before leaving.

"You sure you don't want a ride to work?" he asked.

"No, I'm good." She put her final book in her bag, her locker almost completely emptied out for the break. "If you take me now, you'll miss your chance to windsurf. You don't want to be out there in the dark."

"Who says I don't?"

"Well, I'm fine. Anyway, I'll see you tomorrow?" They had planned to go into the city again, this time purely for fun. No crows or models involved.

"Sounds good. I'll pick you up at four." He pulled her close, wrapping his arms around her waist.

She would never get over this feeling of him. As though they created their own magnetic field.

Then, he reached into his back pocket and pulled out a small canvas bag. "An early Christmas present."

Inside was a thin leather necklace with a small pendant carved out of black stone.

"A crow," she said.

"A crow. So you can keep the crows, and me, close to your heart." He wrinkled his nose. "Is it lame?"

Gin shook her head. "No way. Not lame at all. It's perfect."

Then, they kissed.

// Twenty-Six

But Gin didn't see Felix the next day. He had to leave on a last-minute family vacation to somewhere tropical, luxurious, and so isolated he wouldn't even have cell reception. Apparently, it was one of Grant Gartner's quirks to make sure he was unreachable at least part of the year. Felix apologized over and over when he talked to Gin, saying he'd rather stay with her, but that he'd see her as soon as he got back after Christmas.

She was disappointed, but she had plenty to do to stay busy. Like finish her Christmas shopping.

Felix's gift for her had been so nice, so thoughtful, it had thrown her. Hannah insisted that Gin shouldn't overdo it, but Gin couldn't help analyzing all of the options: a hat from a windsurfing company; an old copy of one of Felix's favorite books; a computer-generated ink drawing of him and the crows out in the field.

After hours at the mall and hours looking online, she finally ended up with a pair of canvas slippers for post-windsurfing, and a framed version of an old cartoon of Abraham Lincoln looking at his own memorial and shaking his head, saying, "Where do they think I came from? A palace?" Apparently Felix hadn't been the only one who thought Lincoln would disapprove of his own memorial.

Christmas Eve, after Gin had spent the day reading ahead for class and watching *The Lord of the Rings* movies, Gin's mom bustled in, still in her scrubs, carrying plastic bags of takeout Vietnamese.

"Merry Christmas, Ginny," she said. "I'll just hop in the shower, and we'll be ready to eat. Is Chloe home yet?"

On cue, Chloe burst in the front door. She was wearing a cream sweater dress and purple tights, her long brown hair loose and wavy down her back, her makeup glittery and fresh, even after her two-hour drive.

"Hi, Mom. Hi, Gin." Her voice rang out as she walked in, heels clicking on the wood floors.

The door to their dad's study opened and he stepped out. "My girls are all here!" He hugged each of them, Chloe stepping away quickly before he could get dry erase marker on her dress.

Their mom went to shower, their dad turned on the news, and Chloe hauled in a huge duffel bag of dirty laundry, then set a few packages under the tree, all wrapped in shiny blue and orange paper with big silver bows. She opened one of the Styrofoam containers of food—pork vermicelli—and picked at the bean sprouts.

"So how's senior year? The last year of high school." Chloe dug a plastic fork from the bag and speared a piece of grilled pork. "Sometimes I wish I was back there. No worries. Nothing that really matters, besides sports games and dances and lunch in the cafeteria."

Gin rolled her eyes. "School's good. I sent in all my college applications."

"That's fantastic. Now you can party." Chloe opened another container—this time of summer rolls—and dipped her finger in the peanut sauce.

"Maybe. I still have classes and everything." And a *boyfriend*, she wanted to add. But she knew enough not to tell Chloe anything until she was ready to tell Chloe everything—Chloe would ask for endless details, and likely would tell their parents. "How about you—school's good? And Jackson?"

Chloe pulled her hair over her shoulder and sighed, smiling. "Jackson's fabulous. He's great, we're great. And even though it's college, and classes are important, school is more fun than you could ever imagine. Just wait for next year." She slid out of her heels and sat at the kitchen table, feet tucked under her. "How are your models? Anything new?"

"Kind of. I can show you later if you want."

Chloe took a bite of a summer roll. "Man, I've missed the noodle place. And yes, absolutely. Let's do it soon, though, because I'm driving back to school tomorrow night. There's a huge post-Christmas party, and you know that college only happens once." She looked at her phone, which was buzzing. "It's Jackson. I better take this."

As she left, her voice turned soft and happy. "Hey there. I miss you . . ."

Gin wondered if that's how she sounded talking to Felix. And it made her miss him even more.

With their mom's busy schedule, lots of the regular Christmas Eve festivities hadn't happened, but both Gin and Chloe still got a set of Christmas pajamas: red tops with little reindeer and green striped bottoms, which they changed into before dinner. They all ate in front of the television—*Planes, Trains and Automobiles* was on, which was Gin's dad's favorite movie of all time—then nibbled on store-made Christmas cookies and sipped Swiss Miss hot chocolate. Gin's mom fell asleep on the couch at eight, Chloe went off to talk with Jackson, and Gin's dad went to his office.

Gin called Felix, but as expected, his phone went straight to voicemail. Then she called Hannah.

"Did the Timer model say to call?" Hannah answered.

"Merry Christmas Eve to you, too," Gin said. "And no. Nothing told me to call you. I decided to. Because I wanted to say hi."

"Sorry. It's a reflex, I think. Are you really not using all your models? I was thinking about your outfit Friday and realized I had never seen you in it. So I wondered if your electricity went out and your laptop wasn't charged and you had to figure it out on your own."

"I'm not, I promise." It was kind of funny. Maybe she had relied on the models more than she should have. "I guess I don't need them as much. Or maybe I'm having fun trying life without the aid of logic."

"Sounds very . . . unlike you."

"I'll assume that's a compliment. Anyway, want to come over tonight? We could make popcorn and watch a Christmas movie?"

"I totally would, but Noah's taking me to the midnight Christmas Eve service at his church. And before that, his family does a big fondue dinner."

"Fondue. Sounds romantic."

"Yeah, with his mother and father and brothers all there. And probably grandparents, too. Maybe cousins. At least it involves lots of melted cheese."

"Wow, the whole family. You guys are serious."

"We'll see. But drink some cocoa for me, okay?"

"Absolutely."

After hanging up, Gin checked her phone again, hoping Felix had called or texted or emailed. But he hadn't. So she wrapped her presents: a "Go" set for her dad, an Amazon gift card for Chloe, a gel-filled sleep mask for her mom. She set them under the tree, and pulled a blanket up over her mom, who was still sleeping on the couch.

In her bedroom, Gin opened the window wide to the cold night. The street was colorful with all the decorations. The house on the corner had all of its trees spun round with twinkly lights, bright blue like the crows' bells.

She glanced at her laptop and had the sudden urge to look at the crow data.

But that wasn't something to do on Christmas Eve.

Instead, she shut her window, pulled on Felix's fleece—amazingly, it still smelled like him—and opened her copy of *The Adventures of Sherlock Holmes*, settling on one of her favorites, *The Adventure of the Blue Carbuncle.*

Gin was awake long before anyone else, so turned the Christmas tree lights on, then brewed coffee and made cinnamon rolls, the type that came in a tube. By the time everyone else started to wake up, she had already eaten two cinnamon rolls and watched *A Christmas Story*, which was running all day on TV.

Chloe came down first and dunked a cinnamon roll in coffee while staring at her phone. Their dad stepped out of his office mumbling something about abstraction and perspective. And their mom came down the stairs. She rummaged through the cabinet to find the biggest coffee mug they owned—a UVA mug Chloe had bought freshman year—and filled it to the brim.

"Doesn't anyone else want to sleep until three?" she asked as she sat next to Gin. "I thought that's what you young adults did. Sleep in so late, your parents have to shake you awake."

"Gin doesn't count." Chloe was scrolling through her phone. "She's more like a computer."

"Hey!" Gin threw a couch pillow at Chloe.

"Just kidding, kid sister." Chloe laughed, then grabbed one of the presents she had brought from under the tree. "Here, why don't you do the honors and open this." Chloe handed the blue-and-orange package to Gin.

Inside was a fitted gray UVA t-shirt. "Thanks, Chloe."

"You're welcome. Mom and Dad got them too. That way, you all can properly cheer for the Cavs on game day."

Their mom kissed Chloe's cheek, and their dad pulled his t-shirt over his pajama top. "There," he said. "I'm ready to start cheering now."

He pulled a brown paper giftbag from under the tree and gave it to their mom. "I know you've been busy with school and work, and so I wanted to get you something extra special."

Their mom shook the package. "Let's see—is it an automatic breakfast maker? Or heated slippers that turn on when my car pulls into the driveway?"

Their dad shook his head. "Just open it."

She pulled out a small box first and opened it to find a silver necklace with a blue and green pendant. "This is beautiful." She held the necklace one way then the other. "What is it? It's so unique."

"A refurbished computer chip. Isn't it nice?"

Chloe looked at the necklace. "Wow, Dad, that's actually cool."

Her dad helped their mom put it on.

"Thank you, honey," their mom said.

"But there's more. Don't throw the bag out yet."

Their mom pulled out an envelope, peeking slowly inside. "A gift certificate to the Red Rock Spa? For an entire weekend? You outdid yourself."

"You deserve it."

They kissed, and Chloe and Gin rolled their eyes but smiled at each other.

Soon the rest of the presents were opened. Besides stocking stuffers like ChapStick and lotion and bubble bath and candy, Gin got a hefty gift certificate to TigerDirect, where she purchased all of her computer equipment, along with a new sweater and a set of good headphones. Chloe got makeup and a pair of Frye leather boots.

After the litter of wrapping paper had been picked up, their mom turned on football and started to heat up their Christmas lunch, fresh from a restaurant, while their dad started playing with one of his presents—a large set of old fashioned metal puzzles, which he planned to have solved within the half hour.

They ate together at the table—roast beef and mashed potatoes on paper plates—then their dad turned on the Discovery Channel, and finally, Gin slipped back upstairs to email Felix.

She used a simple graphics interface to customize an electronic card—Christmas lights came on across a small, bucolic town, and at the end, a group of crows flew by, cawing in time to "We Wish You a Merry Christmas."

She sent the card and texted him, then played Speed Solitaire while waiting to hear back. But after an hour, when late afternoon had nearly faded to evening and there was still no word, she went back downstairs.

Chloe was packed and ready to go. Their mom

urged her to stay one more night, but Chloe had never been the sort of person to change her mind because someone else wanted her to.

Gin walked Chloe out to her car. It was dark and cool, a few stars shining. The Christmas lights already felt less magical. Chloe put her coffee and purse in the car and turned to Gin.

"Try to have a little fun, okay?" She looked at Gin, serious—at least as serious as Chloe could look. Her glossy lips were set in a straight line, and her eyes glowed, in part because of her sparkly pink eye shadow. "That's my only advice. There's plenty of time for work. Like, the rest of your life. You need to seize the moment and enjoy yourself. You know?"

She hugged Gin once and climbed in the car. "By the way, I love your outfit. And your hair. Looks like your model thing is working."

She waved and drove off, taillights streaming down the dark street. Back in the house, Gin's dad puttered around, putting stray cups in the sink and humming Christmas tunes, while her mom slept on the couch.

Gin stared at her phone, willing Felix to call. But as promised, he didn't.

// Twenty-Seven

Another day passed, then another, until Christmas break was over and school was starting. Gin still hadn't heard from Felix.

She had tried not to worry at first, but the more time that had gone by, the more frantic she felt. She emailed and texted and called, all with no response.

If something bad had happened to Felix, she wondered how she'd even know. It wasn't like his dad would call her, and she still had never met his mom. Or maybe—and this almost felt worse—he had had second thoughts about whatever it was that he and Gin had started, and he was trying to let her down easily. That seemed unlikely, except that Gin had no point of reference for how these things were supposed to go.

Hannah, who had plenty of points of reference, wasn't worried. She said that if Grant Gartner wanted to be unreachable, there was no way he'd let his son get in so much as a text. And Gin tried to believe it. But when she walked into school the Monday after break, uneasiness had settled into her stomach, coating her insides.

She waited at her locker until seconds before the bell for first period, hoping Felix would suddenly show up by her side. But he didn't. She went to his locker at break, even stopping by his third period class to see if he was there, which he wasn't. And at lunch, she looked around the cafeteria, ignoring her food.

"Look, it's only the first day back," Hannah said, in between mouthfuls of the soft pretzel Noah had bought her. "They easily could've gotten delayed. Or maybe they extended their vacation. They have so much money, they could vacation for the rest of their lives."

Noah, who's hair had been freshly cropped over break, smiled reassuringly. "I bet he can't wait to talk with you. He probably feels really bad about the whole thing."

Maybe they were right. Maybe there was an easy explanation for all of this, and when Felix finally could call, he'd go on and on about how sorry he was.

Or maybe that wasn't the case at all. Right now, the best anyone could do was guess.

Gin could barely keep herself together in Computer Simulations 101—which Felix did not attend—and when the bell finally rang, Gin went straight to Ms. Sandlin's desk.

"Is Felix marked absent today?" she asked. "Did his family call in?"

Ms. Sandlin's hair swung as she glanced at her computer. "Hmmm, I don't have a message. What do teachers usually do, check with the office?"

Gin nodded, and Ms. Sandlin called the office. "Okay, I see," she said, then turned back to Gin. "It sounds like Felix's vacation got extended. His parents said he'd miss the first week back at school."

"The first week?" Gin felt faintly sick.

"That's what it sounds like." Ms. Sandlin was standing now, closing her laptop and gathering her papers. "But I'm sure you can keep the momentum going on your project. And given the progress you've already made, I don't think this will negatively impact your work."

It took a second for Gin to realize that Ms. Sandlin thought she had been worried about the project. "Okay."

"I've got to take off for an appointment. Would you mind getting the lights when you leave?"

After Ms. Sandlin was gone, Gin turned off the lights and stood in the dark classroom. A week was nothing. She could do anything for a week. Even stop thinking about Felix.

But there was one major flaw with Gin's plan: it was easier to decide not to think about Felix than to actually not think about Felix. She did her homework, and halfheartedly looked over her models, but mostly she tried to distract herself: she took walks in the chilly evenings, watched ridiculous television shows, organized and reorganized her room.

All the next weekend, she checked her phone over and over, refreshing her email a thousand times. There was nothing.

Hannah did what she could to help: she talked with everyone she knew, researched social media feeds, and looked at all sorts of vacation spots for the rich and famous, even calling a few to see if the Gartners were there. She didn't find anything, but still reassured Gin that there was nothing to worry about.

On the following Monday night, more than a week back at school and still no Felix, Gin could hear the uncertainty in Hannah's voice. "Maybe something did go wrong," Hannah said. "I mean, if they're really in

some isolated place, how would anyone know if anything happened, right?"

"Exactly." Gin felt something in her settle. At least
if Hannah agreed this was strange, Gin wasn't crazy.

"Maybe you should look into it, you know?" Hannah
said. "You're good with puzzles."

The next day, right after school, Gin sat in her car
in the high school parking lot and called Odin headquarters. She worked her way through a series of re-
ceptionists, until she finally reached Mr. Gartner's
secretary, who politely said that Mr. Gartner couldn't
come to the phone because he was tied up in meetings for the rest of the day.

Gin shook her head, her mouth dropping open in
surprise. "Wait, you mean he's there? At the office? In
meetings?"

"Well, yes. Can I help—"

"No, no, that's fine." Gin closed her eyes, trying to
think. "I'll call back."

She hung up the phone and tried Felix's cell. It
rang this time, but no one picked up, and eventually,
it went to his voicemail.

"Felix." She tried to keep her voice steady. "I think
you're back. Call me when you get this. We have another check-in with Ms. Sandlin soon."

It was a curt message, but she'd already left messages
about how she missed him, and if he was back in town,
he likely had heard them all. He just hadn't called.

Her chest was tight, her hands trembling. She
didn't know whether to be worried or angry or both.

But she did know what she was going to do next. She started her car and left the school, taking one deep breath after another, steeling herself. Because she wasn't going home.

She was going to Felix's.

// Twenty-Eight

Gin stood at the thick iron gate. It was securely locked, the tall brick fence looming above her on either side. For all she knew, security cameras had already captured her image. Anyone inside could know she was there.

But she wasn't going to think about that. She wasn't going to think, period. Otherwise, she'd never do what she needed to do.

She reached out of her car, held her thumb up to the fingerprint scanner, then waited. As the January air chilled her cheeks, she was suddenly sure this idea—this coming here, to his house—was a bad one. But slowly, the gate opened.

Her stomach seemed to twist on itself. It was hard to breathe. She hadn't expected it to work, and she stood there debating what to do next. It wasn't like breaking and entering: Felix had added her prints to the list of allowable guests. Not that she had tried coming in before. Or ever planned to. But given the circumstances, it might pass as appropriate.

And if she didn't try . . .

She drove forward, slowly, hands clenched around the steering wheel. The leafless trees and wintry lawns passed by too fast, and soon she was there, at the mansion. She glanced over to the gray barn and saw a flash of black feathers as a crow flew up to a perch. It steadied her. Of course the crows would be there.

She stepped outside and shut the car door quietly, then walked up the brick steps. And with one shaky finger, she rang the doorbell.

A maid Gin hadn't seen before answered the door. The woman smiled politely, but concern flashed across her face.

"Hi." Gin tried to push her nervousness back down in her stomach. "I'm a friend of Felix's. He hasn't been at school, and I needed to get in touch with him. You know how it is. Everybody always expects to be able to reach anybody at any time." She held her phone up, apologetically. "But it's been more than two weeks now. And we have this big project we're supposed to be working on. So I thought I'd stop by to check in."

She shut her mouth to stop the words from pouring out.

The maid nodded. "I understand. And I'm sure that Mr. Felix would appreciate your concern. But unfortunately, he is not accepting visitors right now."

Gin's heart beat harder, but her entire body felt suddenly cold. So he was here. Close. Not halfway around the world, stuck in a jungle somewhere. But here.

"I just wanted to see him once. I'd be quick. I

think . . . I think he'd want to see me. Could you ask him?"

The maid glanced behind her. "Okay. I will check with Mr. Felix." She opened the door wider, so Gin could step in. "Please wait here."

The maid looked around again and hurried up the stairs. Halfway up, she glanced back, making sure that Gin hadn't moved.

Which, of course, she hadn't. Gin felt frozen, arms uncomfortably clasped in front of her, trying to slow her breath, telling herself there was probably a simple explanation for everything.

There was a clatter of footsteps down the stairs, and for a second, Gin's heart leapt, sure it was Felix. It definitely wasn't the maid—this person was too fast, too heavy. But then she saw the shiny leather loafers and pressed slacks.

And by the time her mind finally understood that it was not Felix skipping downstairs to see her, to give her a hug and tell her he had missed her, Mr. Gartner was there, standing in front her. "Hello, Gin. I have to say, I'm surprised to see you here."

His words were sharp, his eyes steely.

"I'm sorry. I . . . I . . ." Her voice was too small.

Mr. Gartner narrowed his eyes, face emotionless, as though each of her words was wasting his time.

"I just wanted to see if . . . if everything was okay," she said. "With Felix. Because he hasn't been at school. Or texted, or anything. And I was worried."

"I'm sorry, I assumed Felix had called you. Let me assure you, you have no reason to be concerned." His

voice was calm and controlled as though it were ridiculous for Gin to even ask. "Felix is fine. But he has
had a change in his schooling and will not be at
school for a while, possibly the remainder of the year.
Again, I regret that he wasn't able to tell you himself."

Gin felt her stomach drop. "But, we have a project."

"Yes, the *project*." Mr. Gartner stepped closer, drawing out the word "project" as though it were a silly
child's game. "Felix has informed me of this project.
And I have made it clear that neither he nor you will
be allowed to pursue it further. The data that you
were using is private. Proprietary knowledge. The
only moral and legally sound course of action is for
you to delete whatever files you may have and accept
that this work is no longer an option. Then, you begin
a new project."

"But," Gin said, her face flushed, "the model was
going to be good. We spent so much time on it already. And, it'd be useful, something that someone
might actually want to see. And—"

"That's quite enough, Ms. Hartson. I am sorry for
the inconvenience. But if you take any further steps
on this model, I can promise you that there will be
repercussions. And due to the reach of my little company, those repercussions might impact more than
you."

All the fight and energy drained out of Gin, leaving
a thick, sticky fear.

He gave a quick smile, the type that didn't touch
his eyes, and opened the door. "Now, I don't know the

nature of your and Felix's relationship, but I mean to make this clear as well: Felix is not interested in seeing you right now. I apologize if that sounds harsh."

Gin's face was burning, and the ground suddenly felt unsteady. Like it would buckle up and toss her to the side.

"I'll give Felix your regards. And there's no need to try to let yourself in again. I wasn't aware that Felix had added you to our guest list, and I'm afraid that list needs to be updated." He was walking closer to her, and she had no choice but to back up and step out of the house. "Oh, and I'll look forward to meeting with you for your Harvard interview. I don't believe they've let you know yet, but you've made it past the first round of reviews. Congratulations."

The door closed, the dark heavy wood still and secure. As though it would never open again.

Maybe she was going crazy.

As Gin drove out of the estate, along the wooded roads, she knew she needed to talk with someone. But there was no one to call. Hannah was at a movie with Noah and her phone was off. Gin's dad was still at work, her sister was no doubt at a party, and her mom was working or studying or both.

Not that she could talk with any of her family about this. But they at least cared about her, which counted for something. Her mom would be understanding, she was sure of it. And her dad was usually logical, so could maybe tease out some reason in this situation. Even if it was all unreasonable.

Mr. Gartner's threats. His admonition about using the data, as though there was something there, something no one should see. The way the maid had watched her. The crows, which, from the beginning, may have been the strangest of all.

But worst of all, worse even than the fact that Felix may not come back to school, was that he didn't want to see Gin. It was logically possible that Mr. Gartner had exaggerated that part. Except for the fact that Felix hadn't made any effort to reach her.

Gin's chest ached. Tears ran down her face, slipped off her chin. She had to get herself together.

She pulled off on a side street. There were no houses around, just rolling woods as far as she could see. And she set her timer. Five minutes of breathing. She started, one shaky breath at a time, trying to calm herself. Count to four on the inhale, count to eight on the exhale, again, and again.

But it wasn't working. It was too quiet. And it was darker since the sun was almost down. The horizon blushed with a light pink-orange, split by black silhouettes of trees. Her tears blurred everything. She couldn't stop them, not inside the car, with her stupid timer counting down the seconds that she wasn't with Felix.

She opened the car door and the cool air was a relief. Gravel crunched under her feet, and without knowing what she was doing, she walked into the woods. She pulled her sweatshirt tight around her and sat down on the ground, which was thick with old, dry leaves. The trees towered above her, their tips catching the last bit of light until they, too, were wrapped in hazy twilight.

The woods seemed to grow around her, expanding as darkness fell. She listened to the forest: rustles, scampers, clicks of branches. It smelled like wet dirt and decaying plants and winter. The sky darkened.

Somewhere in the back of her mind, she knew that this was not the sort of thing a girl should be doing—to park off a side street and sit in the woods, alone, at dusk.

And that's when she noticed the bird.

It was perched further back in the woods, maybe ten yards away. Shimmery black, with a wide chest and thick beak. A crow.

It tilted its head so one black eye peered down at her. Their gazes held, girl and crow. Watching each other. The woods were so quiet, as though everything else had faded away.

And then the bird pulled back its wings and opened its beak wide.

"CAW! Ke-AWWW! CAW!"

Gin scrambled backwards, her hands pressing into the leaves, into the dirt, moving herself away, fast.

The bird cawed again and opened its wings. In a whoosh, it took off into the settling night, flying away.

Gin sat there, watching it go, her heart pounding in her chest. Then she ran to her car. She slid inside and turned the car on, the engine roaring in the quiet night. She switched on the headlights, did a tight U-turn, and headed back to the main road. Only once she was there did she venture a quick glance back at the woods. And all she saw were shadows.

// Twenty-Nine

That night, Gin barely slept. Her dreams were littered with crows. Clouds of crows that filled the sky, swooping down and grazing her with strangely sharp wings.

When it was early morning, still dark, she opened her laptop and moved the crow data file into the trash. There was no way she could touch it now, not after what Mr. Gartner had said. She brewed a pot of strong coffee, poured a mug, and drove to Hannah's house.

It was 6:05 a.m. when she got there. Early, but Hannah's mother was always up early. And sure enough, it was Hannah's mother who answered the door. She was dressed in yoga clothes, her blonde hair pulled into a low side ponytail. Her face knit up with concern when she saw Gin.

"Gin, how are you? Is everything okay?"

Gin made an effort to relax her face. "Everything's fine. I'm sorry to come by so early. I just needed to see Hannah. Is that okay?"

"Of course, come in." Hannah's mom glanced up the stairs. "Hannah's still sleeping. But she could use an early wakeup call. Why don't you go ahead and go on up. Unless you'd like breakfast first?"

"Thanks, but I'm good." Gin started up the steps, suddenly feeling calmer. Hannah would make sense of everything.

Hannah's room was still dark, and it took Gin a second to see Hannah in the pile of sheets and blankets.

"Hannah," Gin whispered, but Hannah didn't move. "Hannah," she said louder, shaking Hannah's arm. Finally Hannah groaned and turned to her side.

"What? Is it time?" She mumbled the words, her eyes blinking open, and falling back heavy.

"Hannah, wake up. I need to ask you something."

Hannah rubbed her eyes and scrunched her face as she looked at Gin. Then she sat up, fast. "Oh my gosh—something's wrong. Are you okay? What happened?"

Gin shook her head. "No, it's fine. Don't worry. I just need your opinion."

Hannah scooted over, and Gin sat next to her, pulling the comforter around her.

And Gin told her everything. About how she called Mr. Gartner's secretary, only to learn that the Gartners were in town. About how she went to Felix's house. About how Mr. Gartner said Felix may not come back to school, and that Gin had to stop using the crow data. And how Felix didn't even want to see her. At that part, Gin's eyes teared up.

"I don't get it," Gin said. "I don't know if I did something, or if Mr. Gartner is even telling the truth, or . . . It doesn't make sense, does it?"

"It doesn't." Hannah's eyes were wide. She pushed her tangly hair out of her face. "It's really, really weird. But, maybe it's in the realm of possibilities. I mean, Felix changed schools before, right? And his whole lifestyle, it's different. His family could take off and live anywhere at any time they wanted." She paused, quiet. "I think you need to try to talk with Felix. And maybe, be prepared for whatever he says. I mean, nothing happened with you guys before, right? He didn't act upset or mad or—"

Gin took a sharp breath and shook her head. "No way. There was nothing."

"And you've been dating for only a few weeks, right?"

Gin cringed. They had only been dating for a few weeks. Not long enough for Felix to owe her explanations about his life.

"Look, Felix doesn't seem like the type of guy who would disappear and not even say a thing. Maybe he's grounded or something. What's your gut say?"

"My gut? Right now . . ." she paused, put her hands on her stomach. "Nothing. My gut says nothing."

"Hopefully he'll call you soon. I'd give it another week."

The way Hannah said it, it sounded halfway reasonable. Maybe Gin had blown everything out of proportion.

"I'm sorry, Gin. Are you okay?"

"Yeah, I think so. Thanks. I better head home. Can't go to school like this, right?" She looked down at her pajamas.

"Who says?" Hannah squeezed her arm. "It could pass as '90s grunge. Flannel pajama pants and all."

Gin gave a small smile.

"I'll see you at school," Hannah said. "Okay?"

For that moment, at least, everything did feel possibly okay.

The moment didn't last. All week, everything was off. Gin was forgetting tests and papers and homework. Leaving her laptop at home. Oversleeping. A few teachers asked if she was sick. Even her mom had skipped part of a class so she could take Gin out for sushi and ask her question after question about whether anything was wrong.

Of course something was wrong. Not that she could tell her mom. Even if she could, she wouldn't know what to say, because she didn't know what had happened. And she hated not knowing.

If Felix had called or texted or emailed—anything—she'd at least know something. Like whether he was okay. Whether Mr. Gartner was a jerk or actually was hiding something about the crows. And whether everything that had happened between Gin and Felix was even real.

She checked her phone constantly. Each time, her heart beat a little faster. Each time, when there was nothing from Felix, she felt let down all over again.

Friday night, her dad made popcorn. "I know that Mom is better with this stuff." He set the bowl of popcorn, which smelled of hot oil and melted butter, on the coffee table. "But she's not home until tomorrow morning. So, is there anything going on that you want to talk about?" The light from the television flickered on his face, over his worried eyes.

"No, everything's fine. I'm just overloaded with school. It's nothing to worry about." Then she had a thought—maybe her dad *could* help. "Actually, remember how I told you I was doing a project with Grant Gartner's son?"

"That's right. He's the one you've been hanging out with, right? How's that going?"

"Not well. Felix had to leave school, and now I'm stuck with a project I can't do—Mr. Gartner said we couldn't use the data—and it's kind of a mess." She rubbed her eyes, hard, and tried to keep her voice from cracking.

Her dad tapped his chin. "What was the project about?"

"Crows. The ones the Gartners train. We had all this great data, and the model was almost finished. But now I'm going to have to start over. And I still don't get it—why would Felix suddenly be yanked out of school?" Her voice was rising, turning nearly hysterical, and she felt her eyes tearing up with frustration. Even her dad noticed; he leaned closer and narrowed his eyes, trying to better understand.

"Anyway." She made her voice calmer. Everything would be worse if her dad got worked up. "I didn't know if you had heard anything about the Gartners. If anything had changed, or . . ."

"No, I haven't heard anything like that." Gin's dad

put a hand on her shoulder. "That's too bad about your project. I'm sorry, honey. I'm sure Mr. Gartner is challenging at times, but that does sound a bit unreasonable. I could try to get him a message, if that would help?"

Gin shook her head. That would only make everything worse.

"Well, you're smart. I'm sure you'll think of something." He glanced at his phone. "Pizza should be ready. I'm going to pick it up—and I'll grab some frozen custard on the way back. Vanilla and chocolate? Oh, and I think you got a message. Maybe Hannah called?" He set her phone on the table and left.

The message was bright in the dark living room. Gin's heart stopped as she read it once. Then again, and again.

Because it was from Felix.

// Thirty

He had written. Actually thought of her and typed a message and sent it. That was a good sign, wasn't it? If only his words made more sense.

Gin, I'm so sorry I had to disappear. My dad changed up the rules—he's good at doing that. Everything should calm down in a few weeks, but for now, I'm laying low. No technology for me—imagine that. I found a way to send this, but you won't be able to text back. I wish I could explain every-

thing. And see you. But I can't. I just want you to know that I wish I could. I'm sorry. And, I'm sorry I can't help with the model. Good luck. Felix

She stared at the words, wondering what they meant. Grant Gartner keeping his only son from all technology. Felix not being able to call her, much less see her. And even though he said he wanted to see her, it didn't feel like enough. He sounded so casual about the model. Of course, she needed more than good luck. She needed an entirely new project.

She texted back, right away. *Felix, if you're there, call me. Please.* But the message didn't go through. She tried a second time, and a third time. And she tried to call. Nothing worked.

The room suddenly felt too small, but there was nowhere to go. That's when she started crying. Crying for the fact that she still had no idea what was going on with Felix. Crying for what wasn't in Felix's text: that he missed being with her so much, he'd do whatever it took to make sure they could still be together.

Minutes passed, one after another, until her face was wet and her throat was raw. Crying made everything worse. And it made her mad. Mad at Felix for disappearing. Mad at Mr. Gartner for making her abandon a good project.

She went upstairs and sat in front of her computer. And before she could change her mind, she was dragging the crow data file out of the trash and onto her desktop. Maybe the answer to everything was in the data. Maybe she hadn't looked hard enough.

The data went back five years. There were time-stamped GPS coordinates for all the birds. Details on their body temperatures and weights. Records of every training session, every movement. Piles and piles of numbers.

She had already analyzed the data. But this time, she would keep her focus tight: the movements of one bird during one day.

Minutes later, she had built a map. A simple one that overlaid Catherine's movements over the course of one day a few months earlier onto a satellite image of Northern Virginia and DC. The first part of the day wasn't surprising. Catherine was in the aviary, her movements confined to the woods around Felix's house. She covered a wide area but returned often to what seemed to be her favorite spots.

Late in the day, in one long, steady arc, Catherine moved into the city. Clearly, she was driven there— her path stuck to highways and roads, and her speed hit seventy miles per hour.

Gin enlarged the portion of the map that showed Catherine's time in the city. The first few hours, Catherine's flight pattern seemed almost erratic. She'd stay in one city block for a few minutes, then take off for another area. It was interesting, but it didn't seem odd—the movements mirrored what she did in the aviary.

But at 9 p.m., Catherine stopped moving. She was almost perfectly still, staying exactly in one spot. Almost like she had gone to sleep.

Finally, at 11:00, Catherine flew a few blocks, then must have been collected in the car and driven home.

Gin focused in on the address where Catherine had stopped. It turned out to be a large office building—an entire compound, really. So she googled it.

And the result made her gasp.

She was looking at an image of a satellite office of InTech, one of the biggest high-tech companies in the world. It couldn't be a coincidence that a crow owned by the CEO of Odin was hanging out at an InTech office.

And Gin realized one scenario that could help make sense of everything: perhaps the crows were spies.

Maybe Catherine had a tiny microphone to record conversations, or a video camera to take images of people entering passwords. In some ways, the idea was ludicrous: surely it'd be hard for Catherine to get any information by sitting outside an InTech window. But on the other hand, it would explain everything.

Gin's heart beat fast as her fingers flew over her keyboard, pulling up more data on the other crows' movements. She needed more than one crow stopping at one location: she needed a trend, something that showed lots of crows stopping at the same spot over time. Maybe she was on to something. Maybe her gut had actually led her to a truth. She held her breath while the equations ran.

And that's where the link dissolved.

In thousands of other flights, the birds stopped at hundreds of other places around the city. Not only at InTech's office. They stopped near houses and parks and warehouses and other office buildings. The InTech office was one of the least frequent stops.

Whatever complex training scheme Mr. Gartner had set up, it was not focused on InTech.

She rubbed her eyes and turned off her computer. Nothing was clearer, nothing was answered. She'd been waiting so long for Felix to reach out, but now that he had, she didn't know much more, besides that he was alive. It felt like information purgatory. And she needed to get out.

She tried to call Hannah, but Hannah's phone went straight to voicemail. And so Gin called the one person she knew she'd be able to get a hold of: Lucas.

It didn't take long for Lucas to get to her house. He was surprised she had called, then ecstatic when she asked if he knew of any gaming events she could attend, because—just her luck—there was one that night. He insisted on picking her up and bringing her to it. Before she had time to rethink the soundness of this plan to distract herself, he was at her house, opening the door to his blue Volvo.

"You know, it's fortunate you called when you did," he said. "Because this is one of those nights that you wait for all year. And look, you decide to get into it, and this is what's going on. Pretty cool, right? I think it's a sign."

The car smelled like vanilla air freshener and was meticulously clean. And Lucas drove slow. To his credit, he didn't drive below the speed limit, but unlike everyone else in the greater-DC area, he held steady right at it. Gin wanted to move fast—that was the whole point of getting out—and now she was stuck, inching along, having to think.

That's when she saw it: Lucas's cell phone.

"Lucas, could I borrow your phone for a quick call? My battery's almost dead."

"Sure, no problem." He handed her the phone without a question.

Her hands shook as she dialed Felix's number and pressed the phone against her ear. Street lamps flashed by, and she bit her lip as she listened to one ring. Then another.

She didn't know what she'd do if Felix picked up. But maybe it was just her number that he wasn't answering.

A third ring. A fourth. Her whole body was tense, her heart racing in her chest as though it would squeeze out from behind her ribs to get closer to the phone, closer to possibly hearing Felix's voice.

Then an automated message. *The mailbox is full and cannot accept any messages at this time. Goodbye.*

There was a beep. And silence. Gin listened for a few seconds longer and hung up.

She put the phone back and looked out the window, pressing under her eyes to keep any tears from spilling out. "How far away is this place again?" she asked.

"Not that far. A few more miles. We'll be there in T-minus ten minutes. Hey, did I ever tell you about that time I clunked the goblin?"

"No." She did her best to steady her voice. "But I'd love to hear about it."

When they got to the bar, Gin found herself wishing Hannah was there. Hannah, at least, would've gotten Gin a drink. And this time, Gin wouldn't have turned one down.

People and computers were jammed into the bar so tight, Gin and Lucas had to push through bodies to find a table. As they walked, Lucas gave her an apologetic look and grabbed her hand. "I don't want to lose you," he shouted. "I'd never find you in here."

She didn't mind holding his hand but hoped it didn't give him the wrong idea. She felt her body tighten, the dread building in her chest, when she realized maybe that's what Felix had done with her— given her the wrong idea.

And then, in the middle of the flashing lights and focused gamers, she was thinking about him. Again. Which was so frustrating that for a second, she wished she had never met Felix. If only they hadn't had modeling class together. If only he hadn't transferred to her school.

Maybe she *could* start over. Right then, she could pretend they'd never even met. She'd just have to find a way to make her brain believe it. And if she couldn't trick her brain, she would busy it.

They finally sat down—Lucas must have been somewhat important in the gaming realm, because there was a console reserved for him—and Gin immersed herself in the imaginary world of castles and goblins and machine guns and moons.

"Oh, that's a gunderlick," she said, pointing.

Lucas smiled, obviously pleased. "That's right. You're a quick study. Now watch what I do here."

And she did.

// Thirty-One

By the end of the weekend, even the smallest decisions were too much—Gin stood at her closet trying to get dressed, and when she saw a shirt Felix had complimented, she actually started to cry. She didn't feel like doing or eating anything. So she did the only thing she could—she used her models.

She reviewed all of the logic, made a few tweaks, and ran each of them throughout the day. *TimeKeeper* gave her a schedule and provided things to do during any downtime. *Outfitter* ensured she got dressed. *HungerStriker* confirmed she was eating somewhat balanced meals—or at least eating, period.

She even ran *Decider*.

Scenario: Your so-called boyfriend disappears and doesn't call. Recommended course of action: Sounds like a good time to move on.

Hannah came over Sunday afternoon—a good time to be social, according to *TimeKeeper*. Gin still hadn't told her about Felix's text. Maybe if she'd been able to reach Hannah on Friday, Gin would've said something. But the more time that went by, the harder it was to bring up. In a way, she felt stupid. If Felix had actually liked her, he would've done more than sent a nebulous text.

Hannah asked how Gin was doing. But Gin just shrugged. And soon Hannah couldn't help talking about Noah. How they were really good together—similar, but different in the right ways. Hannah was toning down her excitement, Gin could tell, but it still bubbled through.

Gin got ready for work while Hannah talked. Finally, when Gin glanced in the mirror—*Outfitter* had recommended gray slacks and a gray blouse, as though it knew how Gin was feeling—Hannah sat up and looked at her.

"Wait," Hannah said. "Something happened. I can tell. Are you okay?"

Gin looked away.

"No, really." Hannah stood next to Gin, looking closer. "Did something happen with Felix?"

Gin could see Hannah was worried. And she imagined a scenario in which she broke down and cried. And Hannah would hug her and say that it would be okay. Maybe even that Felix was stupid, and Gin could do better. That there were dozens of other guys—better guys—out there. But then she realized that telling Hannah wouldn't fix anything.

"Felix texted." Gin bit her lip. "He said he was sorry about everything, but that he couldn't talk about it. I mean, he was nice, but it didn't sound like he really missed me or anything. And if he did, he would've found a way to come by, or call, or something. Maybe we're officially broken up. If we were ever dating in the first place."

"What?" Hannah looked alarmed. It was exactly how Gin had felt, but it was worse seeing it on Hannah's face. "Even if he does have to go to another school, you could still see him, right? Why wouldn't he be able to call or email or something? He likes you. This doesn't make sense at—"

"Well, it's the reality." The words came out all wrong—too fast, too harsh. But Hannah's concern was making Gin feel worse. Like Gin had to feel everything all over again. And she was suddenly sick of it. "Sometimes reality doesn't make sense. But it's reality. So by default, it has more weight than any other imagined scenario."

Hannah held up her hands. "Okay, sorry. I just, I think it'd be good to talk about. Maybe we can figure something out."

"There's nothing to figure out." That was an understatement. Hannah could hardly figure out her own love life, much less help Gin with a situation like this. Gin was shoving things in her bag now—cell phone, water bottle, granola bar. "I've considered all the scenarios, and they're all dead ends. I'm not that girl who will go running and crying after him. I tried that, and I can't even get through to him. So, obviously, it wasn't meant to be. Anyway, *Love Fractal* never even put us vaguely together."

Hannah chewed her lip. "Gin, it's okay to be upset," she said in a quiet voice.

"I know that." Gin paused, checking her bag for the third time.

"I mean, you don't have to be logical. *Love Fractal*—it's good, but it's not everything. It can't predict *life*. And Felix, that was real."

It was easy for Hannah to say. She'd had dozens of boyfriends, and if things didn't work out with whomever she was dating, there'd always be another one. Gin hadn't found anyone who *liked* her. It was stupid to think a good-looking, popular boy in school would. The more she thought about it, the more she realized that the best thing she could do was to move on.

"Anyway." Hannah put a hand on Gin's arm. "You don't have to rely on computers for everything. It's not like you're Steve Jobs."

Gin looked down at her bag, her face burning. Hannah knew better than to say something like that. Because Hannah remembered when, at the beginning of sixth grade, Gin answered the teacher's question "What do you want to be when you grow up?" with two words: "Steve Jobs." It was a truthful answer, but it had come across as immature and silly. Even worse was that she'd been teased about it all year. And now, Hannah made it sound like a joke. Maybe everything about Gin's life was a joke.

"I know I'm not Steve Jobs. I'm not trying to be Steve Jobs." She pulled her bag over her shoulder and looked straight ahead, anywhere but at Hannah. "I better go."

"Wait, Gin—don't be upset."

Gin paused at her doorway. And without another word, she left.

At work, Lucas was slumped over in his chair, asleep. A first for Lucas. The gaming competitions must've done him in. Friday's winners had gone on to a second round Saturday night that could last for hours. Apparently, he'd been a winner.

Gin sat at her computer, trying not to think about what Hannah had said, wondering if maybe it had been true. Maybe she'd been trying to make herself something she wasn't, something she'd never be.

Hannah texted. *I'm sorry, Gin. Let's go see a movie or something. Screw Felix.*

But Gin didn't text back. Instead, she stared out her window at the damp, gray city.

Lucas sat up, startled. "What? Where am . . ." He looked around, worried. "I must have drifted off. It gets so quiet on Sundays, you know?" He started typing fast, pausing to rub his face as if to be sure he was awake. "Got to make up for lost time," he mumbled.

After a few hours of work, the code was swimming through Gin's mind. Every now and then, she'd glance at her phone, thinking that she should text

Hannah back. But Hannah was the last person she wanted to talk to.

Suddenly, like a dark wind, a crow fluttered onto her windowsill. Shiny beak. Clawed feet, legs free of tracking bands. Not one of the Gartners' crows, but a wild one. Its head tilted, so it was staring right at her, its round black eye tracking her own.

It felt too close. As though crows would be following her for the rest of her life.

She hit the window with the heel of her hand, hard. The thump scared the crow away. She watched it, wings smoothly paddling through the air, and turned back to her work.

"Those birds," Lucas said.

She turned, surprised to see he'd been watching her.

He shook his head. "They seem like such a nuisance. But you know, they're actually quite smart."

On Monday, Gin steered clear of all the places she'd usually see Hannah. Instead of going to the cafeteria for lunch, she headed to the library, sneaking bites of her granola bar while looking through her modeling notes, ignoring the worry in her stomach. She knew that Felix shouldn't disappear. It wasn't normal for someone to be in school one day and pulled out the next.

But her logic took over, reminding her of the facts:

she barely knew Felix, she still didn't understand why he liked her, there was a chance he regretted everything and was letting her down easily. The best thing to do was to give it a little time—another week, maybe. Anyway, she had enough to think about: she had to create a new model, one that was worthy of a good grade, and quickly.

Maybe Ms. Sandlin would let her team up with another group or give her a ready-made model idea that would be easy to do. Maybe it'd work out to Gin's advantage. The only way to find out was to ask.

With ten minutes left in lunch, Gin headed to the computer simulations classroom. Only Ms. Sandlin was there, working at her laptop. Gin cleared her throat. Ms. Sandlin glanced up and waved Gin over.

"I hope I'm not interrupting you," Gin said.

"Oh, not at all." Ms. Sandlin tucked her hair behind her ears and closed her laptop. "I was just working through the logic for a new airport security system. I'll show you sometime. But I'm glad you stopped by." Ms. Sandlin patted a chair near her desk, and Gin sat down.

"As you may already know, the Gartners have informed the school that Felix won't be returning." Ms. Sandlin paused, as if to gauge Gin's reaction.

Gin closed her eyes for just a moment, steadying her breath. Then it was final. She may never see Felix again. She squeezed her hands together and stared straight ahead, just past Ms. Sandlin to the empty white smartboard

"Final projects are due in less than three months.

This work is the majority of your grade and is critical in determining who will be a part of my summer internship program."

Gin gave a small nod.

"And with Felix gone, I'm afraid you'll have to finish on your own. But the work you and Felix have already done is so intriguing, I know you'll be able to finish well."

Gin grimaced, trying to collect her thoughts. She had to set aside the part about Felix not coming back and deal with that later. For now, she had to focus on her final project. Or rather, her lack of a final project. If only she had emailed Ms. Sandlin first. She could have laid out her points neatly, logically, instead of trying to stumble through them now.

"Well . . ." Gin started, taking a deep breath. "About the model—I think there's a problem with the data. Not that it's bad. Just that, it's data the Gartners don't want us—or me—to use."

Ms. Sandlin furrowed her eyebrows. "The data on crow behavior?"

Gin nodded.

"Why wouldn't they want you to use it? I wouldn't think data on crows would be sensitive." She leaned back. "Would you?"

Gin shook her head.

"And you have this data?"

Gin bit her lip, trying to decide how best to answer. "Yes, I still have it. But it's proprietary. Or at least, that's what Mr. Gartner said."

Ms. Sandlin tapped her nails on her desk. "Well,

that is disappointing. I had high hopes for your model. Do you have other ideas?"

The truth was, Gin had zero other ideas. Unless she could use *Love Fractal.* "I have one I started over the summer. A dating program."

"I saw that in your application for this class. But you wouldn't be able to use it for this project. This has to be something new. Look, it's always hard to shift from working as a group to working as an individual. But it happens. Not only in academic settings, but in the work world as well. For some, it becomes an excuse; for others, it's an opportunity to shine. I hope you will be one of the latter."

Gin wanted to be exactly that. But she had no idea how.

"I believe you're talented, Gin. You have skills that good modelers need, all of which I highlighted in your college recommendation letters. And I would still like for you to be a part of my summer internship program. But I need to see your commitment. Your ability to think outside the box and make something happen when the road blocks go up. To be honest, this could be a perfect opportunity. Don't you agree?"

Gin's mouth was so dry, she couldn't answer.

"Frameworks for the models are due this Friday. Let me know if you need an extension. We could possibly push it out a week, given the circumstances."

Gin didn't need an extension. She needed an entirely new project.

The clock ticked past another minute and a bell rang. The halls grew louder.

Ms. Sandlin turned back to her laptop. "I'll look forward to seeing what you come up with," she said. "And I'd be especially excited if you found a way to continue with the crows."

Gin glanced at her table, the empty seat that wouldn't get filled, and stepped outside into the hall. She walked to a corner, away from the hustle of students, and opened her laptop. The data file was there, looking innocuous on her desktop, ready for her to use. If only that were an option.

// Thirty-Two

>>*Hello. How are you?*

    Fine. And you?

    >>*I'm fine, too. Fine is such a bland word, though. How are you really?*

    Not so good.

    >>*I'm sorry to hear that. Would a movie help?*

An image of *Harry Potter and the Sorcerer's Stone* flashed on Gin's computer. She sighed. It was a nice idea, but the reality was, nothing was going to help. Things had gotten so bad, she was talking to her computer. Technically to herself, as she had written *Cheer-Upper*. Not that she had anyone else to talk with. Hannah had called and texted a dozen times, but Gin hadn't called back, and Hannah had finally stopped.

Gin was surrounded by mounds of schoolwork— tests, papers, projects—and the final project for computer simulations was looming over her. She had a list of ideas, but none that seemed great, not compared with the crows.

I don't know. Probably not.

>>_You could try watching for a few minutes._

The movie started, with its familiarly mysterious music. The owl, the cat, Dumbledore, McGonagall, Hagrid. Baby Harry Potter. And Dumbledore's line: "There, there Hagrid. It's not really goodbye after all." Maybe it was making her feel the tiniest bit better.

OK. I'll try it. Thanks.

>>_Any time._

The nice thing about computers was that they, at least, would always talk to you.

// Thirty-Three

Gin's mom made her favorite meal for dinner—homemade macaroni and cheese, buttered toast, and fruit salad—but even that couldn't calm Gin's nerves. Because it was possibly the most important night of her life.

Earlier that day, she had received a call from Mr. Gartner's secretary, saying her interview for Harvard was scheduled for that night, in Mr. Gartner's office.

"You'll do fine, honey," her mom insisted, clipping on her hospital badge and setting her dishes in the sink. "They'd be crazy not to accept you at Harvard."

But it wasn't just about Harvard. It was about the fact that Gin would have to see Mr. Gartner.

Everything about the interview felt odd. Usually interviews didn't happen until closer to the spring. Usually they were planned more than a few hours in advance. Usually you'd be interviewed by a couple of people, not by the father of your sort of ex-boyfriend who you had barely heard from in more than a month.

It was enough to make Gin sick. Her breath was shallow, her forehead damp. All she wanted was to go back in time and have a do-over. To change everything.

After dinner, Gin got dressed in an *Outfitter* approved combo of gray slacks, a white collared shirt and a black sweater. She brushed her hair straight, cleared her throat, and practiced saying "Hello, Mr. Gartner," until her voice sounded steady and calm. Exactly the opposite of how she felt.

Her dad drove her to the interview—her mom had already left for work—and it was so quiet inside the car that the click of the car's turn signal seemed to echo.

"You'll do great," her dad finally said. "It's an honor that Grant Gartner is interviewing you. I can't imagine he does this often."

Gin didn't answer, knowing it had nothing to do with an honor.

They were meeting at Odin's headquarters, inside Grant Gartner's expansive office park, which was filled with towering buildings, green lawns and mature trees. Her dad pulled up to the entrance and squeezed her shoulder.

"Sometime soon, I'll take you to the new math sculpture downtown. It sounds fascinating. And it'd be a way to celebrate all of your hard work."

It was a nice thought, encouraging enough to give Gin the motivation she needed to get out of the car.

Odin's main building was massive, with glass walls and a modern rock-fountain in the front. There was a security desk inside the entrance. Gin walked through a metal detector as her bag was checked, then a guard looked at her license and made a call to confirm she was supposed to be there. Finally, he motioned for her to go ahead.

Grant Gartner's office was on the top floor. Even the waiting area for his office, where Gin sat for a long five minutes, had impressive views. Gin could see a swath of dark woodland below.

"One more minute, Regina." The secretary looked up from her desk and smiled, her bright red lips setting off her pale skin. Gin recognized her voice. She must've been the one who had told Gin that the Gartners were back in town. "Mr. Gartner is getting off a call."

The door to the office opened. Mr. Gartner stood in the doorway, his presence seeming to fill the room. "Janie, set a meeting up with Max Weatherly for one week from now. And has the research on the new SIM software come through yet?"

"Not yet, sir, but it should be here by tomorrow morning."

"Okay, good. I'll get you that analysis for tomorrow shortly. We'll only be talking for a few minutes." He turned to Gin and smiled as though they were long-lost friends. "Regina. It's so good to see you again. Please, come in."

He seemed so different from how he acted at his house, she didn't even know how to reply. He ushered her into his office and motioned for her to sit on a sleek leather couch. It was growing dark outside, and she could see their faint reflection in the floor-to-ceiling window. Mr. Gartner stood at his desk and poured himself a drink—bourbon, it looked like—then sat across from her.

"Can I offer you a drink?"

She shook her head fast, wondering if they were already on to the trick questions. "Oh, no, I don't drink."

He laughed. "Of course not. But I have other options—tea, perhaps? Or a soda?"

He tilted his head as though he knew how she had asked Felix for an orange soda. She shook her head, faster this time. "No, I'm okay. But thanks."

He leaned back in his chair and swirled his drink, then took a sip and set the glass on the table. "I've read your application." He leaned forward and rubbed his hands together. "Very impressive. It's clear that you know your way around computers."

"Thank you." She refolded her hands in her lap, her arms suddenly feeling awkward. "I've always enjoyed working with computers. And math. And numbers." She took a deep breath, trying to focus.

"Now, I could ask you about some of your models, some of your work . . ." He paused, and Gin held her breath, wondering whether he'd bring up the crow model. "*Love Fractal,* for instance. Or we could talk about your life experiences, perhaps touch on something you've had to overcome. Or even why you'd like to go to Harvard. But let's start with a simpler question. Tell me something I'd find interesting." He leaned back and watched her, waiting.

Gin bit her lip as she searched for an idea. Something Mr. Gartner would find interesting. Her mind, unsurprisingly, went straight to Felix and the crows. Both of which were off limits, and both of which Mr. Gartner knew much more about than she ever would.

"Well, um . . ." She was certain that this was the moment when her dream of going to Harvard—a dream she'd had for more than a decade—evaporated. When she'd set off on the path to becoming just another computer programmer sitting behind a big screen in an open office, shifting through the minutiae of cumbersome software applications, lost in insignificant code.

"It's much, much more likely you'll take a handful of randomly distributed M&M's and end up with ten of one color, than that you'll win the lottery." Her face burned as soon as she said it. It was a ridiculous thing to say.

Mr. Gartner leaned back and took a slow sip of his drink. "That is intriguing. Do you know this from a study you've read?"

"Yes, kind of. Basic probabilities. And I've been testing it. At work."

"Always good to choose a test subject that you enjoy eating. It is an interesting idea. Helpful, perhaps, in showing people the futility of buying lottery tickets."

Gin felt the tension in her back release. Maybe this *was* just a Harvard interview. Maybe it had nothing to do with Felix.

"Except that it's human nature, isn't it, to pursue the long shot? To try to buy a bit of hope, no matter how improbable something actually is." He let the silence sit there between them.

It felt, for a moment, like the air was being slowly sucked out of the office. Because she knew then that Grant Gartner was telling her again that everything with Felix was over.

"And your modeling class at school—that's been going well?"

The abrupt change of topic made Gin's head spin. She refolded her hands in her lap, wishing she had asked for a drink. At least then she'd have something to do.

"Yes, very well." Gin didn't know if he expected her to acknowledge the crow model and Felix, or if it was better to act like nothing had ever happened.

"Have you found a suitable topic for your final project?" He waited for her answer.

Gin cleared her throat, trying to read his expression—it seemed easy and open, but she knew better.

"I think so. I'm going to model traffic. Specifically around the Beltway. I'd like to create a functional model that drivers actually use, and so it would have logic to account for their reactions to information the model provides." Now, she just had to create the whole thing.

"Good." He tapped the side of his glass and finished his drink. "You know, I stopped in to see your dad the other day."

"Oh?" Gin froze. Her dad hadn't mentioned Mr. Gartner's visit. It couldn't be good.

"I like to do that from time to time. See what people are working on in other parts of the company. It sounds like he has an updated version of *Streamliner* coming out."

"Yes, he's been working on that at home."

"Well, we're glad to be able to support his work. He is a good thinker, an excellent logician. I have no doubt that you'd be able to follow suit. And I'm glad that you understand the value a company such as Odin provides in encouraging people like your dad to be creative."

"Yes, of course."

"Good. Then we're on the same page."

Gin had no idea what it meant to be on the same page as Mr. Gartner. Except that she couldn't so much as think about the crow data.

He looked at his watch. It had been no more than ten minutes. Probably less. "Now, barring any questions you might have for me?" He paused for a moment. Gin had a list of questions prepared, but it seemed like Mr. Gartner preferred for her questions to remain unasked. "I suppose this concludes our interview."

He stood, and Gin followed. "Thank you, Mr. Gartner. I appreciate your time."

He shook her hand, hard. "Always happy to assist the younger generation. It's good to know our future is in good hands."

As Gin left, the secretary smiled warmly. "Have a great evening, Regina."

Gin managed to say a quick, "Thanks." But that was all she could get out. Her face was burning, and her chest felt like it was clamping down on her heart. At least she could still put one foot in front of the other, though she barely felt like she was moving. Her chances at Harvard were clearly gone. There was no way Mr. Gartner was going to give her a good recommendation. He didn't even take her seriously.

The elevator opened. She got on, standing in the back corner and looking at her phone, trying to ignore the fact that her eyes were blurring with tears.

She messaged her dad before the doors opened: *Finished—I'll be outside. It was good.* As clueless as he was, even he would realize that a college interview that was over in less than ten minutes definitely wasn't good.

Her phone pinged a minute later. *I'll be right there. Getting ice cream.*

She walked to the corner of the building and stood near the curb. As she waited, a single crow flew overhead. She watched it, her breath stalled as she wondered if it would stop outside of Mr. Gartner's window. But it kept going, past the building and towards the woods, until it was out of sight.

// Thirty-Four

Gin was finishing an outline for her final project—
she had decided to stick with the traffic idea, because
the Department of Transportation had easy-to-access
data, and at the moment, easy was good—when her
phone rang. She stared at the unknown number and
almost let it go to voicemail. Instead, she picked up.

"Hello?"

"Gin, hey. I'm glad you answered."

It was Felix.

Gin didn't even know what to feel. She'd been waiting for him to call for so long, she'd practically given
up. And now, part of her wanted to hang up and toss
the phone out the window. After all, it'd been exactly
three weeks since she last heard from him, three
months since she had seen him. Her Christmas presents for him were still sitting neatly wrapped in her
closet, and she'd long since put the crow necklace in
the bottom of her jewelry box. The probability that
she'd get a good grade in Computer Simulations was
in the single digits. And her chance at Harvard was
virtually shot. All because of him.

There was no way it should have taken him that
long to call. And he shouldn't sound so relaxed.

But all the same, she couldn't help the desire that
was climbing through her. And all she wanted to do
was reach in and pull him through the phone, to her.

"Oh, hi. I thought you couldn't talk." She tried to
sound nonchalant to match the tone of his voice. As
though she knew "boyfriends" disappeared all the

time. Her heart, however, was racing, her palms already sweating.

"I can't. Not really. Don't even ask me how I got this phone. Or where I am right now. But I wanted to say 'hi,' and let you know again that I'm sorry."

She found herself analyzing his voice, searching for a clue as to why he'd disappeared. He sounded surprisingly fine. Healthy and happy. Not like he was stuck in some stone tower somewhere with only bread and water for nourishment. And yet, the situation was still entirely strange. For a high schooler to have no phone, no email—something had to be wrong.

"I . . . I've been worried about you." It was all she could get out. It would've been more accurate to say she'd literally been sick with worry. And that she needed to know, really, if he was okay. But just talking to him was making every neuron in her brain fire all at once, and it was impossible to think.

"I know. And I'm so sorry. I messed it all up."

It was silent for a second. "It's okay," she finally said. Of course it was far from okay, but somehow, Felix did sound genuinely sorry. A small part of her couldn't help wanting to make it better.

"No, it isn't. To hang out, and kiss, and then suddenly disappear. I'm sorry." He was quieter, more serious. "It was all my dad. He flipped out about us modeling the crows. And maybe I had skipped out on school one too many times, too. But anyway. I messed up—again—and I'm sorry it hurt you too."

As far as apologies went, it was a pretty good one. She felt like she could breathe deeper.

"So, you're okay? I mean, really okay? This whole thing, you have to admit, it's just so . . . odd."

He laughed, and it sounded so much like him that she couldn't help smiling. But there was something else there, too. Insistence, maybe. Or anger.

"That's my dad. That's what happens when you have the ability to control everything in the world. Now you see why I don't love money, right? It messes with your head."

Her next question came out before she knew what she was saying. "Can I see you?"

He was quiet. "I wish. I want to see you, too. It's just, I can't do anything right now. But when that changes—as soon as that changes—you're the first person I want to see. I really like you, Gin. And in the meantime, I'll do whatever I can to call. If that's okay?"

She felt her chest lighten. Because it sounded real. Like he did miss her. He did like her. And most important, it sounded like he was actually okay. "Yes, of course. If it's okay with your dad."

Felix sighed. "Nothing normal is okay with my dad. But he doesn't have to know."

"He interviewed me, by the way. For Harvard."

"He did? Wow, that's good—they usually send him students that are a sure bet for getting in. Was he okay?"

Gin made herself take a deep breath. The last thing she wanted to do was cry. "Not really. Interviews aren't my strong suit. And your dad wasn't exactly interested. The whole thing lasted for maybe seven minutes."

"He's like that with everyone. Quick and to the point. He's not one for chitchat. Look, I bet you did really well. You're smarter than 99 percent of the other Harvard applicants. They'd be crazy not to take you." Felix's confidence, if overly optimistic, was nice. "So how's the model?"

"The model? You mean the final project that I'm scrambling to outline? It's okay, I guess. I'm going to look at traffic patterns. Not as exciting as the crows, but it's something."

"Wait—what happened to the crow model? We were almost finished with it." He actually sounded surprised.

"I thought you knew. I stopped by to try to see you." Her face burned as she remembered the whole en-counter, which felt humiliating in retrospect. "And your dad said not to use the data. That I'd be in big trouble if I did. Then, in the interview, he asked what I was doing for the final project, and I told him I was modeling traffic now."

"You came over here?" Felix's voice rose, suddenly strained.

"Yeah, about a month ago."

"He never told me. The jerk." Felix breathed out, loud, as though trying to calm himself. "I mean, it's one thing to mess up my life, but to do this to you? He's crazy. Completely, totally crazy."

Maybe Felix really had wanted to see her.

"I'm sorry, Gin. That's really, really awful. But, you know, I think you should do the crow model anyway."

Gin's skin prickled, and her breath quickened. It

was exactly what she wanted—to continue with the crow model and end up with an incredible final project. But she knew it was exactly what she couldn't do. "He was pretty clear that I couldn't. Proprietary data and all. I—we—could get in big trouble. And I don't want to make him mad. I mean with Harvard and you . . ."

"I hate him," Felix said. "He makes everything impossible." There was another long break, and Gin waited, eyes closed, trying to make sense of everything.

Finally, Felix spoke, his voice more rational this time. "Here's the thing about my dad. He gets all upset about stupid things. I get that he doesn't want the data out there in the world. But it's only numbers on crows hanging out. You can't build some big AI program by watching crows—you have to know AI. This is a high school project. And even if something crazy happened, like we published a paper, we wouldn't have to make all the data public. Anyway, he'd never need to know. It's for school. How would he even find out?"

A pit swirled in Gin's stomach. It wasn't right, she knew that. But Felix made it sound so . . . easy. "I don't know."

"I could still help you. We need to find some way to share files. Give me a few days to figure it out. Look, my dad has taken pretty much everything away from me. I don't want him to take this, too."

Gin closed her eyes, picturing Felix. His eyebrows knit up in concern, his mouth set straight with determination. She tried to consider his proposal logically, but all she could think of was the fact that if he helped, he'd have to stay in touch. And that felt impossible to turn down.

"I'll think about it." Maybe Felix was right—maybe Grant Gartner had overreacted to the whole thing. "I'd like to. And I guess I could always work on both. The traffic model and the crow model."

"You need to do the crow model. It's going to be good. Exactly the sort of thing you should have on your resume, that will let you accomplish all of those awesome goals. Unless of course, all you want is an orange soda. That would change everything."

She closed her eyes, wishing he were there.

"Look, I have to go, but I'll be in touch. One way or another, I promise. It might take a few days. So keep working on the model. And I miss you. Okay?"

"I miss you, too."

He hung up, but she kept the phone to her ear for a second, listening to the silence, as though to capture those last few soundwaves coming through the phone line. And she opened up the files for the crow model and started to work.

At her internship Friday, Gin felt lighter. Her stomach churned with worry about Felix—after all, he was still officially cut off from the regular world—but it felt easier to accept now that she'd talked with him. She'd heard his voice and he had said that he was, all things considered, okay.

The office was quiet as the full-timers had left for the day. Streetlights popped on, their light dull in the early evening, while scattered windows across the street glowed.

Lucas rolled his chair to the side of her desk to ask for help with an equation, but before he rolled back, he paused.

"So I was wondering about that dating model you were writing. Any chance it's ready for testing?"

"*Love Fractal*?"

"Yeah, *Love Fractal*. Just the other night, I was talking with my friend Allen, and he was going on and on about how he knew there was a girl out there who would like to date him, but he didn't know how to meet her. And I mentioned that you had this model, and that it might need to be tested, and . . ."

He paused, waiting for Gin's reply. She knew *Love Fractal* wasn't completely ready. But maybe nothing was ever completely ready. That was the point of testing. And talking to Felix and considering the possibility of working on the crow model made her feel gutsy. Plus, if it did take Felix some time to call again, another distraction wouldn't hurt.

"Sure. I think that would work."

Lucas clapped his hands together. "That'd be awesome. The guys will be so excited."

"You think they'll want to try it?"

"Absolutely, they'd be happy to do it. You know gamers, they love testing out programs. And these guys could definitely use a date. Or at least the hope of a date. Or the hope that there might be the hope of a getting a date." He stopped. "You know what I mean, right?"

Lucas's excitement was catching. Maybe this was exactly what she needed. "I do. You think Sunday is too soon?" If she waited a whole week, she might change her mind.

Lucas cracked his knuckles and turned back to his computer. "No way. That works. I know the perfect place."

Within minutes, Lucas had posted to three local gamer sites, inviting high schoolers to test a prototype of a scientifically based meet-up service.

Once it was published, Gin pushed any second thoughts out of her mind. "You think anyone will show up? It is last minute."

"These groups are so big, last minute doesn't matter. Someone's bound to come. It might only be a few people—"

"Which would be perfect." She felt more settled. A few test runs might not be so bad after all. "All I need to start the verification process is a handful of data points. Thanks."

"Anytime. We gamers are always ready to help each other out. Just let us know, and we're there."

There was still no word from Felix by Saturday. But Gin ignored her building worry by focusing on *Love Fractal*. She made a few changes to the model, even tried to add in a few "soul bits." She wrote a waiver for each participant to sign, saying that they knew results weren't guaranteed, that they wouldn't pursue matches who weren't interested, and that they agreed not to hold her accountable if anything went wrong. The information in the database was all public information—the sort of stuff businesses might use to figure out who would want to buy anything from Gatorade to Gucci bags—so a simple waiver should be enough to cover her.

Lucas would be there to help check people in and explain the test, so Gin could oversee the testing process. With a half-dozen test subjects, they'd be done in less than an hour. It'd be simple.

When she arrived at the coffee shop on Sunday afternoon, there was a line of people out the door and down the block. She shook her head—leave it to Lucas to choose a popular meeting spot.

She pushed her way inside and spotted Lucas at a table in the corner. As soon as he saw her, he ran up.

"Can you believe it?" he asked.

"Believe what? That we picked a super busy time at a super busy place?" She couldn't help sounding annoyed.

"No, it's just this afternoon." He was talking too fast.

"Then I guess we chose a good time."

"You're not getting it." Lucas turned Gin around,

so she was looking at the line of people. "All of these people are here for you. To try out *Love Fractal*."

The people in line were mostly male, probably ages fifteen to eighteen. A disproportionate number wore black t-shirts with obscure logos and had shaggy hair and pale skin. Gamers.

"Wait. All of these people are here for the test?" Gin's mouth was suddenly dry.

"They sure are." Lucas leaned forward and back, almost bouncing in his shoes. "I told you that gamers like to support research. Or maybe they all really need a date."

Gin felt the blood run out of her face. It was way too many people. *Love Fractal* wasn't ready for this, not even close.

"Lucas, I—"

"Need some help? I know." He was checking power connections on three laptops set up on a series of pushed-together tables. "But with these extra laptops, I figured we could have several people going at once. Keep the line moving."

"Okay, but—"

"Don't worry about anything. If it takes too long, they'll leave. And if you get enough data in the first hour, we'll say the test period is over. This is your thing—you can make it whatever you want."

Lucas made it sound manageable. And maybe it was. It wasn't like she had anything better to do. And a bigger data set never hurt anything.

"Okay." She kept her focus on the laptops, not on the huge line of people. "Let's start. You're okay doing the check-ins?"

"Definitely. And my friends can help." He pointed to the line, and two guys near the front waved. "You sure you don't want to charge anything? You could make some money."

Gin shook her head. "Definitely not. This is still the prototype phase. The results they get could be terrible. And be sure you let them know that none of this is guaranteed."

"Got it." Lucas gave two thumbs up. "Nothing guaranteed."

Gin took another deep breath and glanced down the line. There were dozens of guys, all hoping that her program would show them their ideal date. All of them could be disappointed. But maybe the hope of finding someone was enough.

After hundreds of cups of coffee and a sunset that had mellowed into a steely sky, the last test subject finished. It was black outside, and Gin stood near the window, almost pressing her face against the glass as she looked for any stragglers.

A total of 224 subjects had taken the test—212 guys and twelve girls. It was astounding. Actual research projects often got fewer participants.

All of the participants were gamers, which meant the data would be skewed, but at least it would be representative of a particular population. It could be a goldmine. She'd have regular check-ins with willing participants—a week later, a month later, six months later—which meant the data would keep coming in.

She shut down two of the laptops but kept the third open to review the data. Each test subject had been matched with three potential dates from the pool of high schoolers. The test subjects didn't receive any names or email addresses—first, Gin would contact each match to see if they wanted to participate, giving them a photo and profile on the person they had matched with to help them decide.

Even if no one wanted to participate, Gin would still have scores of data to use. Already she could see how the test subjects had judged the photos. There were some images that were generally pleasing, but other than that, there was a range of looks that people liked. This would be fascinating.

Lucas sat down and pushed a latte and bagel towards her. "I thought you might be hungry."

"Yum. Thanks." Her stomach growled as she took a huge bite of the warm bagel, which was spread thick with cream cheese. "And thanks again for all of your help. I couldn't have done any of it without you."

Lucas blushed. "I was happy to do it. So what do the numbers show?" He leaned over her laptop.

"It's hard to say now. But you can see here how everybody rated the different images. Interesting how varied it is, right? And I have a great pool of answers to the questions. It's going to be amazing."

"If you wanted, you could tweak your program to cater to gamers. They're obviously interested in this stuff."

"Not a bad idea." Gin stared at the data, rows and rows of it. Then she looked at Lucas. "Wait, did you ever take the test?"

He fidgeted with an empty coffee cup. "No, but maybe I will." He looked down at the table, almost like he was nervous. "It's just that . . . I might already know what I want the result to be."

He looked up at her and she saw it in his eyes— hope. Her stomach fell. This was not at all what she had planned. And now that she wasn't even talking to Hannah, the last thing she wanted was to lose the one friend she did have.

"Because," he continued, gaining confidence, "I'd want it to be—"

"Well, the offer is always there." She closed her laptop and stood. "You can take the test anytime. I know there's a great girl out there for you." She glanced at her phone, and hastily packed her bags. "I've got to get going, my parents will be worried. But thanks again for all of your help."

Before Lucas could say anything else, she left.

This test works. Really works. I'm seeing this girl who actually likes me. We click. Five stars for Love Fractal.

You should sell this stuff—it's legit.

Like Corky says when he passes level 500 of Thronesville: This is for real. Nice work. Ellie and I both thank you.

Two weeks out, the feedback was coming in constantly. Email after email, even a few calls. There were several unhappy users, but for the most part, people liked *Love Fractal.*

It should make Gin overjoyed, but she couldn't ignore the fact that it had been two weeks since she last heard from Felix, two weeks without a text or an email or a call. She kept her phone on her all the time, the volume turned up even while she slept. She studied images of the Gartner estate on Google Earth, read articles about Odin and Grant Gartner, and even trolled through Felix's social media pages, looking for any activity, any clue as to what was actually going on.

There was nothing.

So, in an effort to keep herself from going completely insane, she dove further into her work. She coded her traffic model, line by line, making it as robust of a model as any she'd ever built. She worked on the crow model, too, tweaking the rules and running scenario after scenario, even though there was a good chance she'd never even show it to Ms. Sandlin. And she spent days and nights analyzing the *Love Fractal* data, until she was deep in the world of numbers, all of which were aligning to predict one thing—love.

Even if *Love Fractal* never found her a match, at least she was proving what she always knew to be true: that love and logic did go hand in hand.

// Thirty-Five

It was late on a Wednesday night. Gin was sitting on her bed, finishing a write-up for an AP Chemistry lab, when she heard the tap at her window.

She jumped, heart racing. But then she smiled, the anticipation rising in her chest.

It had to be one of Felix's crows.

She walked to the window, collecting herself, and slowly opened the shade. And there, perched on the windowsill, her feathers catching a bit of shine from the streetlights, was Catherine.

Gin took a quick breath, her hand fluttering to her chest. "Oh," she said, careful to keep her voice to a whisper.

Gin pushed the window open, and Catherine ruffled her feathers. Gin crouched down, moving slowly so she wouldn't startle her. "Hello there," she whispered.

She panicked for a second—surely Grant Gartner would notice that Felix had sent Catherine to her house, and surely that would be grounds for getting Felix in even bigger trouble—then she saw that the slim metal tracking band that should have been around Catherine's leg was missing.

Catherine cocked her head to the side, as though to get a better look at Gin, and dropped a small paper triangle down on the windowsill.

Gin reached out, slowly, and the bird hopped to one side.

Taking a deep breath, Gin opened the paper to find Felix's small, block print.

Sorry it took me so long. I'm in the technology dark ages here. Dad says it's "good for me." But I've found a work-around. You can message me at the website below. And attach the latest model—I'd still love to help if you haven't finished the whole thing yet. I miss you, Gin. Still hoping we can talk soon. Felix

She ran her finger over the words, imagining him scratching them out in pencil, letting her finger pause on the part about how he missed her.

She copied down the web address, and on the other side of Felix's note, she wrote him back.

I'll send something over right now. Are you okay? I think you are, but let me know. I'm still worried. This is all just . . . different. I could tell someone—Ms. Sandlin maybe?—if you need anything. As for the model—I've made progress, but there's more work to do. I'd love your help. And I miss you, too. Lots. Gin

She folded the note back up into its tight triangle and dropped it on the windowsill. Catherine hopped closer. Then in one fast motion, she dipped her beak down to collect the note and took off.

Her dark shape nearly disappeared in the night, but Gin could see her, beating her wings toward Felix. And for a moment, all Gin wanted was to be that bird.

If she could *see* Felix, it'd go a long way to calming her nerves. Then she'd know—really know—that he was okay.

She sat at her computer and went straight to the URL. She messaged that she missed him, asked him to let her know if anything was wrong, and explained what she had done with the crow model so far. She attached the latest version and waited.

She did a quick calculation on how long it would take for Catherine to get back to Felix and figured thirty minutes was a good guess. But there was no guarantee he'd be able to get online right away.

She refreshed the URL a few times, just in case, and googled things like "controlling fathers" and "children grounded for a month." Nothing was helpful, so she busied herself with some mindless homework. An hour later, with still no response, she turned on a movie. And when that was over, she started to read.

She fell asleep at some point, waking at four in the morning, her bedroom lights still on. She stumbled to her computer and refreshed the URL one more time. There was a short message.

Got it. This will be fun to work on with you. Though anything would be fun to work on with you. And yes, I'm 100 percent okay. I promise. No need to call social services. It's just my dad being himself. I'm sending a photo for proof.

Felix had included a selfie. Raised eyebrows, goofy smile, as cute as she remembered, if not cuter. It looked like he was in his room. Most importantly, he seemed entirely okay. Happy, tan, strong. Like Felix.

Maybe there was nothing to worry about. She breathed out, long. And she wrote back: *Thanks for the proof. It's good to see you. I miss you. I agree—this will be fun. Though it'd be even better in person.*

She took her own selfie—not her best picture, as it was four in the morning, after all. But she did pull off a slightly sad yet cute expression. Like she was pining for him.

With a click, her message and photo flew back to him. She only wished that she could do the same.

// Thirty-Six

Green grass was pushing up through the muddy March earth and flowers popped in pinks, whites, and yellows. Maybe that's how everything was with Felix. Like spring.

Except for the fact that he was still virtually missing. Gin asked him every chance she got whether he was still okay, and he always said he was. And she figured the fact that he was still writing to her was a good sign.

They wrote back and forth on his secure site at least twice a day. Felix described his new tutor, who was following his dad's "Platonic" study program that required lots of old books and virtually no time with technology. Gin wrote him about school and her models and her cat. It didn't feel like they were dating—they hadn't even been in the same room for months—but it felt like something. Which was better than nothing. When it came to Felix, she'd take whatever she could get.

The crow model was coming along extraordinarily well. Each time Gin looked at it, she felt a squeeze in her heart, like she knew it was going to be big—even if no one else ever saw it. And working with Felix was almost too easy. Like a choreographed dance. Every time Gin puzzled through the results of one scenario, Felix would figure it out. Then he'd run more scenarios and try more logic, until he ran out of ideas, and Gin would take over.

Gin was deep into the data now, and she kept expecting to stumble on an odd pattern, something that would explain all of it: the crows, Mr. Gartner's reaction to their project, Felix's virtual disappearance. But the only pattern she could find was the same one she already had seen—that in training, the crows would stop at different locations, staying up to an hour or two at a time.

The crows had to be doing something. If eagles could be trained to take down drones, and rats could be used to sniff out land mines, it wasn't farfetched to assume the crows had a purpose. But she still didn't know what.

The spy theory seemed unlikely now that she knew the crows were stopping all over the city. Maybe the training was research for the AI program. Or maybe the crows just liked certain areas and hung out at those for longer periods of time.

But she had more to worry about than an unlikely crow conspiracy. There were plenty of things that she did know—such as the fact that *Love Fractal* data was still coming in. So far, thirty-one users said the results had given them the courage to ask someone out, eighteen said that they had been pleased with their first dates, and 112 said they would recommend the program to a friend.

Even more exciting, word of *Love Fractal* was spreading. Gin hadn't done any advertising, but already, a few high schoolers had found her and asked if they could give it a try. Several offered to pay. She couldn't help mentally running the math: if 10 percent of the high schoolers in Fairfax County schools alone each paid twenty dollars, she could fund her college education, or at least cover tuition at Harvard if she got in.

One night, after she had posted an updated version of the crow model, her phone lit up—Lucas. She started to let it go to voicemail—she hadn't talked with him much after that day at the coffee shop, and they'd danced around each other at work—but if she didn't answer, she'd just have to call him back.

"Hello?"

"Gin, I'm glad you picked up." Instead of sounding awkward or shy, Lucas was excited. "I know no one actually uses phones. But I knew you were gonna want to hear this. And this way, I can hear your reaction, which I'm sure is going to be good. You know?"

"Sure, Lucas." His enthusiasm made her smile. "So what's the news? Did they finally bring peanut butter M&M's to the snack table?"

"It's better than that. Exponentially. Literally exponentially."

"Okay?"

"Okay. So, *Love Fractal* has gotten popular. Like anything in social networking when it starts to take off. It turns into this crazy curve you can't get off even if you wanted to."

"That's nice to say, but how do you know? It's not like it's been written up in magazines or anything." She walked over to her window and opened it wide. The evening air was heavy and damp and smelled like lilacs.

"I know because there's this huge hacker convention in DC this summer. People come from all over the country. The guys in charge heard about your model and liked what they heard. So they want you to come and present it."

She put a hand on her desk. "Wait, what?"

"And it pays. A few thousand dollars, at least. They'll call and give you all the details. I said I thought you'd do it. But I'm sure you'll do it, because it's one of those opportunities that, statistically speaking, is very improbable."

Gin paused, closed her eyes, tried to think. It *was* good news. The chance of a lifetime.

"Gin? You still there?"

She opened her eyes and felt the phone in her hand. "Yes," she said. "I am. I just . . . I guess I can't believe it. This is good. Right?"

"Exactly. Really good. And well deserved."

She sat down on her bed, trying to think. The doors this could open, the opportunities this could create, not to mention the money she could make . . .

"Wow, Lucas. I don't know what to say. Except thank you. You helped make it all happen."

"Anytime," he said. "So, if you want help getting ready, let me know, okay? I can be available anytime. Besides when I'm at school or at work or doing home-work or at a gaming meetup. Otherwise, I'm free."

"Okay. I will."

"I'll see you at work, okay?" he said. "And Gin? Congratulations."

After she hung up, she sat by her bedroom window, looking out at the broad grassy lawns and aging colonial homes. She still felt an ache in her chest—to see Felix or at least talk with him. Or maybe it was for things changing. For family she barely saw—her mom, her sister. For the fact that she hadn't talked to Hannah in forever.

She grabbed her phone and started texting Hannah. But she couldn't get past the first line. Too much had happened. Too much time had already passed. She couldn't bridge all of that with a short message.

And she didn't have time to worry about all that. If anything, she should be more focused than ever. She could tweak *Love Fractal*, inputting details on whether different matches worked and running other series of algorithms. By the time she presented the model, it'd be better than ever.

In fact, she could start immediately.

// Thirty-Seven

"In the spirit of the second-largest Christian holiday, today we'll be watching a movie." Mr. Ryan was at the front of the class, half-lunging to one side, chalk in hand.

A movie was exactly what Gin needed. She was supposed to find out about Harvard soon and had been checking her email over and over, so often she could barely think. She finally had to stash her phone in a zippered inner pocket of her bag. It took all of her discipline not to pull it back out. Maybe, during the movie, she'd let herself check once.

"But first, let's consider our quote of the day."

In the corner of the board, Mr. Ryan had written the quote in neat yellow letters, all caps:

"Shortly before dawn he went out to them, walking on the lake. He was about to pass by them, but when they saw him walking on the lake, they thought he was a ghost. They cried out, because they all saw him and were terrified. Immediately he spoke to them and said, 'Take courage! It is I. Don't be afraid.'"—*Mark 6*.

It was quiet as everyone read. Quiet like a lake, like a ghost.

"A man who can walk on water." Mr. Ryan hopped up just enough to sit on the edge of his desk. "Who can defy the natural order of things. Who heals people, performs miracles, and later rises from the dead. Think about that. Has anything else ever risen from the dead? Cells that had stopped working, had shut down and started to decay—just started moving again?"

"That's crazy," someone said, and the class laughed.

"Exactly." Mr. Ryan clasped his hands together, pointing to the student who had answered. "And many feel it is just that: crazy. But it is also intriguing, isn't it?"

He paused, looking around the class. "Not only these claims of this man—or God, depending on what you believe. But the claims of all the great spiritual leaders of the world. Anyone who has ever searched for more than the material world and believed that they found it. On one hand, it's crazy. But on the other, it's the only sane thing around."

Mr. Ryan sighed, his lean frame slumped for a second. "Look. I'm about to put this movie on. And you'll watch it for the next forty minutes. We'll learn a little more these next few weeks. And then the year will end. You'll be on your way. Off to summer jobs, to college, to your lives."

Someone whistled, and there was a splatter of claps through the room.

"But here's the thing. You owe it to yourselves to think through these questions, just like all of the ancient people we've learned about did. Is there something more than the material world?" He paused, looking at them one by one.

"Do the work. No one's going to do it for you, and it might be the most important work you ever do. Because, if there is this whole other world, a world that many people long ago based their whole lives on—the immaterial, or spiritual, or whatever you want to call it—don't you want to know?"

The class was silent. And suddenly, all Gin could think of was Felix. If he were there now, he'd be nudging her. "See," he'd whisper. "This is what I'm talking about. A whole other dimension. It feels right."

But Felix wasn't there. And as though a boom of

thunder had rolled through her body, Gin felt fully what she'd been trying to ignore. This whole situation—Felix disappearing from school, not calling her, barely staying in touch; Mr. Gartner warning her not to use the crow data, not to talk to Felix—it really, truly was wrong.

There had to be something else going on. And she had to figure out what it was. Because no one else might ever even look.

The email was there after sixth period. Harvard admissions.

So this was it. Her future was right in front of her.

Her finger hovered over the screen, and she paused. Maybe she should wait. At least until school was over. She could sit in her car, somewhere private.

Then again, whether she had been accepted was already determined. A solid, immutable truth. This was no Schrödinger's cat. Ignoring it wouldn't make it go away or change. And she wanted to know.

So she stepped back under the stairwell, as much privacy as she could get, and clicked.

Dear Regina Hartson,

On behalf of the Admissions Committee, it is my pleasure to offer you admission to Harvard University . . .

She clapped her hand over her mouth.

And she knew—as sure as her bones, as sure as the concrete steps clamoring with students above her—

what she needed to do. It was only a first step. But that was exactly how everything began.

// Thirty-Eight

It was nearly ten at night. Gin's dad had fallen asleep in the chair in his office; her mom was on her way to her shift at the hospital. And Gin was sitting in her bedroom, clicking through Harvard's website, trying to calm her nerves.

Because Felix was coming over.

She had messaged him as soon as she got home from school, after everything had clicked that afternoon, and told him that she had to meet with him. That it couldn't be delayed, that they had to make it happen. Not only because she wanted to see him, but because she had to talk with him about the crows. And he had said yes. That, somehow, he'd find a way to make it work.

It had settled in her, like an itch that wouldn't go away, this idea that the crows simply were not normal, were not a hobby—but were something more. She just didn't know what. And she needed Felix's help to figure it out. Even though Felix's private share site was set up with multiple layers of security, she had to tell him in person.

She glanced at the time, which was exactly ten, and heard a small ping at her window. Not the light tapping of a crow's beak, but more like a pebble hitting the glass. She clicked off her desk light, set her computer to sleep, and closed her laptop—it was dark outside, and she needed to be able to see—then opened up the window to the warm night air.

There, standing below her, with his hands at his sides, wearing loose jeans, a thin hoodie, and leather flip-flops, was Felix.

He waved, and she waved back. He pointed up, made a climbing motion, and shrugged. It wasn't like the movies—Gin had no tree or sturdy trellis leading to her bedroom window. She held up one finger, asking him to wait for a second, and tiptoed down the stairs to the front door.

Her dad was a sound sleeper, and he likely wouldn't even care if Felix came over. But even so, she peeked in his office to be sure he was still asleep. Then she opened the front door slowly and motioned for Felix to come inside.

He stepped in gingerly, and they stood there. It was all Gin could do to keep from leaning in, holding him tight. He took her hand, the feeling fluttering through her, and she silently led him up the stairs.

They didn't say a word until they got to her room, where she closed the door, quietly.

"So this is it?" he whispered. "Your pad."

To have him there, in her room—it felt tingly and charged and impossibly good.

He walked around, quietly laughing at her "I'm So Meta, Even This Acronym" poster and her *Far Side* comics and even her Weird Al poster—"Who else can sing a cool song about shapes, right?" he said—

then he studied her computer set-up. "This is nice. You put it together yourself?" he asked, still whispering.

She stood by his side and whispered back, "Yeah."

"I like it." His face was soft, his eyes crinkled at the edges. He reached a hand out and touched her cheek. Gin put her hand on his, and they tangled their fingers together and leaned even closer.

"I've missed you," he said. "Really, really missed you."

"Me too."

He kissed her, soft, on one cheek and the other. And then her lips. And every bit of Gin rushed with feeling, as though a current was storming through her, stealing her breath with it.

He pulled back slightly and ran a finger along her eyebrow, her cheek, her lips. She closed her eyes—it felt so good, she couldn't even look.

"Is this okay?" he whispered.

She let out a quiet laugh and nodded. Because it was more than okay. It was exactly what she wanted. Everything she'd been missing.

She knew then that no matter what happened, she wouldn't be able to just forget about Felix. It was the same with the crows. They were all stuck in her mind, her heart. "Yes," she said. "It's really, really nice."

He held her arms in his hands, tight, and she wrapped her hands around his waist, setting them at the curve of his back.

They kissed again, harder, as though the months they had spent apart required a close, insistent urgency.

Felix ran his fingers under the hem of her shirt, overwhelming her body with warmth. She let her hands slide up his back, which was taut and strong, traced the long, smooth curve of his spine. They shuffled towards her bed—still kissing—and for a second, she panicked, wondering if he expected anything more, worried she wouldn't be able to turn him down even though she knew it wouldn't be what she wanted, not when they weren't even together. But when they got to the bed, he sat down and tugged her towards him so she was facing him, sitting. They held hands and looked at each other, smiling.

"So, Gin Hartson. How are you?"

She laughed and shook her head. "It's so good to see you. I forgot . . . I mean, not really, but it's just . . . it's good."

He held her hands, rubbing his thumbs over them, and her stomach squeezed into itself.

"I'm sorry again. About everything. I wish I could make it different."

She pressed his hands tighter. "Me too. Do you think it ever will be different? Or, will you be working on your Platonic studies at your parents' house for the next decade?"

He smiled, his eyes bright. "Well, I'm almost 18. And, believe it or not, I'm planning to go to college too. And there's only so much my dad can do once I'm there."

"So a few months . . ."

"A few months, and I'll be free. To go anywhere."

"I got in, by the way."

"To Harvard?"

"Yeah."

He pumped his fists in the air, then he leaned back and shrugged. "Well, I'm not surprised. I always knew you could do it."

She grinned but rolled her eyes. "You were the only one. But thanks. And you can tell your dad 'thanks,' too. I guess."

"He didn't do anything. Besides tell all those Harvard admissions people what they already knew. That you'll do great things."

A nervousness bubbled up in her stomach, and she looked down at her quilt, pulling at a loose thread. The longer she waited to tell him why she had wanted him to come, the harder it'd be. "So, there was something else."

"Yeah?" He raised his eyebrows. "This wasn't just a way to see me? Which, by the way, I should've made happen much earlier. I just needed a little time for my dad to relax about everything. But, what is it?"

"It's about the crows."

"The model's looking good, isn't it?"

"Really good." She could breathe easier for the moment, thinking about the model. At least it was simpler than the topic she needed to bring up. "I still can't believe how well it's coming together. Ms. Sandlin is going to be impressed, you know? If I show it to her, that is. Which I probably won't."

"You have to show it to her." He squeezed her hands and leaned closer, his eyes seeming to glow. "It's good. Unique and interesting and logical, if I do say so myself."

"But the data is proprietary."

He groaned. "Proprietary. Another word for 'pay money to use it.' Seriously, I thought we had gotten over that. Anyway, this model might be the deciding factor in whether you get that internship. Like I said, my dad wouldn't have to know."

"Think you'd still take the internship? If we got it? Because if I do, you'd have to."

"I'd consider it. Anything if you're part of the package."

It made her blush. And it gave her the confidence to keep talking. "You know me, I'm all about internships. But, about the model . . ."

"Is there some code that's not doing what it should? Or a scenario that doesn't make sense?"

She sighed and looked at him. "Felix, I don't know how to say it, but I don't think they're . . . just crows. I think—I *feel* like—they're doing something else."

He let go of her hands and leaned back, so he was resting against her headboard. "Look, you know I'm all for feelings. But, did you see anything in the data?"

She shook her head. "Nothing. Not yet. It just doesn't seem normal. It doesn't seem right."

He put his hands behind his head and sighed. "Welcome to my world. Nothing my dad does is normal. And probably most of it isn't right, either."

"But what about you? What do you think?"

"I've found with my dad it's better not to think too much. And anyway, I like the crows. To be honest, they're like my friends—the only consistent ones I've had since I was a kid. And if my dad enjoys working with them, I'm not going to push it, because there isn't much he enjoys."

"So that's it. You think they fly through the city and stop at certain spots, all for training?"

"I don't know. You're right, that surprised me, too. Maybe there is some purpose for it. But it seems like they stop all over the city. And they're crows. How much harm can you do with crows?"

Gin sighed, the certainty draining out of her again. "I guess. It's just strange. And your dad's business— how he's always ahead of the competition. At least that's what my dad says. There was that newspaper article about how Odin unexpectedly beat everyone to the launch of that quantum cryptography phone. I just thought . . ."

"My dad's good at what he does. He's not perfect, but he's good at his work. And he gets good people to work for him. Like your dad." He bit his lip and looked up, his face softening when his eyes met Gin's. "Look, I know it seems strange. I have no idea what they could be doing, if they're doing anything at all. Do you have theories?"

"They could be helping with research for artificial intelligence. Or they could be trying out new security cameras." She looked down at her bed, then back at him. "Or they could be working as spies."

"Spies?"

Her face pinkened. "Yeah, I mean, maybe it's far-fetched. And I don't know what information they'd be getting. But they could be getting something. No one pays attention to crows. And a few of them

stopped at InTech. Not many in terms of overall statistics, but still."

"Don't give my dad too much credit. He's smart,
but . . ." He looked up, thinking. "Unless."

"Unless what?"

"It's probably nothing." Felix rubbed his hands
over his eyes and shook his head. "But one time, he
had to leave the aviary suddenly, and I glanced at the
computer he was working on. It was pulled up to an
InTech site."

"Like, their website?"

Felix shook his head. "More like an internal site.
With folders of files and stuff. I knew it was strange.
But I didn't think much of it at the time."

They sat on the bed, silent. Gin's desk lamp glared.
The window with its drawn shade seemed suddenly
flimsy. As though anything could burst through. Or
anyone could listen in.

Gin shivered. "So you don't think I'm crazy?"

Felix shook his head. "No, not crazy. I'm not saying
I think you're right, but you're definitely not crazy."

"So what do we do?"

"We still have the data. We can keep looking at it.
If there's something there, we should be able to find
it. And if not, we can let it go."

"What if we find something?"

Felix didn't answer at first, the question lodged
into the space between them. Finally, he sighed.
"Then we find something. It's like truth—it's there
whether you want it to be or not. All we're doing is
looking for it. And it's never a bad thing to look for

the truth." He sat back up and pulled her hands toward his face, resting his lips on them.

"Okay." Gin felt her shoulders relax, her breath sink through her.

"Okay. Anyway, you should totally, always trust your gut. For instance, what does your gut say about this? About me?"

He was looking down, and she studied his face—how his eyelashes curved to touch his cheeks, how his lips opened slightly.

"That I like you. A lot."

"I like you too. More than you know." He leaned closer and kissed her, again. She closed her eyes and kissed him back, breathing in the moment as though that would make it last for days, weeks, even months.

"I better go," he finally said. "But I'll get on our site once I'm home. And we can sort through the data together. And I'll come back soon. I promise."

They tiptoed back downstairs, and Gin walked Felix outside. She was surprised to see the street was empty, Felix's beat up 4Runner nowhere in sight.

"Wait, do you need a ride? How'd you even get here?"

"I've got my methods. One of the first things you learn as Grant Gartner's only child is how to sneak out."

"Are you walking? It's going to take all night to get home."

"No, I've got a ride nearby. I'll hike the last bit of it, though. Believe it or not, there are some back entrances into the Gartner estate."

"Call me if you need help?"

"Of course."

They kissed once more on the porch, and Felix slipped away, walking briskly down the shadowy street.

// Thirty-Nine

You have anything yet?

Gin sent the message and watched her cursor blink, waiting for Felix's response. She felt exhausted, but also wired, as though she had drunk an entire pot of coffee. Because Felix didn't think she was crazy.

They'd been looking at the data for the past three hours. Gin had started as soon as Felix left, and Felix came online two hours later. They hadn't found anything yet. But it was exhilarating. Looking, following her gut. Not to mention the fact that Felix had been there. In her room. The thought of it stung her body, making her chest ache.

Of course, it was all tempered by the fact that they were looking for something possibly illegal that his dad might be doing with the crows.

A message popped up from Felix, and Gin blinked once, hard, before reading it.

Nothing on my end. But I'm glad we're looking. We should keep looking. At the data. And other stuff, too.

She typed back, quick. *I was going to pull more research about animal training. Birds, in particular. And about AI. And . . . what else?*

That's a good start. I'll do the same.

You think there's something? She held her breath as she waited.

Maybe. Probably? I don't know. I'm just annoyed I haven't looked at it before.

There might be nothing. I hope I haven't pulled you off course, on some crazy tangent.

No. Nowhere's a crazy tangent . . . if you're there.

Gin sighed, letting the words sit there, close. *I miss you. I better go soon—my mom will be home. And she likes to see me sleeping.*

Me too.

She waited for him to explain. When he didn't, she wrote back. *You, too, what? Need to sleep? Like to see me sleeping?*

All of the above.

I really miss you.

You too. Sweet dreams. I liked seeing you tonight. Let's do it again. Soon.

Any time you want.

No more messages came from Felix, and Gin finally lay back on her bed, trying to sleep, but uneasiness crept through her chest. She felt like she was perched on a cliff, looking out into the horizon, waiting to see something, with no idea of what she was waiting for.

And she wondered if it'd be better simply not to look.

Over the following days, Gin continued her research. She studied the numbers, searched scientific journal articles, and reread everything she could about crows. She dug deeper into the world of training animals, intrigued to find that chickens could run obstacle courses and "helper monkeys" could assist their owners with daily tasks, such as washing up and opening bottles. But none of it helped.

She spent most of her time on her final projects. She pieced together her traffic model, but her focus was on the crow model. Felix worked on it, too, and they messaged each other through the share site, posting scenarios they'd run and new ideas on what the data was showing.

They may not have found out what Felix's dad was using the crows for, but they were uncovering something about crow behavior: there seemed to be three unique sets of rules that individuals followed—one that fit for the bulk of the population and two others for two distinct subsets of birds.

They set up a new model with that finding. Gin ran it three times before she believed what she was seeing: one of the subsets became leaders; the other subset became *secondary* leaders. Flock leaders had been studied—but the idea of a secondary leader was new. It was like there was a whole other level to the order. It was a real finding, a discovery. Exactly what she'd been hoping for.

She messaged Felix, immediately, attaching the latest version of the model. *Check this out. Do you see what I'm seeing? It's incredible.*

Somehow, amazingly, he was on the site and messaged back. *Hold on—pulling it up . . . Got it . . . waiting . . . Oh, cool. I see it.*

Can you see how the groups split? How there are leaders AND secondary leaders?

Yes, exactly. This is incredible. A new insight to how groups function.

It's the real thing. A discovery.

We DID it! I mean, you did it. It wouldn't have happened without you. Even if it means I'm grounded for the rest of my life.

Will your dad be mad? I don't have to show Ms. Sandlin or anyone else. I have my traffic model. It's not terrible.

No! Not an option! This is science! Where would we be if Isaac Newton or Louis Pasteur kept their work under wraps? We have to share it with Ms. Sandlin. And it's just a high school class. I'll talk with my dad at some point. I promise. He'll understand.

Point taken. I'll think about it. If you're sure. Thanks for working on it with me. And for encouraging me to stick with it. I miss you.

Miss you too.

The data had shown something much better than a crazy conspiracy. Surely Mr. Gartner would reconsider letting them use it. Maybe he'd even want them to use it. Science, after all, was about discoveries. And to make a discovery like this, sometimes you had to take a chance.

There were exactly three weeks left until the final models were due. On Friday, Ms. Sandlin had a check-in for every group. Gin had both models on her laptop—the traffic model and the crow model. When it was Gin's turn to talk with Ms. Sandlin, she hesitated for a moment, took a deep breath, and opened up the crow model. There was a knot in her stomach the whole time, as though she could feel Mr. Gartner's disapproval. But she reminded herself of Felix's assurances. Anyway, Mr. Gartner hadn't given either of them details on why they shouldn't work with the data. He, of all people, should know that Gin and Felix were scientists—and scientists needed facts.

"This is interesting," Ms. Sandlin said after Gin had finished. "May I play with it?" She pulled the laptop closer and started inputting scenarios.

It was beautiful to watch. Thousands of little bird-shapes zoomed around the computer screen in different directions and at different velocities. Slowly, they started to shift. A group of two or three would form in one corner and join up with a few more, and another group would start to grow somewhere else, until the chaotic movement became orderly. Entire groups of birds flying together.

That was always the punchline with a model like this. How you could start with thousands of individuals that all followed a set of localized, individual rules but with no guiding principles for the group as a whole, and then a group-wide behavior—order itself—would emerge. As if it had been designed in the first place.

"And this is where you're seeing the leaders and secondary leaders?" Ms. Sandlin pointed to the front of the flock that had formed on the screen.

"Exactly. We still need to analyze it, but we're hopeful that it's real. Because it could impact—"

"All sorts of things," Ms. Sandlin broke in. "Social structure, how networks form and collapse, decision matrices. The possibilities for a finding like this are endless. Gin, this is excellent. And to think, a few months ago, you felt that you wouldn't be able to do this work. Even more than coming up with a good project, I value your persistence."

Gin squeezed her hands in her lap, the relief washing through her.

"And I've heard that you've been accepted to Harvard. Congratulations. I'll be back there next fall. After your work this summer through the internship program, I'm certain there will be some research opportunities during the school year."

Gin felt it. It had all been worth it. Following her gut had taken her exactly where she wanted to go.

// Forty

The cherry blossoms were nearly ready to bloom, and the city bustled with life.

Gin and her parents were celebrating her Harvard acceptance with dinner at a new dim sum place in the city. But first, they were stopping by "Angles and Lines," an outdoor art exhibit featuring a mathematical sculpture of the Hilbert curve. Gin had first learned about the Hilbert curve in the third grade. It was a continuous fractal space-filling equation: let a Hilbert curve loose in an empty square and the pattern would grow denser with each iteration, until you couldn't even see the lines. If Gin couldn't fall asleep, she'd imagine a Hilbert curve running along her bedroom wall, trailing a gold or blue line behind it.

Most importantly, Hilbert curves were useful, coming in handy for things like mapping a picture of a range of IP addresses and compressing data warehouses. And now Gin would get to see one built out in three-dimensions.

They strode past the Washington Monument, and along the Vietnam Memorial, with its sobering black walls of names. There was a light breeze, and since the sky was cloudy, it wasn't too hot. The day already felt like a fitting celebration.

Gin tried to focus on the moment instead of wallowing in the fact that she probably wouldn't get what she wanted most for her birthday: first, to see Felix; second, to figure out what—if anything—was going on with the crows. The more time that had passed, the more impossible both of those felt.

Felix hadn't messaged Gin once for the past three days. Which wasn't too long when compared with his months of silence, but it still felt strange. And for the crows, Gin had come to the conclusion that Mr. Gartner was so smart that even if something was going on, it'd likely be impossible to find.

Soon they were walking along the wide lawn of the National Mall, near the old carousel, with its colorful circle of painted animals. Gin spotted the aqua blue horse that, when she was young, she had always felt was faster, even though she knew better.

To the side of the carousel, tucked back near a stand of trees, was the sculpture.

A big metal cube made of interlocking lines that went up and over, up and over, in the Hilbert curve pattern. Gin already knew what it would look like from photos. But somehow it was different to see it in person.

"That's pretty cool." Her mom shaded her eyes with her hand. "What's it mean again?"

Her dad looked up, studying the sculpture. "Basically, it's a formula that runs and runs, filling up a predefined space in a particular pattern. It's pleasing to the eye. It's useful. I can show you the equation." He pulled a piece of paper and pen from his shirt pocket, scratched a few notes, and held it up so Gin's mom could see.

"Huh. That is interesting. Reminds me of all those long study nights in college." She leaned towards him, tucked her head on his shoulder. "When I'd watch you scratch out rows of numbers on a white-board. Or was it a chalkboard?"

"That was exciting." They smiled at each other, then kissed.

Gin groaned. "Come on. We're looking at art here."

"With a soon-to-be Harvard student, at that." Gin's mom ruffled Gin's hair. "I think I'll admire the art-work from that bench over there. My feet need a break. You two enjoy."

Gin and her father looked up at the metal statue. "Have you found the point where they had to deviate from the formula, to make the two-dimensional pat-tern into a three-dimensional shape?" he asked.

Gin scanned the metal lines and pointed. "Right there, near that corner."

"Yes, that's right."

They stood quietly for a few minutes. There was something appealing about a simple formula worked out in space, turned into a metal solid, weighty and real.

"Everything has a pattern," Gin said. "From cells and trees, to the videos we watch and the food we buy— there are patterns everywhere. Life likes patterns."

Her dad rubbed his chin and squinted up at the statue. "That is true. Patterns are important. And when looking for them, you must remember they like to be exclusive. Sometimes, there's more than one, and if you want to see them all, you must forget about each prior pattern."

"Which means . . ."

"Find one, and you won't necessarily see another. For instance, if you see a line of cars that alternates color—black, gray, tan, red," her dad motioned to the street, with its line of parked cars for as far as Gin could see, "you might miss the fact that there's a second pattern, such as that every sixth car is from out of state."

"So when looking for a pattern, you have to look at your data constantly, over and over, with fresh eyes." It was a simplistic point, but interesting all the same.

"That would be a good start."

The breeze blew stronger, rustling nearby tree branches. A cloud shifted, and the sun popped out, throwing a dark shadow of the sculpture onto the grass.

"Look at that," her dad said. "From 3-D back to two."

Gin studied the lines of the shadow, but her mind was stuck elsewhere: on the pattern of the crows' flights. She had looked for one pattern without any success. That didn't mean that another one wasn't there.

Late that night, full of doughy dim sum and ice cream cake, Gin sat in her bedroom, her window opened wide, staring at the file of crow data.

She had studied the crow data for weeks, searching

for a pattern. But what if she'd been searching for the wrong pattern?

Her plan for the night was simple: she'd brainstorm all possible patterns—not only the crows' most common stops, but how long they stayed at different stops, impact of year and day of the week, sequence of their stops. Maybe a pattern was there—just not the one she'd been looking for. And maybe it would finally tell her what was going on.

It was nearly one. Gin still hadn't found anything significant or meaningful. She closed her eyes for a second, feeling annoyed about all the wasted time, and suddenly an image of Catherine flashed in her mind.

Catherine. How interesting it was that the crows all looked alike initially, but the more time she had spent with them, the more distinct they had become. Maggie, Rufus, Frederick. All individuals, like people.

She lightly tapped her fingers on her keyboard, thinking, and remembered Felix saying that his dad had bred the crows to enhance certain traits. One of the first things she had done when studying the crows' patterns of movement was to build an immense spreadsheet combining data on every individual crow. Her goal had been to find trends in the group of crows as a whole. It was a sound practice—more data points meant it'd be easier to find actual patterns.

Unless . . . She closed her eyes for a second, think-ing. Unless the pattern was different for each individ-ual. Then she'd need to look for trends within individuals, not the entire group.

She started writing a quick analysis of how often the crows visited each location. But this time, she kept individual crows separate.

She sat back as the program calculated, and a map with brightly colored dots appeared. Each crow was now represented with a different color. Most of the colors and symbols were small points, splattered around the city. But there were four colors—the ones that represented Catherine, Maggie, and two crows she hadn't met named Storm and Ollie—that were concentrated more at three locations.

Gin ran some statistics and found the pattern was, in fact, real: those four crows stopped predominately at three locations, for longer periods of time. No other crow had a pattern like that.

Gin pulled up the address of the most common stop. Then, she gasped.

InTech's satellite office. Where she had seen Catherine stopping on that first flight she mapped. How had she missed this?

Except, of course, she knew how she had missed it. InTech had barely registered for overall stops. But these four crows had clearly been dedicated to stop-ping there.

There was an altitude coordinate, and when she added that in, she found the four crows, invariably, were stopping on the twentieth floor of InTech. A quick search of InTech's employee website showed that floor was for creative development, where much of the technical innovation took place.

It was too much of a coincidence. Specific crows owned by the CEO of Odin, Inc., hanging out at InTech's offices.

She had to tell Felix. She posted the analysis on their message board and wrote a short note—*Take a look at this. Strange, right? Can you meet?*

When he didn't write back immediately, she felt the worry swirl through her stomach. Maybe she'd been too hasty to share the finding with him.

But there was nothing she could do about it now. The website wasn't hers, so there wasn't an easy way for her to delete a posting.

Maybe he'd have an explanation for all of it. Gin typed in the second most-common location, which was for a set of multimillion-dollar row houses in a fancy, downtown neighborhood. According to property records, one was owned by a dermatologist, another by a couple connected with the wealthy Fireton family, and the third by the managing partner of an immense law firm.

None seemed to have any connection to InTech or Odin. Until she found the list of InTech's board of directors online. The lawyer was on the board.

This finding was more than a coincidence. No statistical model would give any probability of this scenario actually happening. It had to be exactly what Felix's father didn't want her to see. And she was staring right at it.

Every hair on her arms stood up, a prickly wave starting at her shoulders and running down to her wrists. She froze, fingers poised over her keyboard. Everything was silent, but she had the strange sensation that someone was watching her.

She clicked out of her computer programs, quick. She stood up, looking around her room. It was empty. Of course it was empty. But it felt different. The light from her desk lamp glared on the wall; her worn blue quilt looked strangely neat on her twin bed; the whiteboard in the corner, covered in her compact handwriting, almost glowed.

She glanced at the window, its shade open. It was black outside, and with the light on in her room, she couldn't see out. But anyone could see in.

With her phone in one hand, as though it offered some protection, Gin walked to the window. One step and another, trying to slow her breath and fill her lungs with oxygen.

She paused. Then she pushed up the wooden frame, fast. Before she had a chance to feel the dread churning in her stomach, she thrust her head outside, into the night air.

The front lawn was shadowy and pale. The empty street was shiny and still. Cars were parked and motionless.

No one was watching her.

Something rubbed against her legs. She jumped, hitting her head, hard. But it was just the cat. Einstein wove back and forth, stopping to press his chin into

Gin's calf. Warm and soft. He sat down, looked up at Gin, and flicked his tail.

Gin closed her eyes and leaned back against the wall. And in one swift movement, she closed the window, pulled the shade down, and picked up Einstein.

"I know, that was ridiculous." She put her head in the cat's fur, breathing in the warmth. "That crazy data got the better of me."

She refreshed the URL, but there was still no word from Felix. She quickly typed in the third location, but it was for a large condo complex with no obvious connection to InTech.

Two locations that were linked to InTech; one that seemingly was not. Maybe the buildings had something else in common besides InTech. Maybe they just had good roosting sites. Or maybe her calculations were off.

The Principle of Occam's Razor flashed in her mind. She needed to start with the most sensible, least farfetched assumption. Not a wild conspiracy theory.

She steadied herself with that logic and decided to look at the data later with fresh eyes. She shut down her desktop computer and her laptop, just a precaution, and lay down in bed. Her desk light still glared, but she didn't turn it off.

Finally, the room bright around her, she fell asleep.

The next morning, Gin still hadn't heard from Felix. Maybe her analysis had been entirely off-base. Crows stopping at a few spots in DC wasn't a crime.

So she turned on music and picked up an optional book for English. She was a few chapters in when the door opened, and her dad peeked inside.

"Got your pancakes." He nudged the door open, holding a plate with five pancakes in one hand and a pitcher of syrup in the other. "For a second there, I thought you had slept in."

"Thanks, Dad. I don't know how I forgot." As she slid out of bed, her stomach growled. She took the plate to her desk and started to eat.

But he didn't leave. "Everything okay? You don't usually miss pancakes."

"Yeah, sorry." She was suddenly starving. Maybe she just needed food to think clearly. "I've been stuck on this data problem. I keep looking for something that probably isn't there. But somehow, my mind won't let it go."

Her dad smoothed her comforter and sat down on her bed. "And why do you think it isn't there?"

"It's not logical. And numbers should be logical."

"Hmmm . . . Illogical." He held up a finger. "But is it interesting? Is there a pattern to the illogical finding?"

"Not really." As soon as she said it, she knew it wasn't the truth. "I mean, maybe one. One that's *really* strange. So strange, it's probably a silly hunch. Nothing a few pancakes and a talk with my logical father can't take care of."

Her dad tilted his head, looking like a spry professor, with Gin his only pupil. "You know . . ." His voice was quiet, but steady. "Hunches are important."

She sighed in frustration. "You've always told me to start with logic."

"That's true." He leaned forward and rested his chin on his hands. "But you also have to follow hunches. That's how all of the great scientific discoveries happen. People set off on their logical work, doing everything in an orderly, analytical way, then they have an accident or a wild idea or a hunch."

"But that's not how you work." She was feeling slightly indignant. Like a child who never believed in Santa, but whose dad was now saying he was real. "You're always outlining and researching. Proving things. Using numbers."

He rubbed his chin. "Yes, Yes. That is important. But so is all the other stuff. The feeling. The idea that there's something underneath. You have to allow your brain to work. To make connections on its own. To have a feeling, or a sense of something, all in the blink of an eye. That's why I collage."

Gin's mouth dropped. "That's why you what? *Collage?* With, like, magazines and scissors and glue?"

"I do it at work. On breaks. I don't talk about it much—it seems to take something away from it. But I pull out images and words and paste them together in new ways. It helps me figure things out."

Gin was speechless. It felt like the world had twisted onto itself.

"I'll show you sometime, if you'd like."

She didn't know how to answer. This was not where she had imagined the conversation going.

"So, follow your hunch. Sorry, I'm not the best at advice. But that's a good nugget, I think."

After her dad left, Gin forced herself to take another bite of a pancake, but it was lumpy and dry in her mouth. And slowly, like a sun rising, she realized why she didn't want to look at the trend. It wasn't because she thought it was absurd or unproductive or trivial. It was because she knew it was possibly the opposite of all of those things—important.

And because she was afraid of what she might find.

// Forty-One

Two places: a giant tech company's satellite office and the home of a board member for the giant tech company. Nothing strange or odd about them. Except that, fairly frequently over the past few years, they had been visited by crows.

Gin set her pancakes aside, the curiosity swelling up in her like a wave, and decided to review everything again. First, she'd check her calculations and confirm that she hadn't somehow messed up the original data. Once she knew that her model was sound, she'd see where a few more online searches took her.

But before doing anything else, she went straight to Felix's messaging board. Her heart sank. Still nothing. Her insides felt as clammy as her hands. If Felix hadn't known about the crows and somehow his dad found out what they'd discovered . . .

Hello? You there? I'm sure it was nothing . . . but it'd still be good to talk. Message me?

She shouldn't worry. After all, she hadn't ruled out a mistake in her original work. She started checking her analysis, almost hoping to find some little issue that explained it all away, but a few hours later, she was virtually certain nothing was wrong with her logic or the data.

So she started on her research. By early afternoon, she had pages of notes on InTech and Odin. There were links to articles, with key sections pasted in, photos of the attorney and other InTech board members, annual reports from both InTech and Odin.

But she still didn't know who from InTech, if anyone, lived at that third location. And she didn't know what the crows were doing, if in fact they had stopped at the three locations for a purpose.

Unless the crows were working as spies. All it would take was a tiny recorder to listen in on conversations happening inside. Or, with access to a wireless network, it'd be possible to download data slowly so regular security measures wouldn't pick up the breach. If a person or even a drone tried to do the same thing, it'd be too obvious. But no one would notice a bird.

She searched "animals trained as spies" and two results came to the top. First was the CIA's "Acoustic Kitty" project from the 1960s in which a cat was implanted with recording devices to spy on the Russian embassy. The program was considered a failure—the first time the cat was released, it walked off because it was hungry; the second time, it walked into the street and was hit by a taxi. Cats, officials had decided, were too unpredictable for that sort of work.

Unlike crows, Gin couldn't help thinking.

The second result was about cyborg insects that had been implanted with tiny recording devices, with a similar aim: scientists could control where and how the insects moved, guiding them to stay outside a window or inside a particular room, and record what was shared, literally "bugging" the place.

There was a chance the crows were doing the exact same thing. The feeling crept through Gin, sending goosebumps along her arms. Then she shook her head, frustrated.

All of these *feelings*. She was tired of them. They were taxing—they fluttered through her, pulling her breath and her logic with them.

She switched back to the crow data. She examined it closer, parsing the data out by groups of birds, by time of year, even by average temperature. The more she looked at the numbers, the clearer the story got. The four crows were stopping at the three locations regularly, staying upwards of two hours at a time, a feat which must have required incredible discipline.

When she closed her eyes, she could almost see them. How they'd tilt their heads, their eyes inquisitive, or lift off into the sky, wings flapping powerfully. And she could picture Felix, out there in the middle of that field, the crows circling around him, working even then. All that training, whether Felix knew it or not, wasn't just a hobby.

It was time for her to get ready for work. She considered calling in sick, but she knew work would be a good break. Anyway, she could bring her laptop and the crow data with her. Maybe she'd show Lucas. She wouldn't have to give him any details. But she was curious to know whether he would see the trend.

There was still the chance that someone else would look at her analysis and tell her she was crazy. Maybe she'd made a simple mistake. Maybe her hunch wasn't anything more than a flip-flopped equation or a group of data points that got copied and pasted. Maybe it was nothing at all.

"Hmmm," Lucas said.

It was the fifth time he had said it in the last five minutes. His mouth was set, and his glasses dropped low over his nose.

Gin had waited until early evening to bring out her laptop. She didn't even feel bad about distracting Lucas from his work: the office was quiet—it was a Sunday after all—and they didn't have any pressing deadlines. And Lucas was always happy to do her a favor.

He'd been playing around with the model for more than an hour, looking through her code, manipulating the raw data. He asked a few questions at the beginning, then hadn't said a word.

"Okay." He cocked his head to one side, finally looking at her. "You know, your hair has gotten long. It's nice."

"Oh." She pulled her fingers through her hair. She was long overdue for a cut. "Thanks."

"You're welcome. Anyway, I think I understand the model." He leaned back, drumming his fingers on the desk. "And I appreciate that you don't want to give me any details about it, to ensure a pure analysis process. For a thorough opinion, I'd need a little more time. However, I'm ready to tell you what I think."

"Okay." Gin clenched her jaw, preparing herself.

"First, it's clear that this model is on the movements of some sort of bird. Or possibly drones . . . no, scratch that, they're birds, right?"

"Yes. How'd you know?" Gin's body felt suddenly chilled.

"The elevation metric was a giveaway. Anyway, I think I see why you've shown me this. Because, while the flocking behavior works seamlessly, the raw data has an oddity. This is real data, right?"

She nodded, her words suddenly frozen. Maybe Lucas was seeing it, too.

"I can't exactly put my finger on it." He narrowed his eyes, looking harder at the screen. "I'd need more time. But there's some trend that's a bit off."

Gin took a deep breath. "Certain cr– . . . individuals

seem to like to stop in a few specific areas, fairly regularly," she said. "Look at the frequency of the stops for individuals three, eight, fifteen, and thirty-two."

He graphed the data, several times to get it right. "I see it now. Yes, that makes sense."

"You don't think that's a mistake? Something I did?"

Lucas shook his head. "No. It seems pretty straight-forward. Do you know why they do that?"

"No. I don't." Her words came out haltingly. "I mean, not really."

"Have you plugged the addresses of the stops into the search engine?"

Gin grimaced. "Well, sort of."

"What'd you find?"

"Two places have a connection to InTech."

Lucas rubbed his chin. "And the third? Which one was that?"

"It's this one. I couldn't find any link there."

Lucas mapped the condo complex, then pulled up resources like city property records and minutes from homeowners' association meetings. He scanned back and forth, between the lists and public records. Then he clapped his hands together.

"What about this guy?" Lucas brought up a photo of a young man, possibly a teenager, with cropped hair, big glasses, and a serious expression.

"Martin Schlesker," Gin read. "What about him?"

"He lives in that building. His condo is on the floor where the birds stopped. And he was a big programmer at InTech. The sort of guy they'd have on special projects."

Gin pulled her arms around her tighter. "Wait, how'd you find that out?"

"I looked at the names of people on that floor, and his name rang a bell, so I searched for him in the AAG site—"

"AAG?"

"American Association of Gamers. When I put him in, I remembered. He's the real deal. A savant or something. One of the best gamers alive. Totally legit. And he started working at InTech when he was 16. He's 20 now."

"Wow."

"Yeah. He worked there for a few years, then must have gotten another offer from someone else." Lucas flipped through the screens, shaking his head. "It's amazing. Now we know where he lives. I might have to go introduce myself. That'd be wild."

"Yeah. Wild." Gin's head was spinning. Every site the crows stopped at had been connected to InTech. And they were all important links, important people.

"You might want to show this to someone else. Not that they'd care too much—these are just birds after all." Lucas pushed up his glasses. "Well, I guess we should pack up."

"You're right—it's late." She stuffed her laptop in her bag as she stood. "Thanks again for your help, Lucas."

"Any time. In fact, if you want to talk more, I'm free any night this week."

Her laptop felt heavier on her shoulder, the strap digging into her shoulder, weighing her down. "That'd be fun."

The city streets were busy—cars clattering, walkers jostling, lights flashing—and it took Gin a second to orient herself. She headed for the Metro station, walking briskly, but before she turned the corner, she glanced back at her office window.

She held her breath, as if expecting a crow would be there. Perched at her window. Waiting. Watching.

But she saw only the city, shiny in the damp night, and the empty windowsill.

// Forty-Two

"All right, class." Ms. Sandlin leaned against the edge of her desk, her gold bracelets catching the light. "This is it. Final check-ins on your models."

Gin scrolled through her model's code, not really seeing it. Because she was debating whether she should tell Ms. Sandlin about the pattern.

She had wanted to hear from Felix first. But for the past week, there'd been nothing. Not even a quick hi on the messaging board. She tried his cell, but it was disconnected. It was like he had disappeared—again.

It was worrisome: if Felix was hurt or in trouble, she might be the only one who knew. Then again, maybe he was annoyed at her for wanting to look at the data more.

She rubbed her face, hard. There were too many scenarios, too many unknowns. Impossible to determine the right thing to do.

"Gin? Time for your check-in."

Ms. Sandlin was motioning her forward.

Gin pulled the model up on her laptop, her hands so damp that her fingers slipped off the keys.

"Very interesting." Ms. Sandlin slid the laptop over and ran the model several times. She played around with the inputs—velocity, rate of aversion, rate of coherence. Every time, the little kite figures flew and flew, randomly at first, until they finally formed cohesive groups. Every time, it was beautiful.

"This is still so intriguing," Ms. Sandlin said. "I see you're almost done now. And the secondary leader phenomenon still holds." She paused the model and pointed to kites in several groups. "Clearly, this work is excellent. I look forward to seeing all of the statistics."

Ms. Sandlin started the model again, letting it run for a few more seconds, until all of the kites were in one group, a flock.

"Perhaps we can even get a journal article published." She leaned toward Gin, hands folded on her desk. "It'd all be under your name, of course, but I could help with the process. I have to say, I'm so glad you continued with this work. Aren't you?"

Gin clenched her hands in her lap. "Actually, there was something strange with the data."

There. She had said it. She was going down this road, and in that moment, it suddenly felt good. If

Felix needed help, this might be the only way to get it for him. And pulling in Ms. Sandlin would take at least some of the responsibility off of Gin.

She pulled up the raw data and explained the trend she thought she was seeing. Then she described how four crows had stopped predominately at three locations, all of which were connected to InTech.

"And the Gartners, who trained the crows that generated this data, own Odin, Inc.," Ms. Sandlin said, quickly connecting the dots that Gin had set out for her. "And Odin's main competition, arguably, is InTech. You know that, right?"

Something about Ms. Sandlin's face—the way her eyebrows were knit together, the intensity of her gaze, made Gin feel even more worried. "But it may not be anything."

Ms. Sandlin narrowed her eyes, looking harder at the data. "Maybe. But, you wouldn't mind if I took a closer look, would you?"

"I guess not." Maybe Gin had secretly hoped that someone—Lucas, Ms. Sandlin, her dad—would see her reasoning was off-base. But they all seemed to think the opposite.

"Good." In a few quick keystrokes, Ms. Sandlin had emailed the file to herself. "I'll let you know what I think. Okay?"

The bell rang, and Ms. Sandlin was on her feet, dismissing the class. Gin packed her bag, telling herself that whatever happened was fine.

Because the data was there. And so was the fact that

Felix had, once again, disappeared. She couldn't change either of those facts. Like Felix had said, they were truths, realities. Like a car with bad brakes, or cancer in your body—it was there, whether you wanted it to be or not.

And at some point, you'd have to deal with it.

// Forty-Three

All weekend, Gin ran statistics to show the secondary leader phenomenon was real. She had pages of statistics and scenarios, dozens more than she needed for her project. But it was better than sitting around and thinking.

Felix still hadn't messaged her. And Gin had a sinking feeling that maybe he never would. But short of driving to his home and trying to bust in through the gate, there wasn't much she could do.

On Monday, Ms. Sandlin asked Gin to stay after class. "I looked at the data," she said as soon as the other students had left. "But first, I want to be clear that you are not in trouble. Got it?"

She acted like Gin should be happy to hear that, but it only made things worse. Because now Gin knew that something was very wrong.

"The pattern you saw is real. It's significant, according to my calculations. And quite strange."

In a way, Gin felt relieved. She wasn't crazy, she hadn't missed some little mistake. But it also meant there could be something real going on. Something that would impact Felix and the crows.

"I've decided the best next step is to send the data to some associates. There won't be any further action unless they feel it's necessary." She gave Gin a warm smile, the type that was supposed to make everything seem like it wasn't a big deal.

Gin tugged on her hair and bit her lip. "I thought the data would stay in the class."

"Yes, it usually would. But if there's something going on, it deserves to be examined further. I believe you understand that—otherwise, I don't think you would have brought the data to me in the first place."

It was true. Gin could have decided not to turn it in, to keep it to herself, to show Ms. Sandlin her traffic model instead. But she hadn't.

"Now, I would suggest that you don't have any contact with the Gartners at this point. This could be sensitive. Otherwise, stick to your regular routine."

"Even Felix? He's been helping with the crow model, and . . ."

"Even Felix. I'll let you know if there's an update." Ms. Sandlin stepped closer and put a hand on Gin's shoulder. "But I want to be clear, this in no way impacts the quality of your work. You should be proud of what you've accomplished. I'm still looking forward to having you in my internship program this summer, and I'd still like to help you publish a journal article on the scientific findings of this model."

Gin made herself nod. "Thanks."

"Of course. You're talented. If anything, this shows it more."

By the time Gin left, the halls were nearly empty. She watched the last few students hurry to their next class. Then she was alone.

She paused for a second. Her skin prickled, and she felt as though someone were there, watching her. She turned and looked behind her, quickly.

The hall was, unsurprisingly, empty. Rows of lockers, shiny floors, and blaring lights.

Nothing to be afraid of.

Two days later, just after Gin had made her way through two slices of Hawaiian pizza and was getting started on her homework, her phone rang. She didn't recognize the number. Which meant it could be Felix.

She stared at the phone, remembering Ms. Sandlin's warning not to talk to any of the Gartners, even Felix. She answered it anyway.

"Hello?"

It was silent for a second. "Hey, Gin."

Felix's voice broke through, raced into Gin's phone, into her ear, her brain. She closed her eyes and winced. It had been two weeks of silence. Two weeks of worrying about him, wondering if he was even alive. She was relieved to finally hear from him, but she was also tired of it. It all felt like a game, and she was done playing.

"I saw your message. I'm sorry it took a while to call. But, it's been . . . hard." There was a softness in his voice.

"I wish you had called too. You're okay? I've been worried." She sat down on her bed and hugged a pillow to her chest.

"Yeah. It's just . . . my dad doesn't make anything easy."

There was another pause. She didn't know what to say. What to tell him or not tell him. Maybe she shouldn't have answered the phone.

"So this pattern," he paused. "What, um . . . what do you think about it?"

She stood at her desk and stared out the window. "I don't know what to think. Except I don't think I ever expected to find anything. Did you?"

"Well, maybe nothing is there."

Her face warmed, and she shook her head. "That's the thing. I checked it all, and the trend I found is real. I don't know what it *means*—"

"And that's the rub, right?" His voice was suddenly cool, insistent. "Because data and patterns and all of these numbers—they're useless if they don't mean anything. And this finding—maybe it's interesting or different. But it doesn't necessarily mean anything."

"Right, that's true. I know that." Gin felt frozen. She wasn't a novice at all of this. And Felix was making her feel like one.

"Okay, good." He sighed. "I'm glad we understand each other. Because the reality is, all this analysis means for me is a bunch of trouble. So maybe it'd be good to ignore the whole thing."

Gin rubbed her forehead and tried to steady her breath. "Well, I know it might not mean anything, but it kind of came up when I was talking with Ms. Sandlin, and—"

"You showed it to Ms. Sandlin?" Now he was mad. Felix, who never, ever seemed so much as frustrated, was mad. At her.

The pit in her stomach grew. She hadn't done anything wrong—had she? Unless she should've waited to tell Ms. Sandlin.

"But, you wanted me to show her the model. And this part just kind of came up. And I hadn't heard from you."

There was another long pause. Gin tugged at her ponytail, nervous.

"Well, I'm sorry I'm still grounded and can't always get to a computer, but that's entirely out of my control." He breathed out, slow. "I thought you would've waited. This isn't a game. This is . . . my family."

Tears filled her eyes and rolled down her cheeks, but she didn't wipe them away. She didn't even move. It was like she was stuck to that one spot on the bed.

"This doesn't sound like you." She nearly choked out the words. "I mean, you're all about truth. And these are numbers. That's it. Nothing I can change."

She wiped her nose, trying not to sniffle. She didn't want him to hear her so upset.

"Gin." His voice was focused as though each word mattered. "You have to listen to me. You have to be careful, okay? We shouldn't even be talking about this. But, be careful. Okay?"

House lights clicked on outside, bright in the deepening dusk. There was a distant sound of frogs croaking, and the days' last birds flitted around the sky.

"Okay." The word just came out. Even though she had no idea how to be careful or what she needed to be protected from.

"I mean, maybe you had the wrong data." He suddenly sounded practical. For a moment, it was comforting. As though nothing were wrong. "I don't even know what file you're working with. The data could've been corrupt. Why don't you send it to me, and I'll take a look?"

"It's the only one you gave me."

"Right. But it doesn't hurt to be sure."

For a second, she hesitated. She had no idea what Felix knew or didn't know, whether he was trying to protect his dad or actually wanted to help her figure it all out. But he had sent her the data to begin with, and her analysis was safely stored on her computer. Sending it back to him now couldn't hurt.

"Okay. It's coming over." She watched the progress bar grow, and soon the spreadsheet was flying through space to Felix.

"I guess you probably have homework?" he said.

And she knew then. The conversation was over. Even if she didn't know what any of it meant.

"I guess," she answered.

"Okay." He sighed again. "I just—I'm sorry. I know it probably doesn't mean anything coming from me. But still, I am."

"Okay," she said. "Me too."

He hung up, and whatever hope she'd had that things could be made right was gone. Now she knew. It'd never be the same again.

// Forty-Four

Two days later, Gin sat on her couch, her dad at her side. A normal school night, except they never sat together like this. And there had never been two suited men sitting across from them.

The men were from the FBI. They had flashed their badges at the front door and followed Gin inside. Thankfully, her dad had been home.

"Now, Regina—" said the man with the blue eyes, broad face, and hollowed cheeks. Agent Mike Finney. He was the talkative one. The other one seemed to be the note taker.

"I actually go by Gin." She regretted saying it as soon as the words were out. He was with the FBI, after all.

"Sorry. Gin. Tell us how you first came in contact with the Gartners."

Gin sat up straight, hands in her lap, expression calm. But the question filled her with dread. If she had known this would happen, she never would've used the data. Would she have?

"You should know," her dad broke in, "that I work for a company owned by Grant Gartner. Though I don't believe Gin had met the Gartners before this year." Her dad was nervous, talking too fast and shifting his weight on the couch.

"Thank you, Mr. Hartson. That's helpful." Agent Finney turned back to Gin, his muscled body awkward in their old La-Z-Boy chair. For a second, his light eyes made Gin think of Felix.

"Now, Gin, tell me how you met the Gartners."

She took a deep breath. And told them everything. Even how she and Felix had started to date a bit, before Felix was taken out of school. When she got to that part, her father raised an eyebrow but didn't say a thing.

Agent Finney listened without reacting. Not even when she told him how she had found the pattern in the data, how certain crows had been stopping at places connected to InTech, how she had emailed the analysis to Felix weeks ago with no word back until two nights earlier, when he called, upset, and warned her to be careful.

A few times she hesitated. Maybe she shouldn't be telling them what she knew. Maybe she should get a lawyer. But she hadn't done anything wrong.

And for all she knew, the Gartners hadn't either.

The light outside faded, and the sky turned dark

blue, then black. Only the lamp in the corner of the living room shone. Gin's dad didn't seem to notice how dark it was, and Gin didn't feel like she could get up, much less move. So they sat there, in the dim room, shadows lengthening around them.

Finally, after a few more clarifications, Agent Finney leaned back and looked at his partner. "What do you think, Paul—we good here?"

Agent Paul nodded.

"Well, okay." Agent Finney stood, and Gin did the same. Her legs felt creaky, like she hadn't moved for hours. "That was very helpful, Gin. Thank you. We'll continue the investigation, and we'll be in touch."

Gin's dad walked them to the door and paused. "Is my daughter in trouble?"

"No." Agent Finney shook his head, reassuringly. "Gin hasn't done anything wrong. But we do strongly advise that you not have any more contact with the Gartners while this is going on. Is that doable?"

Gin nodded. Everyone shook hands, and the agents left. Gin sat back on the sofa and picked up the remote but didn't turn on the television.

Her dad joined her on the couch, close, so their shoulders touched. He breathed in a few times as though trying to figure out what to say. Then the door burst open.

"Gin? Gin, honey?" It was Gin's mom, still in her scrubs. When she saw Gin in the living room, she rushed over and sat next to her, smoothing back her hair.

"Oh, sweetie. Are you okay?"

Gin sighed, trying to keep her eyes from welling up. "Don't worry about it. It's not a big deal."

"Not a big deal?" Her mom sighed, exasperated. "That's a ridiculous thing to say. FBI agents were here talking to my daughter. Because of something with that ridiculous family. As if they don't have enough money in the world to just live their own lives."

Gin blinked hard, barely holding the tears back.

"It's okay," her dad broke in. "Really. They wanted to ask Gin about some data the Gartners have. About their trained crows. Gin's not in trouble. I asked, and they assured me that she'd done nothing wrong."

Her mom put an arm around her shoulder and squeezed, tight. "Want to tell me about it, honey?"

"Dad kind of covered it. Maybe we can talk about it more tomorrow?"

"Okay. Well, I'm here whenever you want to talk. In the meantime, I'll make popcorn. And ice cream sundaes. And we can watch a movie and forget the whole thing."

Her mom stood up and started bustling around in the kitchen. Gin and her dad stayed seated on the couch. Eventually, her dad took the remote from her hand and clicked the television on.

After modeling class the next day, Gin told Ms. Sandlin what had happened. Ms. Sandlin wasn't surprised.

"My associate took a look and passed the data

along to the FBI. The FBI has been quite interested in the data," she said as she shut the classroom door. "This idea that the birds were trained to wait outside of certain locations, possibly to gather sensitive information is not farfetched. Consider InTech. They have a very secure building with an extremely secure perimeter." She sat at her desk, pulled out a piece of paper and a sharpie, and drew a square in the center. Then she drew a larger square around the first one.

"You need all sorts of credentials just to get in the gate." Arrows were now going on the crude sketch, with big Xs in front. "But even InTech uses a local wireless network. It'd be nearly impossible to hack into. But maybe you could get the access credentials if you spied on someone who worked with the company and brought some work home.

"Now, to get into the network and access information, you'd have to be physically close. You could plant a device, perhaps in a closet or outside on a windowsill, but if you used a person, or even a drone, you'd be flagged by security cameras. A bird, however, could leave a device that connects into the network and pick it back up. Or a bird could just sit there. And you could be working nearby, going through InTech's drives, finding anything you'd like. No one would ever know. It'd be elegant, to be honest."

It made Gin shudder. Because it was elegant. Just like Felix's thought process. Maybe Mr. Gartner was stealing information from InTech. And all anyone had ever seen were a few crows flying around.

"But let's not get ahead of ourselves." Ms. Sandlin sat up straighter and folded her hands on her desk. "Even if the data suggests an illegal behavior, it may not be reality."

The halls were loud with lockers clanging and students talking. Gin couldn't help thinking that she should be there, too, pushing her way through the crowd of students, thinking about starting Harvard in a few months. Not stuck in Ms. Sandlin's classroom, worried about investigations and court cases and high-tech secrets.

"Gin."

Gin's attention snapped back to Ms. Sandlin.

"You still aren't in trouble, and you did the right thing. Okay?"

Gin sighed, her body sinking into itself. "I wasn't trying to find this. I was just looking at data."

Ms. Sandlin's expression softened. "Ah, yes. Looking at data. Funny how a few numbers can lead us to truths we never imagined."

That night, Gin was reading in bed, trying to go to sleep. Lately she'd been too tired to even check in with *TimeKeeper*, anyway, she'd have to rework every single assumption for it to make sense. Her old life had basically dissolved.

Her phone pinged, and Gin sighed. Somehow, her email alerts must've gotten turned on. She reached over to her nightstand for her phone and saw the email on the screen. It was from Grant Gartner.

She sat up, hands shaky.

"Hey, Dad?" she called before opening the note.

"One second," he said. He was in his room. Close.

She hadn't received an email from Grant Gartner before. And though she had no idea why he'd be emailing her now, she was certain it couldn't be good.

She closed her eyes for a moment and took a deep breath, then opened the email.

Dear Regina,

I have recently learned that you did not heed my advice, but instead decided to use my painstakingly gathered, proprietary crow data as part of a school project. That is simply unacceptable. Not only is it illegal, but it shows that your character and morals are to be questioned.

I am disappointed to say that I have no choice but to press legal charges. Your family should expect to be served with a lawsuit in the coming week. And unfortunately, I'm no longer able to support your enrollment at Harvard University. Instead, I must alert the Harvard admissions board to what can only be seen as unlawful behavior.

It goes without saying that you must cease all use of the crow data, immediately.

Grant Gartner

// Forty-Five

Her dad was there, as soon as he heard her crying. Because as much as she hated to cry, there was nothing else she could do.

"Bastard," he said, ushering her into his room. "Here, sit down. I'm calling the police. And Mom."

Minutes later, Agent Finney was there. He studied the email and took a report.

"It's not a threat, and in a way, it's a reasonable response. But given the circumstances and the ongoing investigation, we'll pull a patrol team to monitor your house tonight," he said. "Just as a precaution."

"And that's it?" Gin's dad folded his arms across his chest, his face knit up in concern, a bit of toothpaste still on the corner of his mouth. "That's all we do?"

"For now, yes." Agent Finney nodded. "We've accelerated work on the case. Hopefully, we'll have everything wrapped up quickly."

Gin and her dad watched out the windows as the overnight officers drove up and parked in front of the house. Minutes after Agent Finney left, Gin's mom flew into the driveway and jogged inside.

Before she even set down her purse, she hugged Gin, hard.

"Oh sweetie, I'm so sorry," she said. "This whole thing is terrible. Don't give a second thought to his talk of a lawsuit. He's exaggerating everything. You're just a kid."

Gin sat on the couch while Gin's dad told her mom

everything that Agent Finney had said. Then her mom disappeared into the kitchen, returning with a mug of warm milk in hand. Gin took a small sip, and her mom rubbed her back, just like she used to do when Gin was a child.

"How about it, honey—can you sleep?"

Gin looked at her mom as though seeing her for the first time in weeks. She looked exhausted—dark circles under her eyes, face pinched and dry. Gin didn't know what to say. Now that she'd ruined her dream of Harvard and gotten her family mired in a legal case with the wealthiest man in the country, she'd probably never sleep again.

"Why don't you sleep in our room tonight, okay sweetie? I promise, everything will seem better in the morning."

Gin took a deep breath, resolving not to cry, then went upstairs and lay down on her parents' bed. She felt like she was five. Her dad put on the History channel, which was playing a gray and white movie about advancements in farming. Her parents talked quietly in the bathroom, and Gin pretended to be asleep so she wouldn't have to say anything. Eventually they came to bed, and somehow, after an hour or so of being wedged between her parents, Gin slept.

There was nothing for Gin to do at home besides sit and worry, so she went to school. Though being at school seemed just as pointless: all she could think about was Mr. Gartner's email.

When she got home, she wasn't surprised to see Agent Finney there in the living room with her dad and mom. The other agent, Paul, was there, too, as well as a third officer who stood by the door. Maybe they had news on the case.

From the looks on her parents' faces, it wasn't good.

"Gin, honey, why don't you sit down." Her mom was trying to smile and failing entirely.

"Is everything okay?" Gin asked even though she could see it wasn't. "Did something happen?" Maybe they'd have to enter a witness protection program. Maybe everything was really falling apart.

Agent Finney sighed and leaned forward. He looked too folded up in his chair, like he needed another six inches on every side.

"Nothing yet on the case with the Gartners. But there's another matter we need to talk with you about. About another model you wrote." He gave her an apologetic smile and motioned to Agent Paul, who set a recorder on the table and opened a notebook.

"Another model?" Her voice cracked. She scanned the list of every model she made with Felix. Nothing seemed strange about those.

Agent Finney cleared his throat. "Gin, is it correct that you've been working on a computer model known as . . ." he looked at his small notebook, "*Love Fractal?*"

"*Love Fractal?*" She was surprised that Agent

Finney wanted to talk about *Love Fractal*. It couldn't possibly be connected to the crows. It didn't do anything except match people up for a few dates. It was harmless.

"Are you the creator of this program?" A slight crinkling of his eyes, like he hoped she'd say no.

"Yes . . ." Her answer trailed off, hesitant.

"And would you like to explain to us what it does."

Gin glanced at her parents, and they nodded for her to go ahead. She tried to keep her voice even. "It's a model that matches people together for dates. It uses algorithms, just like other dating services. But it also matches people based on an analysis of facial structure, as well as their gut reactions to pictures of other people. I'm still testing it."

Agent Finney's expression was steady. He paused, waiting to see if she wanted to say more, and Agent Paul finished scribbling his notes.

"And the algorithms in your model are lots of lines of code designed to figure out what type of date someone prefers?" Agent Finney asked.

"More or less."

"So, for the gut reactions—there are photos of real people that flash up on the screen?"

"Yes." Gin felt like she was being led down a long, dark hallway.

"And these real people, they're high schoolers? In this area?"

Gin nodded. "I wanted the photos to be realistic. And there's an automatic database for information on high schoolers, because of yearbooks and school

ID's. I compiled those photos. No names are attached—they're just pictures."

Agent Finney rubbed his chin. His fingernails were short, his hands wide. "Okay, so you have a bunch of photos. And then, to match people up, you must have information on students as well?"

"That's right. Since I don't have a good database yet, I used basic information from the school's connect sites. Like, what sports students play, if they're in any honor societies or clubs or band, things like that. Then I put students into different groups and gave them different characteristics based on their online persona." As she talked more, she started to feel a little more relaxed. Maybe he was making sure she knew enough about modeling to be a valid resource for the case with the Gartners.

"Sounds like a lot of work."

"I guess. I had to come up with the basic assumptions. Then I let the equations do the rest."

"And how did you get access to all of this data?"

Now she understood. That was the issue. The data.

It hit her like a wall. She tried to swallow, but her mouth was too dry. She folded and refolded her hands in her lap. "The data was from the school's databases. I mean, data from my school was easy—we all have access to it. The other schools were a little harder. I had a program to get that data."

Agent Paul was scribbling fast, Agent Finney was watching her, and the police officer seemed to be getting ready to tackle her in case she decided to run.

"And did you ever think that maybe getting data like this from public schools would be . . ." Agent Finney took a deep breath and rubbed his face. "Illegal?"

The word made Gin catch her breath. Illegal. Of course she should've thought of that.

She shook her head, fast. "The data is public to all the students. It's not like I was getting grades or test scores or things like that. I could have gotten all this from public sources—newspapers, class lists—but it would've taken too long."

Officer Finney leaned back on the couch. "I get it. And I hate what I'm going to have to say now, but I don't have a choice. Unfortunately, not knowing something's illegal isn't an excuse for doing something illegal. Which is what you did when you hacked into school databases and accessed photos and information."

His words rang through the living room. This was bad. Really bad. World-falling-apart bad. She had messed up. And she hadn't even known it.

"You have to understand." Her mom put an arm around Gin as though that could protect her. "Our daughter is a very good student and an excellent citizen. She would never knowingly hurt someone or do something illegal. There must be some misunderstanding here. Why did this even come up? Are there charges against Gin?"

Officer Finney grimaced. "Let's just say we got an anonymous call from someone who was concerned. As for charges, yes, unfortunately, there are. And I'm sorry to have to do this, but it's my job. I promise we'll do all we can to get to the bottom of it. I don't think you did anything bad on purpose, Gin. But this is a federal offense. So I'm going to have to arrest you."

// Forty-Six

It wasn't really prison that Gin went to. Just a juvenile detention center. She even had her own room. And it wasn't made of metal bars. Though it did have a window that wouldn't open and a wooden door that locked automatically from the outside. Sparse as it was, it was private and had a stack of books. It could've been worse.

But it still was devastating. Because her entire life, everything she'd worked for, was over.

Her parents were horrified. The shock on her dad's face and the anger when he tried to challenge what was happening, along with the dampness in her mom's eyes—it made everything worse. Her parents went with her to the center and watched her get checked in, promising they'd be back first thing in the morning. But then they had to leave.

Agent Finney was nice enough. He said that taking her in was more of a formality, that he was confident she'd be out by the next day, once a judge could set bail, which he promised wouldn't be too high. Considering everything, he thought the charges would eventually be dropped or at least minimized.

But for the moment, she was in jail.

Gin sat on the thin cot in the bare, cream-colored room. The worst part was that all of this stemmed from a little side project, a stupid goal of finding a boyfriend. And now, she definitely wouldn't be able to go to Harvard or do Ms. Sandlin's internship or ever become a real modeler. A federal offense, even if she was cleared, would make all of that impossible. At least Lucas wasn't in trouble. Gin had managed to keep him out of the conversation.

She should be crying. Kicking the wall. Burying her head in her pillow and yelling.

But she just sat there, eyes dry, body immobile. Her knees were pulled up to her chest, and she listened to the sounds echoing around her—banging doors and low televisions and shuffling feet. And for the first time in her life, there was no logical next step.

It smelled like bleach. And old socks. And sausage cooking.

Gin woke suddenly, blinking her eyes and looking around. She had fallen asleep on top of the cot, its thin white sheets and worn blanket still perfectly in place. The clock on the wall read seven. And she pieced together where she was.

Then she panicked.

Thankfully, there was a knock at her door—that must've been what woke her—and it slowly opened to reveal her parents.

Her dad was unshaven, his hair disheveled, but he was dressed in slacks and a button-down shirt. Her mom's eyes were teary with dark circles underneath.

"Gin," her mom said. "Oh, honey." Her voice was so tender, it nearly made Gin cry. Instead, Gin hugged her, tight.

"We're so sorry." Her dad looked exhausted, like he hadn't slept all night. Which he probably hadn't. "Would you like the good news?"

"Does it mean there's bad news?" Gin asked even though she knew the answer. Of course there was bad news.

"I'll take that as a 'yes.'" He tried to smile, but it came out more like a cringe. "The good news is you get to come home today."

"That is good." She took a deep breath. "And the bad news?"

He rubbed his hand through his short hair, making the strands stick up in peaks. "Well, the charges are pretty stiff. And while Agent Finney is doing everything he can to help, his hands are a bit tied. But we have someone on it. He's an excellent lawyer. And he thinks, given your background and your spotless record, there's a good chance we can come to an understanding."

"Okay." Gin's head felt like it was being pressed in on all sides. She felt the urge to explain everything, to make sure he understood. "I didn't know. I should've. I just didn't think it was wrong. Much less a federal offense. I mean—"

Her mom squeezed her hand. "We know, Gin. We

know you. Look, plenty of really smart people make mistakes. And as far as mistakes go, this is a minor one."

It was a nice thing to say. Only, it wasn't true.

"But Harvard will never take me now," Gin said, her eyes welling with tears. "And there's no way I'll get to do the internship with Ms. Sandlin. It's like everything I've worked for is . . . gone." She wiped her eyes, hating that she was crying again.

"If Harvard won't take you, there will be other options, I'm sure of it." Her mom tucked Gin's hair back behind her ears. "You're smart, Gin. Colleges will see that. Let's get you home. That's the first step, right?"

Gin followed them out the door without a second look back.

Home was better, but not much. Gin lay on the couch in the living room and let an endless stream of crappy shows play on the television. Her mom brought her hot tea and vanilla milkshakes and sliced fruit, none of which Gin touched, while her dad sat in his office, talking on his phone.

When it was late afternoon, her dad left to get Chinese carryout and her mom joined her on the couch. The television was playing some show about people surviving in the backwoods of Arkansas with nothing but a box of matches and a fishing hook.

They watched for a while, silently, and Gin's mom shifted so she was looking at Gin.

"Honey, I want to tell you, I'm so sorry."

Gin shook her head. "You didn't do anything. I did."

"But I've been gone so much this year. Your senior year. I didn't mean for that to happen. It seemed like a good opportunity, but I wish I would've been here." Her mom clasped and unclasped her hands in her lap.

"Really, Mom. It's not your fault. It wouldn't have made a difference."

Her mom put her arm around Gin's shoulders in a half-hug. "Well, even so, I'm going to change my schedule now. I need a break from work anyway. I'll be here more, at least through the summer. How's that sound?"

Gin let out a breath. It honestly would be nice.

"That sounds good." Gin leaned against her mom's shoulder. "And I'm kind of sick of pizza."

Her mom laughed, and they watched as the middle-aged man on the screen used his second-to-last match.

When Gin's dad got back with the food, he was in good spirits. He had talked again with the attorney, who was confident that he could get Gin cleared of the charges.

"Ninety-nine percent sure was his exact estimate," her dad said. "Which is pretty good, considering we don't know anything with 100 percent certainty. Not even that we exist."

The news, plus the smell of hot Chinese food, made Gin feel more awake. Her stomach growled, and she realized she hadn't eaten anything since the day before.

Gin had just started on the Moo Goo Gai Pan when there was a knock at the door. Likely the FBI agents again, holding up another dozen charges that were guaranteed to ruin her life. Or worse, maybe Mr. Gartner himself.

Instead, when her mom opened the door, Gin saw it was Hannah.

Before Gin could say a word, her mom was motioning Hannah inside.

"Hannah, I'm so glad you came," she said. "She's right in the living room. I know she'll be happy to see you."

Hannah stepped in, slowly, looking awkward. Their eyes met, and Gin felt nervous and tired all at once.

Gin's mom glanced at Gin, then Hannah. "It's been a rough day—a long twenty-four hours. But it's looking better."

"That's great, Mrs. Hartson." Hannah walked in, closer to the couch, closer to Gin.

"Well, I'll let you two catch up," Gin's mom said and left.

It was too quiet. Gin knew she should say something, but she couldn't make her mouth work.

Hannah gave a half smile. "Hey," she said.

Just the word made Gin want to cry. It had been so long since she had heard Hannah's voice.

"Hey." It was the best she could do.

Hannah folded her arms. Another long pause. "Can I sit down?"

Gin slid to one side of the couch, pulling her knees up to her chin.

"That looks good." Hannah motioned to the food.

"You want some?" Gin asked.

"Well, maybe. You know me—always hungry, right? And somehow, you always seem to be a good source of food."

It was enough to break the ice, and the girls laughed nervously. Hannah grabbed chopsticks and took a bite of chicken.

Suddenly, everything welled up in Gin. The tiredness and fear and sadness. And as hard as it would be, she knew she had to apologize. "I'm sorry," she said, the words practically bursting out.

"Oh, Gin, no." Hannah dropped the chopsticks. "I should've—"

"No. It was my fault. I should have called and texted you back. I was just so upset about Felix. And now, it all seems silly. It all seems so little. Compared to this other stuff."

Hannah slid closer. "I'm sorry too. I should've called more. Or come here sooner."

Gin started crying, the tears dripping down her cheeks. She had been sure she couldn't make any more tears, but there they were. Hannah was crying, too.

The girls looked at each other, their faces red and teary. Gin sniffed loudly, more of a congested snort, and they started to laugh.

"So, we're okay?" Gin asked.

Hannah scooted closer to Gin and leaned her head on Gin's shoulder. "Definitely okay." She wiped her eyes and blew her nose. "Even if you end up in prison, I promise I'll write. And do whatever I can to break you out. Metal files in cakes and all that."

Gin was laughing again. "Can you believe it?" she finally said. "I mean, I'm in trouble. Like, big trouble."

"I think it'll be okay. These things can blow over. And you do have a good track record."

"That's what my dad said."

"It's not like you're some crazy hacker or anything." Hannah picked up her chopsticks and leaned forward to take another piece of chicken. "If anything, it shows you have skills. Maybe the FBI will want you to work for them."

"But this stuff with Mr. Gartner. I mean, if I really did find something, and he gets in trouble, he'll—"

"Do what? He couldn't hurt you. Not now. He's got bigger issues than a high schooler who knows how to use a computer. He's the one who might actually be spying on other companies." Hannah popped the chicken in her mouth and waved her chopsticks in the air for emphasis. "You want to know what I think?"

Gin sniffled, then nodded.

"Okay, first for the *Love Fractal* stuff, don't volunteer any information. You don't get in trouble for not telling them stuff if they don't ask, you know?"

It was exactly what her lawyer had been telling her: no need to say a single word until they had more in-sight.

"If there's going to be a settlement, it should hap-pen fast, okay? I've seen enough crime shows to know that," Hannah continued. "And you can figure it out from there. I'll help, and we can ask Noah if you want. His dad's a lawyer."

"He could help?"

Hannah smiled wide. "He'd love to help. So, you have a team."

Gin sighed, long and deep. It felt like some of her fear was letting itself out, making room for another feeling. It tingled in her chest, her throat. The sort of thing she never would've noticed a few months ear-lier. The sort of thing she could have written off as her stomach telling her it was time for dinner or her body fighting off a cold. Only this time, she knew it wasn't those things at all. This feeling was real.

"And the stuff with Grant Gartner—you have to let it go." Hannah tossed her hair as though letting it go would be easy. "You're like the whistle-blower, and the whistle-blower is always 100 percent protected."

"As my dad pointed out just before you came, noth-ing's 100 percent."

"You know what I mean. Anyway, you have to de-cide what to do now. What's *Decider* say?"

Gin shook her head. The inputs would be laugh-able: *What to do when you discover your boyfriend's dad might be stealing high-tech secrets and you're charged with a felony for accessing data on school websites?*

"Wait a minute—*Decider* can't help?" Hannah looked surprised.

"Let's just say, even if I did try to make it work, there's no way it could tell me anything real."

"Oh." Hannah was silent for a second. "You know, maybe it's a good thing."

Gin sighed. Her eyes were damp, her body exhausted, and suddenly, everything felt ridiculous.

"Gin, are you okay?" Hannah scooted closer.

Gin looked up so Hannah could see her face. Because for some inexplicable reason, Gin was smiling. Not crying. But nearly laughing.

Hannah started laughing. Her deep, rumbling laugh, which made Gin laugh harder. There were tears in both girls' eyes, and Gin was shaking her head, wondering if she'd gone crazy.

Once the laughter had settled, Gin held up one hand.

"What's the sound of one hand clapping?" she asked.

Hannah raised her eyebrows.

Then Gin opened and closed her hand.

The girls were laughing again. And Gin knew that she definitely wasn't crazy. Maybe she was saner than she'd ever been before.

// Forty-Seven

Being arrested made everything different. It was as though something had broken in Gin, split apart inside her. Freed her.

Maybe she wouldn't end up at Harvard. Or any top-notch college. Or with a summer internship. But maybe those things didn't matter as much as she had thought.

She wasn't in jail. And she was friends with Hannah again. And her mom was home, really home, boiling chickens and baking blueberry muffins and humming around the house. Her mom would still finish her nurse practitioner's program—she'd just take a little more time to do it.

While Gin didn't have a boyfriend, there was time for that later. Of course, she missed Felix—her chest ached every time she thought of him. Even after their last conversation, with his strange words and cool tone, she wanted to see him or hear from him. But all things considered, she was okay.

She took a whole week off of school after the arrest. And though there were a few looks and whispers her first day back, it was mostly uneventful. Like high school should be.

She nearly made it through the whole week feeling like that. But on Friday, as modeling class was ending, Ms. Sandlin asked her to stay after.

The class emptied, and Ms. Sandlin closed the door. "I wanted to give you an update. First on the internship."

Gin steeled herself, purposefully breathing slowly so she wouldn't start crying. She reminded herself that whatever happened, she'd be okay. Even if, in that moment, it didn't feel true.

Ms. Sandlin leaned against her desk. "I'm sure this has been a difficult time. But I have good news. You'll still be able to join my internship program as planned."

Gin looked at her, hard, to see if she was joking. "Wait. What do you mean?"

"I mean that you'll be one of my interns this summer. And we have a compelling lineup of projects to work on. I know you'll be an important part of the team." Her mouth was set, face serious. Definitely not a joke.

"Wow." The word came out shaky and Gin shook her head slightly, in disbelief. "I mean, thank you. I just didn't expect that it'd be okay."

"It never bothered me that you had accessed some data from the schools. It was public information, after all. I considered it . . . clever." Ms. Sandlin held a finger up for emphasis. "But there are lots of policies, and we wanted to be sure to review everything in the proper way. I'm still waiting for the final, official go-ahead, but for all intents and purposes, the intern spot is yours."

Gin let out a big breath and touched her hand to her mouth. This was better than she had imagined.

Ms. Sandlin crossed her arms and shifted forward. "Now, for the other matter. The crow model."

Gin's stomach twisted around itself again. She

looked around for a chair in case she needed to sit down.

"Great work on that as well. At all levels. You made an exemplary model, with some incredible findings. For science and for justice."

Gin felt another breath work its way through her chest. Maybe this wouldn't be so bad, either.

"Now, of course, the consequences that Mr. Gartner likely deserves may not pan out. There's a certain level of proof required to bring charges. Right now, there are lots of connections. But proof is a different story. So I suppose time will tell."

Ms. Sandlin waited, as though she expected Gin to say she was disappointed. But the truth was, Gin didn't even know what she wanted for Mr. Gartner. She just wanted it all to be over.

Maybe, like Ms. Sandlin said, time would reveal the truth. Or maybe it wouldn't.

Maybe time would tell nothing.

She was laying on her bed that night, reading *The Lord of the Rings* when her phone buzzed.

Are you home? I need to see you.

Felix. She stared at the text. She shouldn't see him—it was the last thing she was supposed to do.

But before she knew what she was doing, her fingers were typing one word: *Yes.*

Meet me outside? On your front porch?

So he was there. Now. Maybe it was dangerous: after all, the police had stopped monitoring the house days ago. But police could be back in minutes if needed. Her parents were right inside. And it was Felix.

She shouldn't even want to see him. He hadn't texted, emailed, called—anything—for weeks, during which time she'd been threatened, booked into jail, and more or less disenrolled from Harvard.

But still . . . it was Felix. Just thinking his name made her heart beat faster, her hands turn damp.

Coming now.

With each step downstairs, she felt the nerves shake inside of her. Her parents were in the living room, watching a movie. "I'll be outside for a second," she said, trying to keep her voice steady.

"Okay, sweetheart," her mom answered.

Gin opened the door and stepped out into the darkness. Fireflies blinked near the old pine tree. A half moon was rising, and the street lights were on.

There was nothing at first. She didn't see him or even his car. Just the quiet street. It smelled like warm pavement and cut grass. Crickets chirped.

But then, near the side of the porch, something moved.

He walked towards her, wearing jeans and an old t-shirt. His face seemed too pale, his eyes dark underneath.

"Hey," he whispered.

"Hey." It was such a small word. It didn't capture anything. How angry she was with him. Disappointed.

Devastated. But how she still wanted to tell him everything. Still wanted to touch his face, to kiss him.

"I won't be long." He stood there, hands in his pockets. "I came to drop something off."

Her body pulsed with that statement. She knew exactly what she wanted, what she'd always want: him. But instead of saying that, she just nodded. "Okay."

He stepped closer. The air between them felt charged.

"I hope you know that I didn't want any of this to happen." He whispered the words, but they were so full—of regret and sadness and pain—it made her catch her breath.

"See, I thought the worst thing was for my dad to get in trouble. That they'd take him away, then take the crows, shutting them up in some research place where they'd sit in cages." He reached forward, tentative, and took her hand. "But, I understand now that wasn't the worst thing."

The touch was explosive. But he was opening up her hand, not holding it. He placed two tiny silver circles in her palm.

"What are these?" she asked.

"It's what they need to show that my dad did what you think."

"I haven't thought any—" she started to protest.

But he closed her hand over the circles and shook his head. "No, wait. That's not what I meant. I know you weren't looking for anything bad. The problem with truth is that it has a habit of finding you, whether you look for it or not. These trackers have data on them. And the data shows that my dad did something. I can't turn them in myself. I mean, as much as I hate him, I just . . . can't. He's still my dad. You know?" The glow from the living room windows shone in his eyes, which looked damp from tears.

He blinked hard and held her hands tighter. "It all comes down to one choice. Help my dad or help you. And I choose you."

It hit her with a shudder. "But . . . will you be okay? With your dad?"

He shrugged, his face sad. "Probably not. But I don't think I ever was."

They stood there, close, the night quiet around them.

"Gin, are you okay?" her mom's voice called from inside.

"Yes, Mom. I'm coming."

Felix squeezed her hands once more. "Give those to the FBI, okay? And tell them I have more."

"I will."

Before she could say anything else, he had slipped back into the shadows. And then he was gone.

// Forty-Eight

It was early in the evening on a school night. Gin had finished her final Monday of high school, then gone to her internship and now was riding the Metro home. But instead of taking the orange line all the way, she got off at the Foggy Bottom station and started walking.

It was a beautiful day. The air was warm, the city fresh and green. As she walked, she thought about all that had happened in the weeks since Felix had come to her house. How she hadn't even tried to look at the data. How instead, she had gone back inside and told her parents she thought of something that might help the police, then they called Agent Finney. How, when he had come over, she told him she remembered Felix had left a few crow-anklets at her house—examples of what the birds wore when they were training—and that the drives might have important information. Or they might have nothing. She didn't know.

It had been a small lie, but she wasn't testifying in court, and if they needed to know the truth, she'd tell them. Anyway, she hadn't known whether the data would reveal anything. But Felix asked her to do it. And she still trusted him.

It turned out she had good reason to trust him: there was actual data on the drives, which had been illegally downloaded from InTech servers during times the four crows were there. Virtual proof that Mr. Gartner had used the crows as spies. And the next day when the police had gone to the Gartners' house for more, Felix had shown them a whole case full.

As the days passed, it had become the story of the year. The CEO of Odin stealing trade secrets from InTech by spying with crows. Newspapers slammed the story on their front pages, and the online newsfeeds buzzed with the development. How the crows had been trained for years. How Mr. Gartner had someone bribe a janitor to leave a blue bell outside the right windows at first so the crows would know where to go.

Soon there was a settlement out of court. In a matter of weeks, Grant Gartner was in prison. More of a confined estate for billionaires. But still, he was there. For a long time.

Hannah, always ready to help, had found an old friend who went to Felix's old private school and got all the details that weren't in the papers. Felix's mom was officially at home, no trips in the near future. They'd probably lose the big estate, but Mrs. Gartner had her own money tucked away somewhere, so they'd be okay. And they got to keep the crows. Felix could still work with them. He just had to meet with government scientists and show them what the crows could do. The government might even start its own corvid training program.

The charges against Gin for getting the *Love Fractal* data hadn't been dropped, but they were lessened— with her good track record, she got by with a stint of community service. She had to help in elementary school computer labs for six months. Lucas's involvement, luckily, had never come up. Gin was barred from sharing *Love Fractal* with anyone else, at least with the downloaded high school data. But that didn't matter, because interest in *Love Fractal* had grown so quickly that students all over the country were sending her their information to use. By the end of the summer, she might have a functional site that worked for high schoolers across the entire US. Even Lucas was talking about finally trying it out.

Gin had kept her summer internship at Georgetown, but even with another glowing recommendation from Ms. Sandlin, the officials at Harvard had rescinded her acceptance into the university. The official letter of un-acceptance had said, *Harvard has the highest of expectations for all its students, and unfortunately, with the recent developments, we are not able to continue to extend our offer of acceptance.* But there were other options—the University of Virginia had shown some interest, and even MIT was reviewing her circumstances. While Gin was disappointed, she had decided there was more to life than which college she went to.

Anyway, her internship was starting right after graduation. Her mom was home. And even Chloe planned to come back for a few weeks that summer.

Everything, really, was fine.

Except for the matter of Felix.

She hadn't heard from him, not since the night he dropped off the trackers. And she missed him. A small part of her hoped that if he had risked everything to help her, maybe he missed her too.

But there was nothing she could do. She didn't even have a way to get in touch with him. His phone was always off, his voicemail still full. And the URL they had set up for messaging each other had been taken down. The legal proceedings were all over— there was nothing keeping them apart now. But he hadn't even tried to reach out.

She paused—the mile-long walk had gone by faster than she expected—and then started up the white steps of the Lincoln Memorial. She skirted around the edge of the statue and stood in a corner off to the side, out of the way of photo-snapping tourists. There were just a few groups of people there; after they had taken the necessary shots and walked around the sitting Lincoln once or twice, they left, likely headed on to the next site.

For a moment, Gin was alone.

She looked up at Lincoln, his face frozen in his somber expression, and sat down on the top step, staring vaguely out into the city. There was a boy walking along the lawn below—loose jeans and a yellow t-shirt and shaggy hair. She leaned forward, holding her breath, hoping it was Felix.

But when the boy turned, she could clearly see it wasn't him.

She sat on the marble steps for ten minutes, until another group of tourists arrived—a family, the young kids giggling as they bounded up the stairs. And she started down, knowing that the best thing to do—really, the only thing to do—was to keeping moving forward. And maybe then, she'd eventually be able to move on.

// Forty-Nine

The sun was bright outside, but Gin was sitting in class, watching the clock. Seventh period was nearly over, which meant she was almost done. Her last few minutes in the public school system.

Mr. Ryan's closing quote—the last bit of wisdom etched out in yellow chalk that Gin might ever receive—was stuck in her mind: *There is no time; only moment. Like air, spirit, freedom. Moment is reality.*

It wasn't attributed to anyone, and she wondered if Mr. Ryan had made it up. Before they'd left class, he had erased it, the words swept into nothing more than a light yellow smudge. Then he had told them that they now carried the knowledge from that year's studies within them.

The final bell rang, and Gin stepped outside into the sticky air, the heat heavy over the black pavement of the parking lot. It all felt like a dream.

So when she saw it—the beat up 4Runner parked right in front of school—she thought her mind was making it up. She looked away, then back. No, it was real. Felix was there.

Her breath caught in her throat, and her whole body filled with a desire she hadn't let herself feel for weeks.

She reasoned with herself—maybe he was there to get a transcript or clean out his locker. She stared straight ahead, letting her feet move her forward. When she was a few yards away, she couldn't help giving him one quick glance.

As soon as their eyes met, he raised a hand. A tentative greeting. He half-winced, as if to say that he knew it'd be perfectly acceptable if she gave him the finger and kept going. But of course, she couldn't do that. Because in that moment, everything melted. The line of yellow buses. The cars zooming out of the parking lot. The students walking and laughing. The glaring sun. It all pooled into a puddle and disappeared. And all there was, was Felix.

Her hand was lifting up, waving back, doing it all without the conscious agreement of her brain. There was no option but to walk over to his car. Except that suddenly, she couldn't make her legs move. She felt frozen. As though her feet were cemented to the sidewalk. As though she'd stay there, in front of her now-former high school, for the rest of her life.

But then he was opening his car door. And coming towards her. He wore old jeans, a green t-shirt that made his bright eyes brighter, and his leather flip-flops—the ones that seemed sewn to his feet. The ones that, when he finally did kick them off, would be stained with sweat and imprinted with his foot. As though he had walked for hundreds of miles in them, which he probably had.

She had tried to sweep him from her heart, to move those memories out—how he looked and felt and smelled. But now, with him right there, she realized she had merely stuffed them all back in some dusty folds of her brain.

She knew he'd hop up on the curb; a second later, he did. She knew he'd give her one of his smiles. Though she braced herself for it, as soon as his lips turned up, she felt her heart beat impossibly fast.

"Hey," he said.

She wanted to reach out, pull his body towards her

own, lean into him, and kiss him. But for all she knew, he was here to make sure everything between them was officially and finally broken off. From the corner of her eye, she saw the first bus in the line rev up and push forward in a lurch. A heavy load. How her heart felt.

"Hey," she finally answered, the word coming out as a whispery greeting.

"So." He stepped closer.

His presence flooded through her. Like every bit of her skin was opening. There was a scientific explanation for it—dilation, vasoconstriction, something—but in that moment, she had no idea what it was.

"So," she answered. Their words hung there in the air, poor excuses for all they needed to say.

He ran a hand through his hair and bit his lip, and she saw a pinkness glowing from under his tan skin. "This is harder than I thought," he said, almost to himself.

She looked down at the sidewalk. Her stomach churned, and a sense of worry took root. Maybe the best thing to do, maybe the only thing to do, was to leave.

Gin took a breath, preparing to hear him tell her goodbye, when he spoke. "Want to go for a ride?" He sounded hopeful.

Gin could say that going for a ride wouldn't do either of them any good. That it wasn't what she needed. That it could set her back weeks, months, which was not okay—especially with her internship and, hopefully, college just around the corner.

But instead, she said, "Okay." And then she was following him, staring at the back of his neck, his tan skin, his dark beaded necklace.

They drove out of the parking lot, fast. The air rushed through the open windows; the 4Runner's old shocks bounced and heaved. Nothing about the car was like Felix's wealthy life, but it all felt like him.

She let her arm hang out the window, warmed in the sun, and leaned back, feeling her body relax. She closed her eyes and decided that no matter what, she could have this one moment.

"River sound good?" he asked, pulling onto the main street and flying through a series of green lights.

"Sure."

And that was all either of them said for the entire drive. There were no polite conversations, no formalities, no observations. As though neither one of them wanted to broach what needed to be said.

Soon, they were parking in the lot along the river's bank. The Potomac rushed before them, wide and swollen and murky and deep. No one else was around. As if Felix had reserved the whole place in advance.

They walked to the edge and sat down on the grassy bank, next to each other but not close enough to touch. And Gin remembered the time they had met there. When everything around was dying, getting ready for winter. And now, it had all shifted, turned back to a lush green, offset by the blue sky and bright sun and sparkling water.

He leaned back on his hands and turned towards her, squinting in the light.

"Gin." He was suddenly serious. "I've been wanting to tell you this for months. I just didn't know how. And my dad, of course, had said I was never allowed to see you again. And it seemed right at the time. Only, I didn't know how I'd feel—I mean, really feel." He sighed, deep, and shook his head. "This is way harder than I thought."

Gin felt it sink through her. He was going to officially break up with her. Maybe he felt guilty for pulling her through all of it, and this was his opportunity to lessen his guilt. Make sure they left on good terms.

The realization rolled through her, building until it filled up her chest, and she was suddenly angry. She didn't know why she had agreed to ride out with him. To waste a perfectly good afternoon. She didn't need this—to hear all the reasons why whatever they had no longer existed.

"Don't worry about it." Her voice was clear and matter-of-fact. "You don't need to do this." She stood up, fast.

The shine from the water was suddenly too harsh, the sun too bright, and she wished it was overcast—muggy and gray and miserable. Or rainy. Maybe a storm would blow in fast, and the clouds would pile up and release fat drops of water, plinking on the river and staining the concrete.

She pushed her hair behind her ears and crossed her arms over her chest. "Why don't you just take me back to school. I've got work to do." She turned and started walking away, back to the car.

"No—Gin. Wait!"

She felt his hand on her elbow, pulling her back around. "What, Felix? You've already broken up with me by the simple fact of disappearing. You don't need to make it more than what it already is. And I can't say I blame you. What I did, looking into that data, finding that stuff out—how could you not break up with me? If we were ever dating in the first place."

He wasn't letting go of her arm. She was already planning to get a taxi to drive her back home, when confusion crossed his face, followed by a flash of understanding. He eased his grip on her arm, but still didn't let go. Instead, he slid his hand down, until he was holding her hand, and pulled her towards him. Suddenly, it was all she could do to keep breathing.

"Wait," he said. "You think I'm breaking up with you? I mean, probably it seemed like I already did that by leaving and all, but that's what you think I'm trying to tell you right now? Why I came to school to pick you up and bring you out here?"

A breeze kicked up, and the waves splashed the damp, fishy smell of river water toward them. "I guess. I don't know."

Felix sighed, deep and long.

"Gin." His voice was soft. "I brought you here to tell you that I'm sorry. Really, really sorry. For everything that happened."

Her cheeks flushed. "You're sorry? That's why we're here?"

Felix stepped closer, took her other hand in his, and stood facing her. His hands felt so good, so familiar. He leaned closer, his face near hers, and it felt like he might kiss her. But instead, he smiled.

"Yeah," he said. "That's why we're here. So I could say sorry for being such a jerk. And so, hopefully, you'd accept my apology?" His eyebrows furrowed up, and the sun glinted in his eyes, and his lips—those lips—seemed to dance.

She breathed him in, let the feeling of him rush through her. "Okay," she said quietly, squeezing his hands.

"Okay?" He narrowed his eyes and tilted his head forward, making sure.

It settled in her, steadied her. Of course she would forgive him. "Yes. Definitely. I forgive you."

Felix breathed out and closed his eyes. Then he pulled her closer, so her body was almost against his. Their t-shirts just touched. The space between them was so small, inches, centimeters, it felt like the air itself would spark into a thousand electrical pulses. He took her hands and wrapped them around his waist, pulling them to either side of his hips, and onto the small of his back. Then he wove his hands around her, pressing firmly so her body was touching his.

Touching. Their energy and muscle and heat, pressed together, mingling. And it was better than she had remembered.

There was a flash of doubt, like a cloud across her mind. *Love Fractal* had never paired her with Felix. *Decider* had never said to trust him. Her tools of logic hadn't chosen him.

Unless, her brain reasoned—or maybe this time it

was her heart talking—maybe it didn't matter. Maybe logic would never work with Felix. Maybe whatever they had was untouchable, unexplainable by logic.

Maybe Mr. Ryan was right. That there was more than just the material world. Something beyond what could be seen and touched.

She breathed the idea in, let it sit there, steady. Looked up at him, his lips so close to her own.

"How are the crows?"

He smiled. "They're okay. They miss you. I think they'd like to see you."

"Really?"

"Yep. They told me so the other day."

She laughed. "Felix, really."

"They did. Catherine gave this long croo-ack, croo-ack, then flew right to the spot where you and I sat that first night, and hopped three times. She was telling me she wanted you to come back."

Gin was laughing so hard her body was shaking, but he didn't loosen his grip.

"Oh," she said when she finally caught her breath. "I'm sorry about everything."

He touched his forehead to hers. "You didn't do anything wrong. My father did. But you didn't. So I wanted to bring you here to say sorry. And also . . ."

"And also what?"

He closed his eyes for a second. A lone cloud crossed in front of the sun and cast a shadow over them, cooling the air. Two seagulls flew above, and a sailboat coasted along in the distance.

"Here's the thing. I know I'm not in your results."

"In my what?"

"Your results. For *Love Fractal.* Or probably all the other logical frameworks you've built. And I don't think it's a bad thing, by the way, to have all of those models to figure out what to do. I mean, when you think about it, you've done pretty well so far."

"Felix, wait. It's different now. I was just thinking about this. Literally. A second ago. I—"

"No," he said. "Just let me finish. So I'm not in your models, right? Which some would say is a bad thing. And maybe it is. I'm not going to make that decision for you. But maybe it's not so bad. I mean, how often are models right? And so, maybe, the fact that I'm not in there means we have something even bigger. Something so big, it's more than our brains—more than a bunch of neurons firing, the sort of thing a computer can do. Maybe it's more like our souls are coming into the equation. Because, I don't know about you, but I can't change how I feel about you. It's here. And, to be honest, it feels more real than anything else."

He was sweating, the drops glistening on his upper lip. And he was talking so fast that Gin couldn't do anything but let the words click into her mind, into her heart, one by one.

"So. That's it. My speech." He took a deep breath. "With one more part. I love you."

The sun burst out again, setting golden light and thick shadows around them, warming their backs and their heads. Gin tucked her hair behind her ear and looked at him a second longer. Considered all she knew and didn't know about love. Wondered if she could parse it out, understand it well enough to make an informed statement.

Then she took a deep breath. "I love you too." Once she had said it, once the words were out, the feeling became more solid. More real. Like she had to say it first for it to be anything. And there it was. Something true. She loved Felix. No matter what any model said or didn't say, she loved him.

He pulled her in tight, his hands warm on her face, and kissed her. And she kissed him back, their mouths knitting themselves together, so close and warm, mixed with the breeze and the river and the sun. She breathed him in, deep, and turned her mind off. Because sometimes, things were better without thinking.

"I missed you." He tucked his face against hers.

"I missed you too."

There was this rustling of wings, almost like a breeze, and a small wedge of blackness overhead. A crow was flying by. Strong and steady and beautiful.

"Come on," Felix said. "Let's go back and see them. Want to?"

And of course, she did.

// Acknowledgments

Big thanks to Laura, fantastic first-draft sounding board; computer modeling wizards, including Matt, who helped me understand Gin's world; agent extraordinaire, Beth Campbell, for taking a chance on me; the team at Amberjack Publishing for bringing this book to life; Carolyn and Jerry for unwavering love and support; and Helen for paving the way in the writing world. Extra special thanks to Karen, for her effervescent enthusiasm and tech know-how, and for tirelessly listening to storylines at the beach. To my parents, for making sure my childhood was filled with books, loving me so well, and believing I could do anything. To my daughters, for sharing their mom with her imaginary friends. And always to Tim, who has supported me every step of the way.

// About the Author

Susan Cunningham lives in the Colorado Rocky Mountains with her husband and two daughters. She enjoys science nearly as much as writing: she's traveled to the bottom of the ocean via submarine to observe life at hydrothermal vents, camped out on an island of birds to study tern behavior, and now spends time in an office analyzing data on wool apparel. She blogs about writing and science at susancunninghambooks.com.